Slowly they crep
   pausing often
     sodden leaves

Now the shoreline came into view, and Buffy's eyes filled with Roman legionnaires. Five bonfires blazed, embers floating up into the night sky. Dozens of battle horses paced and whinnied. More than fifty boats bobbed on the water, tied to other boats that had been dragged up onto shore. The men paced, talked, checked weaponry, and gazed across at the island. It was clearly a massive military operation.

"Oh, dear," Giles gasped.

"Not 'oh, dear' again, Giles. Stop it with the 'oh, dear.' What is it?"

"It seems we've landed at a most inopportune time," he whispered, drawing up next to her.

Buffy the Vampire Slayer™

Buffy the Vampire Slayer
(movie tie-in)
The Harvest
Halloween Rain
Coyote Moon
Night of the Living Rerun
Blooded
Visitors
Unnatural Selection
The Power of Persuasion
Deep Water
Here Be Monsters
Ghoul Trouble
Doomsday Deck
Sweet Sixteen
Crossings
Little Things

The Angel Chronicles, Vol. 1
The Angel Chronicles, Vol. 2
The Angel Chronicles, Vol. 3
The Xander Years, Vol. 1
The Xander Years, Vol. 2
The Willow Files, Vol. 1
The Willow Files, Vol. 2
How I Survived My Summer Vacation,
Vol. 1
The Cordelia Collection, Vol. 1
The Faith Trials, Vol. 1
The Journals of Rupert Giles, Vol. 1
Tales of the Slayer, Vol. 1
Tales of the Slayer, Vol. 2
Tales of the Slayer, Vol. 3
Tales of the Slayer, Vol. 4

The Postcards
The Essential Angel Posterbook
The Sunnydale High Yearbook
Pop Quiz: Buffy the Vampire Slayer
The Monster Book
The Script Book, Season One, Vol. 1
The Script Book, Season One, Vol. 2
The Script Book, Season Two, Vol. 1
The Script Book, Season Two, Vol. 2
The Script Book, Season Two, Vol. 3
The Script Book, Season Two, Vol. 4
The Script Book, Season Three, Vol. 1
The Script Book, Season Three, Vol. 2
The Musical Script Book: Once More, With Feeling
The Watcher's Guide, Vol. 1: The Official Companion to the Hit Show
The Watcher's Guide, Vol. 2: The Official Companion to the Hit Show
The Watcher's Guide, Vol. 3: The Official Companion to the Hit Show

The Lost Slayer serial novel
Part 1: Prophecies
Part 2: Dark Times
Part 3: King of the Dead
Part 4: Original Sins
Omnibus Edition
Child of the Hunt
Return to Chaos
The Gatekeeper Trilogy
Book 1: Out of the Madhouse
Book 2: Ghost Roads
Book 3: Sons of Entropy
Obsidian Fate
Immortal
Sins of the Father
Resurrecting Ravana
Prime Evil
The Evil That Men Do
Paleo
Spike and Dru: Pretty Maids
All in a Row
Revenant
The Book of Fours
Tempted Champions
Oz: Into the Wild
The Wisdom of War
These Our Actors
Blood and Fog
Chosen
Chaos Bleeds
Mortal Fear
Apocalypse Memories
Wicked Willow Trilogy
The Darkening
Shattered Twilight
Broken Sunrise
Stake Your Destiny
The Suicide King
Keep Me in Mind
Colony
Night Terrors
Queen of the Slayers
Spark and Burn
Afterimage
Carnival of Souls
Go Ask Malice: A Slayer's Diary
Blackout
Portal Through Time

Available from POCKET BOOKS

Portal Through Time

Alice Henderson

**An original novel based on the hit television series
created by Joss Whedon**

POCKET
BOOKS

LONDON • SYDNEY • NEW YORK • TORONTO

This book is a work of fiction. Any references to historical events, real people, or real locales are used fictitiously. Other names, characters, places, and incidents are the product of the author's imagination, and any resemblance to actual events or locales or persons, living or dead, is entirely coincidental.

Pocket Books UK Ltd.
An imprint of Simon & Schuster
Africa House, 64–78 Kingsway
London WC2B6AH

™ & © 2006 Twentieth Century Fox Film Corporation. All rights reserved.

All rights reserved, including the right of reproduction in whole
or in part in any form.

Pocket Books and related logo are trademarks of
Simon & Schuster, Ltd.

Printed and bound in Great Britain
First Edition 10 9 8 7 6 5 4 3 2 1
ISBN-13: 978-1-4165-2688-9
ISBN-10: 1-4165-2688-9

A CIP catalogue record for this book is available from the British Library

To Norma, fearless history teacher, my stalwart companion, my mother, for your support and belief in me. You gave me my love of history, which shines through in this book.

Acknowledgments

Hearty thanks to Cara Bedick for all her editing work; to Elizabeth Bracken for her assistance in the early stages; to Debbie Olshan at Fox; to all the other writers, cast, and crew who have brought Buffy to life on the page and screen; to Jason, for his endless encouragement, belief, and support; and to Norma and our rainy visit to the Shiloh battlefield.

Portal Through Time

Chapter One

Buffy Summers did not know she was about to die. She entered the gym for cheerleader tryouts, excited to show off the new move she'd perfected. For some reason, she was much better at acrobatic moves than the other girls. It just came naturally to her. And now, during her freshman year at Hemery High, she was trying out for the high school cheerleading team.

With a toss of her blond hair, she entered the gym, confident of placing on the team. She'd bowl them over, do her flips, and then go home and binge on pizza with her parents. When she came to school the next day, the tryout results would be posted.

The doors shut behind her as she entered the gym.

• • •

Ten feet away, two vampires crouched in the shrubbery outside the Hemery High gym. Gold and pink still glowed in the west of the newly darkened sky. They talked in whispers, orchestrating their attack.

The gym doors opened suddenly with a bang, and a stream of girls appeared, pom-poms in hand, tossing ponytails, talking in excited voices. The last one out was Buffy, walking a little slower, a small frown on her face. They knew she'd tried out for the team but didn't think she'd done very well. It was a low moment, a vulnerable moment, and though she was not yet an active Slayer, the vampires hesitated before attacking. They both knew her as the fearsome warrior they'd fought in 1997 during the Master's ascension. Victor, who'd been around since the Crusades, had barely escaped when the Slayer's attention focused on killing Luke at the Bronze. He'd slipped out the back door into the alley. Jason, much younger, was no less terrified when he'd glimpsed the end of his three-hundred-year life as Buffy fought her way through the horde of vampires gathered at the Bronze that night. Somehow, miraculously, he'd been shoved aside by another vamp, and Buffy had staked her instead.

But that was the future they'd left behind. When they returned later that night, everything would be different. If all went well, they'd kill Buffy, and the Master would reign supreme on the surface, rising to ever more power with each passing moon. Victor grinned at the thought of that glorious possible future. But the current reality was far more dire than that. The

Master was dead, and Buffy triumphant. And so they'd crossed time itself, mouths eager to taste the blood of a potential Slayer. The Master would live, and the earth would tremble. The Hellmouth, writhing and alive, spitting out demons to swarm over the earth, would gape open, emitting darkness and chaos and things that fed voraciously on human life.

Victor leaned forward from his crouch behind the bushes, chancing a look at Buffy. She loitered by the stairs, still looking sad, and slowly made her way to the sidewalk. As soon as she turned her back, Victor would strike. He licked his lips, the anticipation of tasting a potential Slayer's blood making his stomach nearly sing with savage delight. He signaled for Jason to follow him, and they started down the sidewalk behind Buffy. Victor fought the rising fear back down into his chest. This was not the Slayer. Not yet. She was an ordinary human that he would destroy.

He and Jason had one simple assignment: Stab her. Slit her throat. Be sure she was dead. Then return to 1998, triumphant.

Victor slunk forward, still at a crouch, moving silently. Jason followed close behind, drawing his knife slowly from its sheath above his boot. Victor reached inside his jacket, felt the reassuring weight of his throwing knife in its holster. Buffy made her way down the street, unaware of their presence. They crept from bush to bush, taking refuge in the shadows of trees and hiding behind parked cars on the road.

Now Buffy walked only ten feet before them. Victor slid his throwing knife out of the holster and rose to his full height. Taking careful aim between her shoulders, he flung the blade with a powerful movement of his wrist. Expertly it sailed to its target, and Buffy Summers cried out in surprise and pain as it sank into her back. She stumbled, pitched forward, went off balance, and landed with a painful smack on the concrete.

Quickly Jason closed in, stepping over her prone body and grabbing a fistful of blond hair to lift her head. He moved his knife low, readying to draw it across her throat. Buffy spun suddenly, rolling over, then cried out in agony as the blade in her back twisted against the sidewalk, tearing her flesh as she landed on it. Her eyes teared in pain but still she fought, kicking at Jason.

Victor's feet turned to lead. There was some mistake. She was already the Slayer. She had to be. She kicked Jason in the groin and he sprawled to one side.

But no. That couldn't be right. It was 1995, and he knew that she would not be activated until 1996. He remembered Lucien warning him that she might still be strong, still quick on her feet. But she was not yet the Slayer.

Victor closed in, tripping Buffy as she rose to her feet. She crashed back down, and he wrenched the knife out of Jason's hand. Trembling, he lowered the knife to her throat, praying she wouldn't spring up suddenly, produce a stake, and drive it through his heart, turning him to dust. But she didn't. The pain in her back looked unbearable, and he could clearly hear from her labored breathing that he'd punctured a lung.

She wheezed and coughed, striking him with her fists in his face and neck. He braced for the blows and moved in closer.

He thrust the blade into her neck and dragged it across her throat, slicing a deep wound that instantly welled and overflowed with sticky blood. He studied her face as she glared back at him with eyes full of hatred and anger. Buffy struggled and punched him as she suffocated. Then she managed to throw him off and get up, staggering down the street with her hands clenched tightly over the gash in her throat.

She lurched out into the street, trying to shout but unable to. She waved her arms, choked, and sputtered. The street lay empty. No cars. No people out walking. Her struggle for life went unseen.

Victor pulled Jason up from the sidewalk, and they watched as she rushed violently into a parked car and slumped over its hood, gathering strength to continue. But they could hear her rasping, failing breath, could see the warm sticky blood erupting out of her. She staggered forward into the street and fell. One elbow came up, trying to lift her, but her head hit the pavement for the second time. This time she lay still, arms splayed, the last of her blood pumping into the street, where it meandered into rivulets, rejoined in the gutter, and flowed away into the storm drain.

Buffy Summers was dead.

Chapter Two

Standing in the center of the cemetery, the two assassins waited. Victor looked at his watch. Five minutes until the rendezvous. He searched the shadows expectantly for Lucien. He should be here, somewhere, observing at a safe distance. After all, Lucien didn't want to risk himself. He was the only one who knew how to work the arcane time magicks. And if they had not succeeded in killing Buffy, he would have had to work them again. But they had killed her. They'd killed the Slayer, even if she wasn't quite the Slayer yet.

As Victor checked his watch again, Lucien crept out of the shadows. Dressed in a white, frilly shirt, black pants, and tall black boots, he looked more like a villain from a gothic novel than a twentieth-century devotee of the Master.

"We did it," he said to Lucien unnecessarily. After all, the spell caster had seen everything.

Lucien nodded. "And now we journey back to 1998 and see how we fared."

Jason frowned. "But she's dead. We did it. When we go back, the Master will have ascended safely. Chaos will rule the earth."

"Yes, yes," Lucien replied. "Maybe." He scowled with one eyebrow up, an expression that made Victor think of a million bad actors he'd seen in his lifetime. And the way he dressed made him look as if he'd just stepped off the cover of a romance novel. He was the Fabio of vampires, no doubt, and Victor couldn't deny that he knew his stuff.

Speaking in a language that Victor didn't recognize, Lucien uttered the words that would open the time portal and transport them back to 1998. At the end of the incantation, a tiny point of light winked into view in the air above them. It swirled, growing and growing in size, sucking in dry leaves, and lifting Lucien's hair to toss in the wind.

The spinning portal was ready for the assassins.

Victor steeled himself for the inevitable seasickness that accompanied the transportation. They all closed their eyes tightly against the brilliant, swirling vortex of light. It descended over them, and Victor felt the pricking of his hair as the portal began to draw him upward. His shirtsleeves tugged up toward the vortex, followed by his chest, and then his waist. He hovered for a moment, arms windmilling as he fell off balance. Then he was sucked violently up and through the whirling bright light, grabbing at Jason as Victor came up beside him. Sheer terror thrilled through Victor's chest, and he opened his eyes wide. They streamed with tears from the incredible velocity of forward movement. In spite of himself, in spite of centuries of playing tough, he held on to Jason tightly, letting out a piercing shriek as the speed increased. Then, just as abruptly, it stopped, spilling them out onto a parking lot in Sunnydale, 1998.

A very sunny parking lot.

Jason's hair caught on fire immediately, going up in waving tendrils of bright flame. Victor's hands smoked, his face suddenly bubbling and hot. He burst into a run with Lucien close behind, not caring what direction he headed in, as long as there was cover. Then, a few feet away, he spotted a manhole. Tearing off the cover with vampiric strength, he leaped feetfirst into the cool darkness. With a splash, he landed in fetid water that coursed by his feet. Not caring about the vile stench, Victor dropped and rolled in it, quenching the flames. Lucien landed next to him, splashing eagerly into the water as if they were at a luxurious spa and not a fecal-matter-strewn sewer. Victor rose to his feet and called for Jason through the small round hole above.

He heard screaming, his friend's unmistakable voice crying out in agony. Then nothing.

Victor turned to Lucien and cursed. "The day? You brought us back in the friggin' day?"

Lucien stood up on wobbly legs, brushing strands of something black and glistening off his once pristine shirt. "I didn't know . . . ," he said pitifully.

"What the hell? Don't you know your own ass from your arcane spells?"

Lucien said nothing, only stared on miserably.

"Are you really that clueless? What if we'd been transported right into daylight before we even killed Buffy? What if there'd been no cover?"

Lucien shook his head. "It was a risk. There's really no way to tell when it will be sunny and when it will be night."

"It was a *risk*?" Anger fumed inside Victor. "You didn't tell me or Jason anything about it!" He punched the curved sewer wall, then immediately wished he hadn't, as pain coursed up his arm. He liked Jason. They'd been pals since the Revolutionary War. Now he was dust.

"No one gambles with me like that!" Victor shouted.

Scowling, he chose an underground course to Lucien's lair and set off, feet splashing in the vile gray water. He didn't care how powerful Lucien was. He'd lost his best friend and almost become a toaster pastry.

Behind him, he could hear Lucien tromping in the water, quiet and thinking.

In less than ten minutes, they reached the lair.

Only it was completely different.

Where tables once stood, covered in books, maps, calculations, historical research, and candelabra, now rested a lush canopy bed full of velvet draperies and piled with soft pillows. A few pillar candles resting on pedestal tables gleamed in the confines of the cavern, creating shifting shadows on the wall.

"What the hell?" Victor asked.

"Something's not right," Lucien agreed. He moved forward, striding around the room and looking for clues.

For a moment Victor wondered if they'd walked into the wrong chamber. But he was sure it was this one. The cave formations were familiar, but nothing else was.

"We need to go topside, find out what's been going on," Lucien explained. "I expected the future to be a little different when we returned, so this could just be par for the course."

Victor was less hopeful. This all felt wrong.

Just as they turned to leave, a tall, attractive vampire strode into the room. He knew her—recognized her as one of the girls who was friends with Buffy. But she was a vampire now, brow creased and raised, fangs glistening.

"Ever hear of knocking?" she asked, frowning.

"Uh . . . ," Lucien began, then trailed off.

"Pardon us," Victor stepped in. "We are new in town, and wondered if you could fill us in on what's been going on in Sunnydale the last couple of years?"

The attractive brunette vampire placed one impatient hand on her hip. "The last couple of years?" she quipped. "Why don't you take your skanky butts over to the library and do some research or something? You smell like a sewage treatment plant. And what are you doing in my place, anyway?"

Lucien trembled with impatience. "Has the Master risen?" he blurted out, all eagerness and no style. Victor couldn't believe he followed this guy. But if it meant putting the Master back in power, he was willing.

"The Master?" She furrowed her brow. "You guys really have been out of town. He was killed right after he ascended."

"By the Slayer?"

"Well, yeah, of course." After a moment she added, "Well, not really. You know, a former Slayer."

Lucien frowned in confusion.

The vampire shook her head, obviously pitying the sadness that was Victor and Lucien. "Clueless and styleless," she said. "It's bad enough I have to live in some stinky old cave because my parents' house has skylights all over the place. But I hardly think I have to chat about the weather with creeps like you." The other hand came to her hip, and she fixed them with a scowl.

"Please," said Lucien. "Please explain."

"Don't tell me you haven't heard of the Slayer and what happened to her?"

Lucien shook his head.

"Kafara. She came to Sunnydale to fight the Master, only her presence allowed him to ascend. He drank her blood and escaped. But some other vamps found her near death and turned her. Man, is she one mean vamp. I wouldn't want to cross her, and she's the only one you'll ever hear me say that about." She smoothed back an errant strand of brown hair and looked down at her nails. "Anyway, she dusted the Master that first night. Rose to power herself. Sunnydale's been great ever since. I used to think vamps were so gross, but I like being one."

"And the Hellmouth?" Lucien asked, pressing her for more.

"Closed. When the Master died. But that's okay. If the world had been overrun by beasties, there'd be less for us to eat, right?"

Victor smiled at her. "What's your name?"

"Cordelia," she answered. "But don't think you can wear it out. Don't ever come here again."

"Of course," Victor murmured. "Have you ever heard of Buffy Summers?"

"Who?" Her expression was blank.

"No one."

Lucien punched his palm with a fist. "Then why did it go so wrong?"

Reaching to take his arm, Victor said, "We're going, Lucien."

"But . . ."

"We're going," he said more firmly, leading Lucien out of the cave.

Darkness crept over them again as they returned to the sewer tunnels. "I didn't count on that!" Lucien cursed. "I thought we'd just have to kill Buffy. I thought no other Slayer would be able to destroy the Master."

"And no other Slayer did. She was a vamp when she dusted him."

Lucien turned on Victor in the darkness and struck him hard across the mouth. "Don't say 'dusted' when referring to the Master. He was too important for such reckless terms."

Victor brought his hand quickly to his mouth,

tasted blood there. His eyes narrowed, anger simmering inside him. Half of him wanted to pummel Lucien into the sewer brick right then. Lucien had struck him, he'd killed Jason, and they'd been unsuccessful. But he stilled himself, forcing calm to spread over his limbs.

"What went wrong?" he said through clenched teeth.

Lucien shook his head. "Maybe we need to go farther back. Kill Buffy when she's just a kid. That will activate a different Slayer. And perhaps that one will be ineffective."

"Perhaps? I don't like the idea of jumping back into daylight for a 'perhaps.'"

"Maybe not," Lucien answered, "but we're going to. And we need to find another assassin."

At that offhand comment, Victor raised his hand to strike Lucien hard, hard enough to rattle his teeth. But he restrained himself. Jason had been his friend for two hundred years, and Lucien treated him as if he could replace him by walking into an assassin mart and picking someone off the shelf. "We won't be able to replace Jason," he said instead of hitting him. "You lost one of the best assassins you could have gotten."

"Yeah, I noticed back there," Lucien retorted, and Victor remembered how Buffy had disabled Jason with a kick. But that didn't give Lucien the right to that dig. Every assassin had his off days. This time Victor did strike Lucien, hard across the face, an open-handed slap meant to humiliate the cocky spell caster. It worked.

Lucien roared with rage and shoved ineffectively at Victor in the confines of the sewer tunnel. Victor evaded his blows and sprinted down the length of the tunnel, outpacing him. "Looks like we have to start all over again!" he yelled back.

He heard Lucien's footsteps slow to a stop. "No," came his voice in the darkness. "I kept a backup of all my research. We only need to get it out of lockup and gather the next team."

"And what about the unique artifact? Where is it?"

Lucien's face contorted in anger. "Damn!"

This did not sound good to Victor. The artifact was what made it all work. When Lucien joined the artifact with his incantations, they could travel through time. Lucien had forged the artifact himself, fashioning it from two different unique relics rumored throughout the ages to hold the power of time travel. It had taken him considerable time just to locate and acquire the relics, and he had traveled as far as Tibet in his search. Once both relics were found, he had incanted and melted and wound the two pieces together to make the Wand of Wells, as Lucien called it. At first Victor thought he meant "wells" as in ancient, sacred places of worship. But it had actually been a tribute to H. G. Wells, author of *The Time Machine*. The wand itself was gorgeous—it gleamed silver along its jewel-encrusted length, and at one end a silver clawed hand held a luminous blue stone the size of a house cat. It wasn't exactly tiny. Not something you could put in your pocket. Of course, they couldn't have carried it with them anyway.

The way the magick worked was that the Wand of Wells always had to stay behind on a time jump. It served as a marker to the year from which the travelers departed. Without it, they could return to the Stone Age, or worse yet, to a time when the sun had gone supernova and there was no Earth at all. To ensure that it wouldn't get misplaced or stolen, they had bricked it up inside a wall in one of the crypts of the Sunnydale Cemetery. As long as it existed when they left a year, it would still be there when they returned, guiding them back to the correct year. It existed in a time bubble of its own. Even if they changed the past, the artifact would still be there in the alternate version of 1998. Even if the wall they'd bricked it up inside didn't exist anymore, the Wand of Wells would still be there, on that exact spot.

But while it was great at returning them to the right date and year, it wasn't so hot at returning them to the right location and time of day, as the previous sunlight incident had proven. They'd departed from Lucien's underground lair, but had returned two blocks away on the surface.

During their test runs, they frequently had to backtrack to the artifact's location. At least it would be there. It always was.

"Let's backtrack to the crypt," Lucien said. "This time we'll kill Buffy when she's a little girl."

Chapter Three

Armed with backup copies of research, Lucien peeked at the artifact he'd constructed, preparing to open the portal. The Wand of Wells was still there, bricked up inside the crypt wall. They always checked for it, every time they readied to travel back in time. If it wasn't there, they wouldn't be able to return to 1998. Seeing it gleam inside its dark hole, Lucien replaced the loose brick, sealing it inside once more.

It had taken him months of constant work, with almost no sleep, to build the artifact and imbue it with arcane powers. At first he didn't even think it would be possible. But the more obsessed he became, and the more he read about time magick, the more determined he grew.

The Master, he knew, simply had to rise again. And though Buffy may have sent him plummeting down onto a sharp protrusion of wood, and broken his bones to powder with a hammer, there was still a chance.

All Lucien had to do was travel back in time and kill Buffy so that she was not the active Slayer at the time of the Master's ascension. Only Buffy, he believed firmly, could have defeated the Master. Another Slayer in her place would not have the fortitude, the necessary skills. At least he hoped not. Unless she turned into an evil, power-hungry vampire. But they were about to erase this alternate future altogether.

He left the secret room, making certain it sealed behind him. Then he navigated down a narrow tunnel and entered his sleeping room. Just as he shut the door behind him, he heard shuffling in the corridor outside and pressed against the door, listening. His biggest fear was the Slayer discovering what he was up to before he had the chance to go back in time and kill her. He quickly breathed a sigh of relief, almost laughed. It couldn't be Buffy outside. They'd killed her. Her life had come to an end at the ripe age of fourteen, and if there was a Slayer out there, lurking outside his door, it certainly wouldn't be her. Not that he didn't feel that deep-down twinge of fear at the thought of another Slayer. It was just that he'd seen Buffy in action and knew she was practically undefeatable.

The shuffling grew louder. Then came a tapping at his door. He swung it open to reveal Victor standing on the other side, cleaning his throwing knife with a cloth. "Ready?" he asked, looking up from his task.

Lucien nodded. He'd just returned from Willy's, where he'd recruited the meanest-looking vamp of all the patrons for this little excursion. The goal this time was 1984. Buffy would be only three years old. Easy pickings. This would hopefully undo the mess he'd made and restore the Master again. He had given strict instructions to the Master's closest followers to keep them from turning any Slayer the Master killed this time around.

His warning had met with strange glances and humoring nods. Most of them didn't understand the power of time travel. They didn't even think it was possible. For them, this change in events, in which the Master was murdered by a vampiric ex-Slayer, appeared to be as it had always been. But for Lucien and Victor, because they'd been the ones traveling through time, events had changed around them, and they could still recall how the timeline originally flowed. They were, in essence, in an alternate 1998, one that Lucien now hoped to alter even more.

"Where's the other assassin?" Victor asked, resheathing his knife. Lucien tried not to notice his clothes. Victor dressed the part of uncivilized ruffian. His leather jacket, at least two decades old, was scored in a dozen places from scuffles and fights. Before he could help himself, Lucien snarked, "Do you always have to dress so . . . low?"

"It's my lucky jacket," Victor said defensively.

"At least we'll be going back to a time period where you'll still be in style."

Victor poked Lucien's shoulder angrily with his

index finger. "A time period when *I'll* be in style? You look like you raided Lord Byron's closet. Your clothes just announce, 'Hey, I'm a vampire, by the way. A dorky one.'"

Lucien waved him off. "We need to meet Gorga."

"Gorga? You got us a guy named Gorga? That sounds like a cheese or an enemy of Godzilla, not an assassin."

"Then you should get along perfectly." Lucien exited, closing the door behind him.

Twenty minutes later, in an alley behind the Bronze, all three vampires met. Monstrous, muscular, and bald, Gorga carried a battle-ax, a crossbow, and a sword sheathed in a belt. Lucien had a feeling Gorga hadn't quite wrapped his head around the fact that they were targeting the Slayer *before* she was the Slayer.

"She's a three-year-old girl, for God's sake," Victor told him, disliking Gorga from the start. But Lucien knew that anyone but Jason would have made Victor angry.

Reciting the proper incantations, Lucien opened the time portal. It sucked the three of them inside, whirling them uncontrollably faster and faster, careening into the past and across space.

They tumbled out into the early evening on a suburban street in 1984. The portal winked out of view. Lucien had gotten pretty good at determining where and when it would spit them out. While he wasn't able to pick a specific hour, he'd become more accurate at figuring out how to land in specific months and years. And for locations he could get within five miles of his target. And now here they were, in 1984 Los Angeles.

Lucien knew it was 1984 because just then a group of teenagers turned the corner. One wore a Michael Jackson *Thriller* jacket, black parachute pants, and a sequined glove on one hand. One teenager's hair, styled in a Jheri curl, positively dripped with shiny product. He produced a spray bottle from his jacket and squirted his Jheri with more "activator." A girl in the group had bleached-blond hair so big that it continually poked her companions in the face and eyes with stiff, hairsprayed tendrils. Her big hoop earrings could have comfortably slept five. Another of the teenagers wore a pastel blue blazer with a coral pink T-shirt underneath. On his feet were white slip-on canvas deck shoes with no socks. Lucien felt the pain deep, deep down.

Victor consulted a map in his back pocket, then replaced it. "Three doors down," he said. "On the left. Not bad, Lucien. I half expected us to land in Paris, going this far back." Sometimes, on test runs, they'd spent days just reaching their target location. Other times they hadn't reached it at all.

Lucien nodded. "I'm getting better." He didn't remind Victor of one of the first attempts, which had landed them in a yak herd in Burma for seven hours, knee-deep in dung, with no coats while Lucien tried to read the incantation as the ink ran during a rainstorm.

This was much, much better, Lucien kept telling himself, as the teenagers passed and he stifled a shudder.

Victor forged ahead, not waiting for the others. The group of friends snuck looks at Gorga and his collection of medieval weaponry, but the vamps kept quiet. They were under strict instructions this time not to interact or otherwise alter the future. Their sole change would be to kill Buffy when she was a child.

As they neared Buffy's childhood home, Victor slowed, peeking over a chest-high wooden fence that framed her backyard. He laughed softly. "We're in luck. She's outside. Looks like they're getting ready to cook something on the hibachi. And she's alone right now."

They glanced up at the sliding glass door that led into the house. Inside, her parents milled around, cutting vegetables and pieces of meat. In the yard, Buffy played with a badminton birdie, tossing it around while she sat on the grass, giggling softly to herself.

Victor rummaged around in his other pocket and produced a stolen photo of Buffy as a kid. He compared it to the little girl. "It's definitely her. Make yourself scarce, Lucien. Meet you down the block."

"Then we can party like it's 1984," Gorga put in, shouldering his battle-ax.

Victor narrowed his eyes. "I really don't think you're going to need that thing."

"Split her in two. Split pea soup," the monstrous giant retorted.

Double-checking the house again and seeing her parents still inside, Victor vaulted over the fence, landing beside Buffy in the grass. Here was the Slayer, the woman he had feared since he'd come to Sunnydale two years ago. Amazing. As he closed in on her, she looked up at him, her smile fading to a frown. "Who are you?" she asked.

Gorga landed with a heavy thud next to him. He swung the ax up, then paused.

"What's wrong?" Victor asked.

Gorga looked down at the little girl. He couldn't kill her. He kept the ax poised but couldn't bring himself to swing it down.

"You're not having a change of heart, are you?"

Gorga relented, bringing the ax down gently beside him. He gripped the handle, meeting the little girl's eyes. "Not because I care," said the monstrous hulk. "Gorga is no softie. It's just that she's only three. How embarrassing is that? How will I describe this kill to the monthly Assassins Club?"

Victor shook his head. "How about, 'Man, that baby came at me with everything it had, but I still made the kill.'" He grabbed the ax out of Gorga's hands and swung it high. The ax blade flashed and swung down. With a sickening *snick* it sliced the little girl in two.

Gorga stood, unblinking. She hadn't even cried out. The badminton birdie, now spattered with blood, rolled out of her hand and described a small semicircle in the grass before coming to a halt near the hibachi.

Victor straightened up and looked at Gorga, who met his eyes. Then he waved one triumphant fist in the air. "Dangerous kill, man," Victor told him. Briefly he thought of beheading the vampire giant. Some use he was. But he decided against it. They might need him again. He handed back the ax, then sprinted up over the fence again. Gorga used the gate, opening and closing it silently behind him.

They hurried down the street. Victor heard the sliding door swish open and a woman's scream so powerful it caused his eardrums to thrum with vibration.

Buffy Summers was dead.

Again.

Chapter Four

Sunnydale, 1998

Thirty minutes later Lucien, Gorga, and Victor whirled out of the vortex into the quiet of night, crashing into a brick wall next to the Bronze.

Lucien leaped up, hopeful, eyes darting down the alley, as if he expected a banner to be strung across the wall declaring THE MASTER ROSE. ALL WENT WELL. WISH YOU WERE HERE.

But of course, they'd have to ask around before they knew if they'd been successful.

Lucien chose the Master's lair as the first stop. They entered through the back of the mausoleum and started down the tunnels. They'd gone only a hundred feet before the tunnel abruptly ended in a cave-in. They tried the other routes in—a sewer tunnel Victor knew about, then a maintenance tunnel on the far side of town Gorga had used once. But all of them ended in cave-ins.

At Willy's, Lucien asked around and learned that a tremendous explosion had shaken that part of Sunnydale so vigorously that huge parts of it had collapsed. When one demon clammed up, not wanting to discuss it further, Lucien moved on to the next. Slowly the story came together.

When he probed about the current Slayer, he learned that her Watcher focused primarily on prophecies, and that he'd figured out that the Master could not ascend if he didn't drink the blood of a Slayer. So the Slayer, who came to Sunnydale specifically to stop the ascension, just sat in her hotel room and didn't go down to confront the Master at all. One night soon after, she and her Watcher dynamited the whole underground lair, burying the Master completely. One vamp who'd barely escaped witnessed the Master's skull getting crushed by a falling stalactite.

Lucien assimilated all of this, downing only half of his glass of blood as he sat at the bar. Anger simmered, then exploded. "Damn it! Why the hell isn't this working?"

Victor shook his head. "Something's wrong. It's the time line. It's as if the Master's destruction is ordained. We need a prophecy guy."

Lucien brought his fist down hard onto the bar, then winced from the pain. He knew Victor made sense, but the sheer frustration made him want to smash his glass and give up on the whole thing. But the minute he finished that thought, he knew better. He could never give up. He'd pledged his life to the Master and would not stop until he was resurrected.

But he couldn't believe this. What a mess of trial and error. So far none of the time jumps had worked. Originally, after several successful trial runs, Lucien had traveled back to 1937. The Master came to Sunnydale that year, intending to open the Hellmouth and invite the old demons to retake the earth. But a violent earthquake shook Sunnydale just as he was finishing his incantation, and he became sealed in a prison of his own making, trapped as the earthquake shifted land and created an impenetrable mystic wall.

At first Lucien thought the matter simple—he would travel back in time and warn the Master not to open the Hellmouth on that particular day. The Master could wait, be successful another day. But when Lucien interrupted the Master before he began the incantations, the great vampire didn't know Lucien. Lucien remembered with frustration that he hadn't entered the Master's service until 1942, when he needed more and more vampires to do tasks for him during his captivity. Lucien explained nonetheless about the earthquake and his subsequent imprisonment. But the Master had not only refused to listen, he was gravely insulted. No mere earthquake, the ancient vampire had reasoned, could trap him down here and disrupt his spell. Lucien obviously just wanted to keep the status quo. He was a coward, afraid of releasing the creatures from the Hellmouth. The Master ignored him and continued the incantations, ordering three vampires to drag Lucien out of the area, for his cries were distracting.

Shortly after Lucien reached the surface, escorted by the vampires into the night, the earthquake began. First a mild shaking shuddered through the earth beneath their feet. Then a more robust wave rolling through the bedrock set gravestones askew and knocked the vampires off their feet. The violent quake lasted a whole minute, then stopped, the rumbling replaced with the crying sirens of fire engines and police cars.

As Lucien wandered the smoldering rubble of devastated Sunnydale, he knew he had to think of a different way to help the Master. Stopping him in that moment, when the Master had traveled so far and researched the perfect incantation to open the Hellmouth, would be impossible. The Master could be stubbornly determined, Lucien knew. And so he quested on, feeling not discouraged but almost self-righteous. The Master may have turned him away in 1937, but Lucien was such a powerful devotee that he would struggle on regardless. His reward would be to see the Master free and the creatures of the Hellmouth overtaking Sunnydale—and then the world.

Now, sitting in Willy's, Lucien's mind wandered over these events. Why weren't his attempts working? Were the events written in stone? The Master's incarceration in 1937? His death in 1997? This couldn't be. If it were so, what was Fate's point of imprisoning him in 1937? Just to keep him trapped for forty years? To teach him a lesson? Why not just kill him in 1937?

There must be a way, somehow, for Lucien to alter the events. Maybe he just hadn't gone back far enough.

Victor was right. They needed a prophecy guy. And Lucien knew just who to see.

Five hours later, Lucien and Victor sat in the waiting room of Zaaargul the Seer. They'd left Gorga at Willy's, needing a break from him. Victor put down the issue of *Celebrity Haircuts* he'd been perusing and exhaled impatiently.

"Is this guy even for real?" he asked Lucien. "He's got three a's in his first name. That's such a cheesy 'creature from beyond' thing to do."

"It's not his first name, it's his *only* name."

"That's even worse."

Lucien turned to him, head lowered and threatening. "You got a better idea? Got another prophecy guy in your Rolodex of the Undead?"

Victor nodded. "Yeah, as a matter of fact. I say we kidnap this new Watcher, torture him, and make him figure out why we can't stop the Master's death."

"I wouldn't want to torture a Watcher," Lucien said. "Those guys can be brutal. You ever meet the last one?"

"Yes, at the Bronze. And he didn't seem so tough."

Lucien shuddered. "That was a front. Believe me. I knew that guy in the seventies in London, and he was one hell of a brutal guy. 'Ripper,' they called him. The kind of guy you don't want your brood to go near when they're young. Or old. Believe me, wherever that guy is, we're damn lucky we're not stuck with him as the Watcher."

Victor restlessly picked up an issue of *Make-Or-Break Looks*. The cover lines read "10 Ways to Please Your Demon," "5 Surefire Makeup Cure-Alls to Cover Your Puffy Tentacles," and "1501 Two-Minute Hairstyles for the Undead." Victor flung that aside too. "Oh, come on! This guy's an evil prophecy reader, right? Well, how come he doesn't have any good magazines?"

"Because he's evil."

"Oh, yeah. See your point."

"And listen," Lucien added. "Don't insult him or anything, okay? I've heard things. I don't know if they're true, but I've heard things."

"What kind of things?"

"Head-squished, dragged-to-the-bottom-of-the-ocean-to-rot-for-all-eternity, toothpick-in-the-eyeball kind of things."

Victor shifted uncomfortably in his seat.

A few minutes later the receptionist, a gaunt vampire who looked like she hadn't eaten in a week, showed them in to see Zaaargul.

She closed the door behind them, and they stood before a massive mahogany desk with a green study lamp. Zaaargul sat at the desk, a bulky, vaguely octopus-looking creature with too many tentacles to count, and huge, luminous golden eyes with curved, horizontal pupils.

In one tentacle he held a quill pen, with which he filled in ovals on a lottery ticket.

"Hello," Lucien said.

One golden eye swiveled in its protruding socket,

and a tentacle emerged from beneath the desk and motioned them forward.

Quietly they took the two chairs sitting before the desk. The unnerving suggestion to take the chairs came silently, unbidden into Lucien's head. He'd heard that Dracula could do that, but Dracula had a lot fewer tentacles and wasn't nearly as disturbing to behold. Next to the ticket an ancient tome lay open, its leather binding decaying, parchment pages stained and worn.

Several moments ticked by painfully. "I can tell you more of my situation, and then we can come back for the solution," Lucien offered, anxious to get out of there as soon as possible.

"Look. You do the waiting in my waiting room, not in here." He placed the quill pen back in its silver holder with one delicate tentacle. "I figured it out on your way here."

Lucien looked amazed. "From the little I told you on the phone—"

"Please don't interrupt. My time is valuable." From a small silver tray, Zaaargul plucked a slice of Gruyère from an array of cheeses and brought it to his beak, nibbling daintily. "A Slayer named Buffy Summers," he continued, "is prophecied to kill the Master toward the close of the twentieth century."

"Yes, and we killed her. Twice. I'll bet you've never even heard of her. Have you?" he added, less certainly.

Zaaargul held up an impatient tentacle. "I assumed she was the destroyed Slayer you spoke of on the phone. Because you have now disrupted the flow of normal events, the prophecy is still trying to fulfill itself, using whatever Slayer is in her place, because she should be the natural Slayer during these years. In the unaltered time line, Buffy was born and should have become the Slayer. Her Watcher should have found her and trained her at an early age, so that she would be ready to become the Slayer when she was activated."

Lucien leaned forward across the desk. "But she was different. Her Watcher didn't find her until she was in her early teens. She lacked much of the usual training and discipline."

Zaaargul lowered his large, meaty unibrow over his yellow eyes. "That is not important now. Because Buffy was born a potential Slayer, and because all the other Slayers before her died just when they happened to die, she was activated at the perfect time to be the Slayer when the Master ascended." Zaaargul paused, opening a drawer and taking out a handful of sunflower seeds, which he munched down, shell and all.

Disgusting, thought Lucien.

"Therefore, if you want to disrupt this prophecy, your only chance is to disrupt the lineage of the Slayers. Take action in the past to ensure that Slayers are activated at different times. Therefore, when it comes to the years in which Buffy Summers is alive, she may never be activated at all. The prophecy of her killing the Master goes out of whack, and the Master goes free."

Zaaargul closed the heavy tome in front of him, then used several rear tentacles, much longer than his front few, to reshelve the volume carefully behind him on a massive bookshelf. He blinked, his large yellow eyes glistening and nearly hypnotic. Lucien flashed back to a time when he had stood in front of an octopus tank at the Monterey Bay Aquarium for hours, convinced that the creature held him in his power. Those glistening golden eyes were the same then. . . .

Lucien shook his head and was unnerved to see Zaaargul make the barest hint of a smile. A smug smile. Darn mind-control cephalopods. Lucien reigned in his thoughts, considered what he'd learned. "So you're saying that I need to go back in time and either kill a few Slayers, or preserve their lives beyond the years they lived?"

Zaaargul nodded.

"I like the killing option better," Victor said, the first words he'd spoken since they walked in. "More room for creativity."

"So we kill some Slayers," Lucien agreed.

Zaaargul's skin flushed to an entirely different tone. The greenish parts turned gold, the reddish parts blue. "I suggest you choose the most documented Slayers. The more details you know of their tendencies and schedules, the better you can hunt them. Three or four of them should do the trick."

"Any idea who those were?" Lucien ventured.

"Not a clue. Not my area. Now," he said, waving a tentacle distractedly, "if you'll excuse me, I have others waiting."

Lucien jumped up. "Of course! Thank you!"

Victor got up too, with a little bow, and they backed

toward the door. Something about those eyes . . . Lucien wanted to get out of there badly. He suddenly felt like a snack.

"And don't forget," added Zaaargul, "that you must go back and save Buffy's life. Twice. You must put the time line right again and then work from there if this is going to be successful."

Lucien licked his lips nervously. "Of course!"

Victor opened the door. "Say, do you always pick your own numbers, or do you ever do quick pick?"

Lucien couldn't believe this. If his heart could still beat, it would be skittering around in his chest right now like a kitten high on catnip.

"Quick pick, on occasion," Zaaargul answered. "Today I'm using the numbers for the date I spawned my daughter."

"Cool." Victor left the room, with Lucien treading on his heels. Lucien didn't relax until they were all the way out of that place, in the cool night air. He looked up at the twinkling stars, glad to be outside. "How will we choose which Slayers to kill?" he asked Victor.

"Simple." He glanced at his watch. "Three hours to sunrise. We find out where this new Watcher is holing up while they're in town, break in, and steal his journals."

"Sounds simple."

"If he's not there," Victor added. "I don't fancy fighting off the new Slayer tonight."

"Nor do I," Lucien put in.

"Let's do some recon."

A half hour later they'd tracked down the

Watcher's hotel. Liam Folsworthy, a graduate of Oxford, they were told at Willy's, was not only an expert on prophecies, but knew a bit of Jeet Kune Do, as well. Victor was not enthused. The last thing he wanted was some English Bruce Lee kicking his ass up and down the hotel parking lot.

The hotel room, though, was dark, and Victor wasted no time in bashing in a window after he'd checked the darkness inside for a sleeping form. The Watcher was out. He reached around to unlatch the hotel lock, and they slid inside. It was fortuitous, Victor realized, that the Slayer and Watcher *were* only visiting. It meant hotel rooms and not houses. They couldn't have entered Liam's house without an invitation, but a hotel room was public, and vampires, though without the right to vote, were still the public.

Lucien and Victor quickly moved to the bed, dumping out suitcases and clearing out drawers. In the bathroom, between two folded towels, Victor found the Watcher journals. He grabbed them, and they left without cleaning up. No reason to do that. In a few minutes they'd travel back in time again, and Liam Folsworthy might never be a Watcher after all.

With the Watcher journals tucked under Lucien's arm, they headed for the caverns beneath Sunnydale, where they would open the vortex once again, this time to save Buffy's life.

Three days later Lucien prepared for his most dangerous mission yet. He had never traveled so far back in time. He had spent the last few days making much smaller time jumps, but he told Victor to stay behind, not sure of the danger of someone meeting themselves in the past. He went alone, avoiding himself and pausing only to talk to Victor in both situations. In 1984 he'd stopped Victor and Gorga from leaping over the fence to kill toddler Buffy. In 1996 he'd stopped Jason and Victor in the bushes outside the Hemery High gym, before Buffy emerged after tryouts.

This last had the added effect of bringing Jason back from the dead, because Lucien warned Jason about the impending sunlight and told him which direction to run to get to the sewer. Lucien's effort was successful, and Jason lived. Victor had been in a good mood ever since. Saving Jason had been an unforeseen bonus, and Lucien played it up, making Victor think it had been as important to Lucien as saving Buffy. He didn't let Victor know it had only occurred to him at the last minute, because frankly, he was a little scared of Victor.

They had returned to a Sunnydale in which Buffy Summers was the active Slayer and the Master was dead.

But that was a temporary situation, Lucien knew.

He'd pored over the Watcher journals, surprised at all the detail, not just about the Slayers, but about many vampires, too, including Darla, Angelus, and the Master himself. After many sleepless days of study, Lucien at last narrowed down his search to four of the most documented Slayers: a Celtic warrior Slayer who lived during the Roman occupation of Britain; a

Sumerian Slayer living in 2700 B.C.E.; an American Civil War Slayer; and an aristocratic Slayer who'd survived the French Revolution.

He'd selected teams of assassins, including Jason and Victor, to tackle these time periods. The assassins received period dress and lessons on how to act, talk, and blend in. He didn't want them getting staked for standing out. They had to infiltrate each time period, find the Slayer, and destroy her.

When they were all finished, the Slayer lineage would be so off that Buffy would never be activated. Instead, the Slayer in her time period might not even journey to Sunnydale. And if she did, they could all band together to kill her. This way the Master could rise, instead of his bones being ground to dust.

Unfolding the incantations before him, Lucien checked them over and over. He'd made three copies. One for himself, one for Victor, and one that he would leave with Gorga in case they all failed. He checked again on the artifact. It was still there. Now he just needed to gather Victor and Jason, and they could jump back in time to kill the Celtic Slayer in 60 C.E.

Chapter Five

Buffy Summers was not dead.

But she did feel like she was. She'd dragged in from patrolling at four a.m. the night before, and she had trouble sleeping because of a painfully bruised shoulder. Buffy was the lucky Chosen One, the one girl in all the world with the power to fight vampires and other creatures of darkness. This usually meant long hours hunting around cemeteries, but occasionally it meant long hours hanging out at the Bronze, their local nightspot, hunting for vampires. Buffy greatly preferred the latter. Occasionally it even meant smooching with Angel, her vampiric love, in a graveyard. That might sound strange, a Slayer in love with a vampire, but Angel was different. He had a soul. Other vamps didn't, which made them free of conscience to do any evil thing they wanted. And they took full advantage of that. But Angel had pissed off the wrong gypsies by murdering one of their daughters, and they'd cursed him. His soul returned to his body, and now he lived in eternal anguish over the terrible things the vampire demon had done in his soul's absence. He was always brooding and tormented, though occasionally he took a break to engage with Buffy in those graveyard smoochies.

But now Buffy sat in English class, slumping forward in her desk, able to stay awake only because of the semiconstant rain of paper pellets flicked at her by her best friend, Willow Rosenberg.

Her head began to sink down.

"Buffy!" her friend whispered sharply. "She's coming this way!"

Buffy snapped awake, ready to stake vamps, and instead saw something far more terrifying. Mrs. Niedermeyer stood at the head of her row, thumbing through a stack of handouts. "Today's quiz," Mrs. Niedermeyer said, "is on Thomas Hardy's *Tess of the D'Urbervilles*. I hope you all read your assignment this week. This covers the basic themes and plot points of the book. And if you rented the film instead of reading it, be warned that there are enough differences to cause you to get an F on this quiz."

Rented the film? That would have been a good idea. Less Cliffs-Notey, more entertainment value. But Buffy hadn't even thought of that. *Tess of the D'Urbervilles*? She thought she'd heard of it before. Vaguely recalled being handed a copy of it a few weeks ago and signing for it. She even remember seeing the book recently—probably beneath her bed—

yes, that was it, under her new pair of boots. Or had she left it at Angel's?

Either way, she hadn't read it.

She hadn't even cracked it open.

The quiz landed on her desk, and Mrs. Niedermeyer turned to inflict her reign of terror on the next row of seats. She looked down at the test. Thomas Hardy. Did he have anything to do with the Hardy Boys? She'd seen a few episodes of that old show on cable recently, starring hottie Parker Stevenson. Then she saw the date of the book's publication: 1891. This was definitely something different.

"Will," Buffy whispered to her friend. She gave Willow the best *help!* face she could muster, bringing her eyebrows up, frowning slightly.

"It's simple," Willow whispered back. "Just write down the most depressing answers you can think of. They're bound to be right."

"Okay." Buffy thought. She scanned the questions:

1. When Tess is forced to baptize her own dying infant, where does she ultimately bury the body?
2. When Tess confesses her unfortunate past to her new husband Angel, he leaves her behind, unforgiven, and moves to what country?
3. When Alec returns for Tess's hand in marriage, what does he use to bribe and coerce her into being his consort?
4. When Tess receives word that her mother is dying, which family member unexpectedly dies instead?

5. What crime does Tess resort to in order to ultimately escape from Alec?

Buffy blinked, taking in the story line, reading the rest of the questions. She got the full gist of this book from the quiz alone. Even with a love interest named Angel, which she could certainly appreciate, it sounded like the most depressing book she'd never read. Dying infants, lonely burials in neglected corners of graveyards, women forced to be with men they despised and hated, family members dying unexpectedly, families turned out into the street with nowhere to go, a woman neglected and then driven to murder. *What was this guy's damage?* The author clearly needed a side of depression with his morning depression.

She glanced over at Willow, eyes wide in disbelief.

"This is pretty bad," admitted Willow in a whisper. "His novel *The Mayor of Casterbridge* is downright cheery in comparison. It opens with the main character selling his wife and baby at a country carnival, and things generally get worse after that."

"Sounds uplifting. I'll get right to reading that one." Buffy glanced up at Mrs. Niedermeyer, who sat at her desk, busy grading homework.

She went back to the quiz.

Following Willow's advice, she wrote down the most depressing answers she could think of, getting quite creative at times, including making Tess into a homeless, impoverished seller of wilted violets. It seemed to fit right in.

The bell rang, and they all filed forward, placing their tests on Mrs. Niedermeyer's desk. She smiled at them all as they passed by. Buffy felt the hot burning of classic I Didn't Do My Homework Syndrome as she walked up. She plunked her test down on the pile and hurriedly left the room.

"So how was slayage last night?" Willow asked, falling in beside her. The Slayer was supposed to have a secret profession, but she wouldn't have lasted as long as she had without the help of her friends.

"Pretty uneventful. Maybe four vamps total."

"Any other vamps show up?" Willow shot her a meaningful look.

"Maybe," Buffy answered, immediately swept away in Angelness.

"Sounds like it was a good night."

Xander Harris appeared behind them, placing his arms over their shoulders. "What sounds like it was a good night?" he asked.

"Buffy saw Angel last night. There were smoochies."

"Buff—the guy's dead. I just don't get it," Xander said, disgusted. She knew he was actually jealous. He'd been crushing on her since they met.

"Yeah, Buffy, what would you see in someone so gorgeous, gallant, and mysterious?" Willow asked.

"You know, Will, I just don't know." Xander was a goofy kind of guy, sort of awkward and a little fashion-challenged. But he was a good person, and he made her laugh. He and Willow had been best friends since they were kids. Willow often reminisced of happy times watching Xander do the Snoopy dance, which he apparently still did upon request. However, Buffy had yet to make such a request.

Since her arrival at Sunnydale High, Willow and Xander had become her best friends. Her Watcher, Rupert Giles, had initially been dismayed that her two new friends knew her secret identity as the Slayer. But they had bailed her out more times than she could count, and Xander had even saved her life once. Buffy shuddered involuntarily every time she thought about it. She'd gone to fight the Master, one of the most ancient and powerful vampires ever to exist. At the time he was trapped in the caves beneath Sunnydale. Despite a prophecy that she would die in the fight, Buffy had challenged him. He killed her. Bit her, drank her blood, then tossed her facedown into a standing pool of water. Her blood gave him the power to break free of his imprisonment, and he rose to the surface. Buffy had drowned. If it hadn't been for Xander and his CPR skills, she would have stayed dead.

Instead, because of her friends, she had lived and killed the Master.

His plans to open the Hellmouth, the evil portal that lay beneath Sunnydale, had been thwarted.

They had won.

So Giles didn't know what he was talking about when he warned her about her friends knowing. She wouldn't be here if they were in the dark, because there were a lot of other things in the dark that wanted her dead.

Of course, Giles would continue being annoyed by how many people knew she slayed vamps. At least her mom didn't know. Buffy wouldn't want her worrying about her daughter staying out all night, staking vamps, beheading demons, and generally getting all manner of supernatural goo on her new sweaters.

They reached the end of the hall and walked into the cafeteria.

"Anything interesting happen last night, aside from the usual vamp slayage?" Willow asked.

"You mean demony stuff?" Buffy asked.

"Yeah."

"Nope. Nothing like that. Just the usual. Fight, dust, brush off the clothes."

They filed through the cafeteria line, and Buffy got some mashed potatoes and so-called gravy, which looked more like slime from a mucous demon than anything edible. "And this is why I keep the world safe," she told Xander. He'd selected the too-perfectly-square chicken patty that for some reason was gray.

"It's a noble job," he answered.

They chose a table and sat down. Willow had somehow conquered the lunch line and emerged with a rather fresh-looking tossed salad.

"Hey!" Buffy said. "How did you pull that off?"

"I bribed the cafeteria lady."

"With what?" Buffy asked.

"Told her I'd help her with her homework."

"She's not in high school," Xander pointed out. "She *works* for the high school."

Willow took a bite of the crisp lettuce. "Night school," she said around the mouthful. "She's studying to be a dental hygienist."

"Maybe she feels bad about all the teeth the school food is ruining through malnutrition," Xander guessed.

"Probably," Buffy said, picking at her mashed potatoes with a spork.

"Good morning, all!" called a chipper English voice. Rupert Giles approached the table and pulled out a bright orange plastic chair. He sat down, the chair legs screeching on the floor as he drew the seat closer. "Oh, sorry."

It was a normal day.

Giles was the school librarian, so he could pull off the look.

"Hi, Giles," chorused the other three.

Buffy smiled at him. "Hey, Giles. What's up?"

"I'm not sure," he said, placing the books on the table. As usual, he wore head-to-foot tweed, gray today. He adjusted the wire-framed glasses on his nose and spoke quietly. "Something's going on. Apparently there have been some very interesting thefts of price-less artifacts. The police have tracked the thief to Sunnydale, though they haven't caught him."

"What artifacts?" asked Buffy.

"Well," Giles said, looking around to be sure no one listened, "I've been researching just that all morning. Both artifacts are reputed to have similar powers."

When he fell silent, Buffy prompted him. "What kind of powers?"

"Time travel."

"What?" chorused Willow and Xander.

"Time travel," Giles repeated. "The first artifact was the Blade of Madrigon, reportedly able to slice holes in the fabric of time and space."

"Holes you can crawl through?" asked Xander.

"Yes. Holes to the past. But supposedly you cannot climb back through once you've crossed over."

"Not very handy," said Xander.

"And the other one?" Buffy asked.

"Ah, yes. The other one is the Gem of Chargulgaak."

"The Gem of Whosamawhatsis?" asked Xander.

"Chargulgaak. Throughout the centuries, it was rumored to transport people forward from the past to the present."

"Sounds like the noise you make when drinking expired milk," Xander said. "So you'd activate this Gem of Garglegok and poof, there would be Einstein? Or poof you'd have Mozart standing in your living room?"

Giles regarded him sternly. "Well, perhaps not as easy as 'poof,' but in essence, yes. A person long dead could be brought to the future."

"Wouldn't they stink if they're long dead?" asked Xander.

"No, Xander," Giles said impatiently. "You would bring them forward from a time when they were still alive."

"Oh, gotcha."

"So why would someone want to steal these two thingies?" Buffy asked.

Willow faced her. "Imagine their power if they were brought together. You could open a hole to the past, climb through, then use the Gem to return to the future."

Giles looked at her proudly. "Exactly."

"And you think some beastie here in Sunnydale wants to use it for evil? What if it's just an eccentric art thief? Or it could be someone collecting them for the purposes of good," Buffy added hopefully. In reality, she wanted to spend the evening at the Bronze with Angel, instead of doing recon work.

"Buffy, how many times has a rare stolen artifact been brought to Sunnydale for the purpose of cheering up denizens of retirement facilities, or finding homes for sad little puppies?" Giles asked her.

"Oh. Yeah. Good point." She glanced around to make sure no one overheard. "So where do I start?"

Giles related a news item he'd found earlier in the library. "The police traced the Gem to a warehouse near the Bronze, then lost the trail. Perhaps you could start there? Do a little reconnaissance after school?"

"Bronze. Sounds like a plan," Buffy told him.

"Wonderful." Giles stood up. "Now I'm going off campus for lunch."

"You're so evil, Giles," Buffy said, convinced now more than ever that her "mashed potatoes" were actually the excretions of a potato demon. Maybe it was a teeny tiny potato demon, who right now was actually living inside the viscous mound of white mush.

"Yeah," Xander agreed. "You're supposed to be one of the good guys, helping us fight the forces of evil."

"Yes," Giles said, cocking one eyebrow defiantly.

"And I'm about to go fight the forces of evil at a nice little French bistro I noticed on my way to work."

He turned and left the room, waving good-bye over his shoulder.

Buffy looked down at her mashed potatoes and waited for the potato demon inside to install cable in his little mashed-potato hut.

Later that afternoon, as soon as dusk hit, Buffy set out. After two and a half hours of creeping through cemeteries, sewers, caverns beneath Sunnydale, and an endless series of warehouses in the Bronze district, Buffy had learned nothing. However, she had overheard more useless vampire gossip than she ever cared to. She dusted most of those she came across after listening in. Who knew the undead could be so boring? Most of them didn't know any good dirt at all. Especially nothing having to do with a gem or a knife. She even questioned some of them directly when she didn't overhear anything of interest. At first they were always swaggering and cocky. By the end, they quivered and pleaded. But none of them had heard anything about the stolen artifacts.

So then maybe some kind benefactor *was* going to use them to save the lives of unfortunate puppies?

Giles was right. No way.

She needed more info.

As she walked down the street in front of the Bronze, she heard a thud, and suddenly quick footsteps closed in on her. She whirled around. Angel stood before her.

"Hey," he said.

"Hey." He looked stunning, all darkness and mystery. *Play it casual. Don't let him see that your heart is fluttering out of control.* Willow was right. He was gorgeous. Tall, with short, dark brown hair and expressive eyes, he dressed completely in black, with a billowing trench coat. It wavered in the slight evening breeze. He looked the part of a hero, a warrior. And he was one fine kisser.

"Going to the Bronze?" he asked.

"Yeah. Giles had some hunch about these two stolen artifacts, but I've dug around everywhere and haven't found anything remotely related."

"You mean the Gem of Chargulgaak and the Blade of Madrigon?" Angel asked.

Her mouth almost fell open. She didn't let it. "Yeah, you heard about those?"

"It's why I was coming to see you."

Buffy felt a pang in the pit of her stomach. Oh. And here she thought it might have been just to see her. But he was in warning mode. She saw that now. A deeper furrow on the perpetually brooding brow. A slight downcast of the mouth. "What do you know?"

"A vampire named Lucien brought the two artifacts to Sunnydale. He joined them together to form a unique object, capable of—"

"Traveling through time?"

Angel gave a slight smile. "Yes."

"And his insidious plot?"

"To travel back in time and kill a Slayer."

"Why?" Buffy asked. "She'd already be dead."

"But he wants to murder her before her natural death."

Now Buffy's brow furrowed. "What would that accomplish?"

"It would mess up the Slayer lineage. Different Slayers would activate at different times."

She still didn't get it. Sounded more like an Ethan Rayne chaos plot.

"Buffy, he wants to keep you from being activated as a Slayer. That way, the Master will rise."

Her head started to hurt. "He can do that?"

"Yes. If he destroys the natural progression of Slayers, you won't be the Slayer when the Master rises and opens the Hellmouth."

"But won't whoever is the Slayer still stop him?" she asked.

Angel shook his head. "Not necessarily. The alternate Slayer could live in Zimbabwe, for all we know. Or she might not be able to defeat him. It's a problem, Buffy. You've got to stop him."

"How did you learn this?"

"Oh, the usual. Slinking around sewers. Lurking in warehouses. Keeping my ear to the graveyard dirt."

"Where is this Lucien?"

"In one of the caverns under Sunnydale, near where the Master was trapped. I tracked one of his lackeys to a fork in the tunnels but lost him afterward."

Buffy took a deep breath. "Okay. I'm going to call Giles and tell him this. See what he can dig up on the time travel capabilities of this new artifact. In the meantime, will you show me where you lost the minion?"

"Of course."

She sighed. No Bronze tonight. Just an evil plot to foil. But Angel was with her. Things could be looking up.

As they walked, Buffy leaned a little closer to Angel, taking in his scent. "Which Slayer are they going to kill?"

"I don't know. The bits and pieces I overheard were never that specific. Mostly just boasting, would-be assassins bragging that they were going to kill a Slayer."

"So they could choose any Slayer, in any time period in the past?" she asked.

"As long as it's before you were alive. That's all they need to do to alter the Slayer lineage."

"This is pretty insidious." Briefly she entertained the notion of an alternate future in which she was just a normal girl who could lead a normal life. Someone else would be the Slayer instead of her. She could have a conventional dating life, and her boyfriends might not get killed by rampaging demons at all.

Of course, would she have Angel then? And would she move here to Sunnydale? She would have had no cause to burn down the gym that got her kicked out of her former high school. She would never meet Willow or Xander or Giles. But she'd have fewer bruises.

Then again, she sort of liked saving the world from time to time, and Angel was right. The alternate Slayer might not even live in this country, might not learn about the Master until it was too late. Or worse, she could even get killed by the Master. Buffy did, after all.

They stopped at a pay phone, and Buffy called Giles at his place. She described the newly forged artifact and Lucien's plot.

"Insidious," Giles said.

"That's what I said."

"I'll see what I can dig up on this Lucien character. I may end up at the library later for some of my books."

"Okay, Giles. I'll come by there after I do a little recon with Angel."

"Be careful, Buffy. We don't know anything about this new player. He could be very dangerous."

Across town, deep under the streets of Sunnydale, Lucien got a paper cut and cursed. He tried folding the incantations again with one hand, bringing his egregiously wounded finger to his mouth.

"Our fearless leader," Victor remarked to Jason. Jason snickered.

"Shut up!" cried Lucien. He finished folding the papers, straightened his ascot, and smoothed his lapels. He looked like a character straight out of *The Importance of Being Earnest,* Victor thought. Didn't he know a Slayer would stake him on sight for being so out of date in his fashions?

Now composed, Lucien handed one copy of the papers to Victor, and one to Jason. "It's very important you hang on to these," he told him. "These are the incantations that will transport you back and forth through time."

"I remember the drill," Victor said impatiently. How many times had he endlessly traipsed through time while Lucien spoke one incantation after the other, honing their landing spots and times?

"This time it's different," Lucien snapped. "It's going to be dangerous in these places. These Slayers are active and trained. We're not killing them while they're still children. All of us may perish. Keep this copy of the incantations in case I am unable to speak them."

"You mean if you get dusted."

"Or toasted," Jason sneered bitterly.

"I've told you a million times I was sorry about that!" Lucien said in exasperation. "But yes. In the event of my death, you must continue on. I've written the incantations out phonetically. You have your copies, and I have mine.

"Now. First we go to Wales in 60 C.E. I've chosen appropriate clothing for all of us so we can blend in. I've worked and worked on this spell, so we're going to land right on the Isle of Anglesey. That was a tough one to calculate. Very tough. It took a lot of hard work."

Neither Jason nor Victor provided the compliment he was fishing for.

"Right. Let's change. We leave here in an hour," Lucien told them.

"You sure we'll land at night this time?" Jason asked. "I don't want to risk a repeat of becoming a Tater Tot."

Lucien threw his arms up in frustration. "You

know I can't promise that. It's not that exact. I run the risk of daylight too, you know." He stormed around the cave, fuming. "Why do I have to work with people who don't appreciate the subtlety of time travel and its alternate future capability? That is what this entire endeavor centers around!"

"We can appreciate the subtleties," Victor assured him. "We just want to avoid your errors."

Jason snickered again, and Lucien ordered them out.

As Victor left the cavern room, the incantations crinkling in his pocket, he shook his head sadly. How did he end up with such a wiener as a boss? It was downright dispiriting.

He and Jason meandered to their quarters, two little rooms off the main cavern that Victor had decorated with some stolen antiquities. On his bed rested their outfits. Two woolen tunics, woolen leggings, leather boots that laced up the front, and two heavy woolen capes.

Victor hated wool.

It itched. It was heavy.

Jason followed him in, eyeing the outfits. He picked up the moccasin-like boots. "No way, nohow. I'm not wearing these things."

"We have to look authentic."

"I don't give beans for authentic. I haven't taken off my lucky combat boots for fifteen years."

Victor looked down at his friend's feet. The combat boots, once black, were now worn, the brown leather beneath showing through in a dozen places. Jason had sewn and resewn the soles in place countless times. They smelled only slightly better than a compost heap on fire.

But he knew that Jason's insistence on wearing them would annoy Lucien, so he encouraged his friend to do so.

In their separate rooms, they dressed quickly, anticipating the hunt. They rejoined each other and checked their knife holsters. Victor had lovingly sharpened and oiled each blade to perfection.

They returned to the rooms beneath the crypt. Lucien was already in a similar outfit. Instantly he sized them up. "What are those?" he asked Jason impatiently, pointing to the boots.

"Those are my lucky combat boots."

"Well, they aren't historically accurate."

"Screw historically accurate," Jason countered. "They're my lucky combat boots. You can either live with that or send Gorga."

Lucien sighed. As much as Jason annoyed him, his intellect was a step above Gorga's. No. He would use the monstrous vampire only as a last resort, if all of them failed. "Very well," he said. "It's time to leave."

Angel stopped at a fork in the tunnels. "This is where I lost him."

Buffy bent low, looking for recent scuff marks in the cave floor. There were too many to count. "Looks like Free Burger Wednesday at the Doublemeat Palace. Dozens of people have passed by here. These passages are definitely being used for something."

They took the left tunnel, walking along a narrow passageway. The cave floor lowered, forcing them to bend as they walked. Buffy felt along the rough stone wall for any sign of a hidden door.

"We're under the cemetery right now, aren't we?" she asked Angel.

"Yes. Under the west side."

His underground geography was a lot better than hers, but then again, she could move around on the surface at all hours. Angel wasn't so lucky.

The tunnel ended at a large cavernous room. A dozen other passageways led off from there. They backtracked to the fork and took the passage on the right. Again Buffy felt along the narrow cavern walls for a ledge or crack, anything that might pass as a secret door. She found nothing.

They emerged into the large room for a second time. "I can see why you lost him."

Angel looked up at the ceiling, then around at the various passages snaking off into the distance. "I don't think he made it as far as this room. I would have seen him, whichever tunnel he took. I ran straight through the left tunnel and emerged here. He was nowhere in sight, and I'd been right behind him."

"So then back to the search for the secret passageway." They turned around, facing the tunnel they'd just taken.

Suddenly a bright light flashed out, blinding Buffy. She brought an arm up to shield her eyes. At first she thought it was a powerful flashlight. It played over the cavern walls. Then she spotted a crack in the tunnel wall. The light squeezed through that tiny space. It coursed blue, then silver, dancing in the dust kicked up from their movement.

It pulsed, then vanished.

Buffy raced to the spot, feeling again along the wall. Her fingernails slid into a barely perceptible crack. She traced the line of it down to the ground, then along the floor and up the other side. A small piece of rock slid to one side as her fingers grazed it. With the grinding of rock against rock, a square door scraped inward. The flicker of torchlight illuminated the room beyond.

Buffy entered, Angel behind her.

No one waited in the small room. One of the walls was brick, the others the limestone of the cavern. Tables littered with notes stood along three of the walls. A worn chair sat before one of them, next to a pile of Watcher journals. She leafed through them. Next to the journals lay a piece of thick parchment paper. An inscription was scrawled on it, in some strange language Buffy didn't recognize. There were numbers, though, and she read those: "60 C.E."

"Look at this," she said to Angel.

He joined her, peering at the paper. "Looks like they picked a Slayer. But I don't know what the inscription says."

"No," she said, pocketing it. "But I know someone who will." She continued her circuit of the room, gathering up any other notes she found. The rest of the material was books, charts, and magickal symbols. She'd have to bring Giles back here.

She stared at the walls, the floor, and the ceiling.

Nothing here could have created that play of light on the walls. *Magick?* she wondered. She moved to the brick wall. "This looks like a foundation," she said, peering up.

"Maybe there's a mausoleum up there," Angel agreed.

"The flash of light . . ." Her voice trailed off.

"Yes?"

"Do you think that was the assassins leaving?"

"You mean in a portal?"

She nodded.

Angel's face turned grave. "We need to get to Giles."

Chapter Six

At the library, full research mode was under way. Buffy and Angel strode in, greeting Willow and Xander at the large center table.

"You guys are here late," Buffy said. She glanced at the clock. Eleven p.m.

Willow gave a slight nod to Giles's office. "Apparently we don't need sleep."

Xander sighed and leaned back in his wooden chair. "Or social lives." He threw his pencil onto the table, where it rolled to a stop.

Giles emerged from his office.

"What'd you find?" Buffy asked him.

Her Watcher walked with a heavy book in his hand, thumbing through the pages as he moved. "It's all quite fascinating," he said. At the center table, he placed the book down, then referred to another one lying open beside it. "Very fascinating."

"Share, Giles."

"There is a record of a vampire named Lucien who hails from the fourteen hundreds. He was a master sorcerer, capable of the most advanced incantations. Not only could he perform spells and enchantments, he could create them."

Buffy pulled out the piece of parchment from her pocket. "Like this?" She handed it to Giles. She told him about the books and charts they'd found in the little room, and about the bright flash of light that could have been a portal.

He studied the note. "Oh, my."

"What is it?"

"Just a moment . . ." Reading the note and walking at the same time, Giles climbed the short flight of stairs to the upper stacks. Moments later he emerged again with a large, dusty volume. He read a few pages and returned to the table. "Oh, my."

"Oh my what, Giles?" Buffy urged him.

"He's created an incantation to go with the newly forged artifact. It's written in an obscure Akkadian dialect. There are two spells here. One will transport the user and his companions to Wales in 60 C.E. The other will bring them back here, to the present." He put down the parchment, then hurried into his office. Buffy heard file drawers opening and shutting, then a brief silence. He emerged, thumbing through some Watcher journals. "60 C.E., 60 C.E.," he mumbled, searching the pages. "Ah, here we are. The Isle of Anglesey, 60 C.E. The Slayer then was Incinii, a fierce warrior who defended her homeland not only from vampires, but from invading Romans." He looked up from the text. "She must be the target. We must stop them before they leave!"

Angel stepped forward. "It might be too late for that."

"What do you mean?" Giles asked.

Buffy cleared her throat. "We think the assassins already left in that flash of light."

Giles nearly dropped the journal, then looked at his watch. "Any moment now, history might change around us. If they succeed, the Slayer lineage will be disrupted, and the time line forever altered. We could all cease to exist at any moment."

"How do I stop them?" Buffy asked.

Giles looked down at the spell. "We must follow them back in time."

"Right on!" Xander yelled, leaping to his feet. "Time travel!"

Willow smiled too, excited at the prospect.

Buffy had a bad feeling, and Angel brooded next to her.

Giles turned to Willow and Xander. "I don't think it's a good idea for either of you to go. This could be a very dangerous endeavor. And time travel could be tricky—anything we do could forever alter the future. You could step on a beetle and cause a plague to wipe out all of Europe."

"What, like the butterfly flapping its wings in

Central Park and causing a hurricane off the Eastern Seaboard?" Willow asked. She liked chaos theory.

"Exactly," Giles said.

Xander shook his head adamantly. "Oh, no way. I'm going. You guys will need an expert in time travel."

"Your expertise," Giles said bluntly, "comes from Arnold Schwarzenegger and Michael J. Fox movies."

"And that's bad?" Xander challenged.

"Oh, dear."

"Giles, look," Buffy said. "I could use all of your help. Who knows what I'm going to come up against in these places?" After a modest pause, she added, "I didn't exactly study a whole lot of history. I could get burned at the stake or something."

"That's no fun," said Willow. "I hate when that happens."

"Wait, wait," Angel interrupted. "What about this artifact? We don't know where it is."

Giles held up a finger, then pushed some books around on the table until he found the one he wanted. "Aha! This is what I learned about the power of the Gem of Chargulgaak. It does not travel through time itself. It acts as a marker, left behind in the present."

"What does that mean?" asked Xander.

"It means," Giles continued, "that Lucien would have to leave it here in Sunnydale in 1998 when he journeys back in time. It would be the only way he could return."

"So then we find it and steal it?" Buffy asked.

"You didn't see it in the chamber?" Giles asked.

Buffy shook her head.

"That's strange. . . ." He took off his glasses, placing one stem in the corner of his mouth, then removing it. "Why would the artifact not be there? It must be there!" He paced around the room, then sat down on the table corner.

"Could he have hidden it?" Angel asked.

Giles shot to his feet. "Of course!" He snapped his fingers, then replaced his glasses. "He would have to hide it. If someone stole or destroyed it while he was gone, it would be disastrous." He met Buffy's eyes. "And we don't even need to find it to use this spell," he finished.

"What?" Buffy asked, bewildered.

"We know it's here in Sunnydale in 1998. Lucien would have to leave it behind." He waved the parchment. "If we use this incantation to travel back in time and stop the assassins, we, too, will return to Sunnydale in 1998. As long as it's here somewhere, we don't need to actually possess it to travel backward in time."

"This whole thing is very confusing," Buffy said.

Willow stood up. "No, I see what he means, Buffy. We just piggyback onto Lucien's spell. We say the incantation and poof, we travel back to 60 C.E. Then we speak the return incantation and we come back to Sunnydale in 1998. The artifact has to stay here."

"Wouldn't the assassins already have beat us to the Slayer?" Buffy asked.

"No," Xander told her, starting to get it all. "We need to think four-dimensionally." He pointed at the incantation. "As long as we use the same incantation, we enter at the exact same point in time as the assassins. They won't have a time jump on us at all, no matter how much earlier they left today. Even if they left last week, we'd still arrive at the same time. Like in *The Terminator*, Reese and the Terminator leave at different times, but arrive the same night—"

Buffy cut him off. "So we speak this incantation?"

Giles read it over. "We can give it a try."

"And we come back to 1998?" she asked suspiciously. "Not to Cro-Magnon times when I'm going to have to fight off pterodactyls for my food?"

"Would you wear one of those little deerskin bikini things that—," Xander began, but stopped abruptly when Angel cleared his throat.

"It should work," Giles assured her.

"I don't like 'should,' Giles."

Xander walked over to her. "Like the 'should,' Buff. Embrace the 'should.' This is time travel. A once-in-a-lifetime adventure."

Willow and Giles waited for her, eyebrows raised.

She stared at her friends, then exhaled. "Okay," she said. "When do we leave?"

Giles excitedly paced again. "We'll need supplies. And period clothing."

"We could raid the drama club's storage closet," Willow offered. "It's Saturday. They won't notice anything missing for a couple of days, and we'll be back by then, right?"

Giles again read over the spell. "We should be back only moments after we leave."

"Moments?" Buffy asked. "How many moments? You mean Angel and I could have stuck around and grabbed this guy when he returned?"

"Perhaps," Giles said.

"But wouldn't that mean that he would have been successful?" Willow asked. "Wouldn't their coming back mean they'd killed the Slayer, and then everything would be different?"

Giles regarded her gravely. "You may be right, Willow. The sooner we leave, the sooner we'll be outside of time ourselves. Right now, if they returned successful in their mission, we could all suddenly disappear. At the very least, Buffy may not be the Slayer. At the worst, the Master would be in power."

"We need to leave now, Giles," Buffy said, her stomach turning sour. "Will, go raid the drama club's closet. Xander, help her. We go now."

Twenty minutes later they rendezvoused in the library, all wearing clothes from a recent production of *Robin Hood*. The outfits weren't historically accurate, but the garments were heavy and woolen, with simple tunics, leggings, and capes. They were good enough on such short notice.

Giles, after practicing the incantation silently, realized it wasn't very specific about the time of day. They could arrive at sunrise, noon, or night. Buffy insisted that Angel stay there and dig up all he could on Lucien and his plot. Angel didn't like it, but he agreed.

He left the library and the four Scoobies gathered, with Giles in the center. He spoke the words aloud for the first time. A bright point of light fluttered into view in the air above them. The library shook. The bright point expanded, growing elliptical, and a wind kicked up in the room. The light swirled and glittered, the wind tugging at their hair and clothes. Buffy felt lighter and lighter, and then she sailed up through the air, her feet leaving the floor. Speeding toward the dizzying display of light, she held her breath and squeezed her eyes shut. Then, unsure of what lay on the other side, not even sure she'd live to see it, she hurtled into the vortex, careening backward through time.

Chapter Seven

Wales, 60 C.E.

Buffy felt her body decelerate suddenly. The brightness flashed and faded, spitting her out onto a sandy beach. She tumbled, landing against a large rock in the small of her back. Wincing, she looked up to see the vortex, spiraling in the air five feet above her. She rolled over onto her stomach, propped herself up on her elbows, and scanned the beach. No sign of the vamps at all. Giles said they would land at the same time. Was it possible they'd landed somewhere else? She tried to get up to run, do a cursory search, but her trembling legs gave out beneath her and she fell.

A flash of brightness pulled her attention back to the vortex. A dark figure appeared in the brightness.

Then Xander, screaming, launched out of the light and tumbled to a painful stop on the beach. Dazed, her head feeling more like a pillow than a place with a working brain, Buffy crawled to him. Two more silhouettes appeared in the light, and the vortex ejected Willow and Giles simultaneously onto the rocks below. Willow landed rolling, managing to somersault up and onto her feet, where she stood, blinking, looking as if any minute she might fall over again.

Giles landed flat on his face, hitting his head on a rock. He groaned, cradling his skull and curling up onto his side. Buffy fought the woolliness in her head. It was day. She had been right to leave Angel behind. If the vampires did land at the same time, they might be dust now. She peered up into the heavily overcast sky. Or maybe not. She scanned her surroundings, searching for the assassins to no avail. Then she spoke to Xander. "You alive?" she asked.

He groaned.

"Good." She looked over her shoulder at Willow. "Are you alive?"

Willow swayed on her feet, eyes fixed on the spot where the portal was. "I think so. But I can't feel my head."

"It's still on your torso. Trust me."

Buffy crawled then to Giles, who continued to lie in a ball. She peeled his hand away from the wound to find a small red bruise forming. It looked minor, with no blood. Poor Giles. Always getting hit on the head.

"Don't say it," he warned her, reading her mind. He rolled over, meeting her eyes. "I travel back in time to Roman-occupied Britain to face legionnaires and Druids, only to be done in by a rock."

"I think you'll live."

"Oh, good." Shakily he rose to his knees, holding his head again. "Anyone else feel like their head is full of sponge cake?"

Xander stood up on trembling legs. "I was going to say Ding Dongs, but that works too."

"Or matzo balls," Willow added. She slumped onto her knees.

"Giles, where are the vampires?" Buffy asked, rolling over on her back.

He scanned the beach, getting to his feet, his hands resting on his knees. "You looked when you first landed?"

"Yes. No sign."

"Interesting." He straightened up.

Her friends were up. Buffy knew she had to get up too. She tried to shake the gauzy feeling from her mind and slowly stood up.

"It's possible that Lucien worked out the time travel, but not the location travel."

Buffy narrowed her eyes at him. "What do you mean?"

"Well, the time magick may be very specific when it comes to what year we land in, but sketchier when it comes down to the location. The vampires may have landed at the same instant we did, but miles away."

Buffy scanned the beach into the distance.

"It's day, too," Xander pointed out. "Any chance they just went poof?"

Buffy looked up into the thick mass of roiling storm clouds above them. "I don't think so. These clouds would have protected them long enough to find cover. They would have smoked and been singed a bit, but I don't think we can count on total incineration."

On shaky legs, she moved to the nearest cluster of trees, then to a jumble of boulders, searching beneath them and in the darker places for any signs of hiding vampires. She didn't see any place that could have afforded them cover for long. Unless they went underwater.

She took in the scene before her. The beach behind them ended at a thinned tree line of oaks and pine, many of which had been cut down recently. Only a few still stood, thin ones. A misty rain began to fall, clinging to her hair in tiny droplets. In the distance a thin, gray column of smoke rose up behind a nearby hill. Buffy turned around. On the opposite side of this ruined forest lay a narrow strait and an immense island full of tremendous old-growth trees. Beyond that lay an enormous ocean. Buffy wasn't positive, but she was pretty sure they should be on the *island* part of the Isle of Anglesey.

"Where are we?" she asked, brushing dirt off her woolen leggings. Her outfit was so scratchy that she couldn't imagine how people could have suffered in it for an entire lifetime. She pulled her thick cape closer around her shoulders as her breath misted in the chilly, wet air.

Giles swayed a bit but maintained his balance. He stared at the island momentarily, then removed his glasses. After wiping mist away from the lenses with a handkerchief, he replaced them. Squinting for a full minute at the vast forest on the island, and then at the ruined one on their side, he said, "Oh, dear."

"What oh dear?" Buffy asked, alarmed that she might be right.

"It seems we've landed on the wrong land mass. If I'm not mistaken, we are on the mainland, and the Slayer we seek is on that island there." He pointed to the land across the narrow strait.

"So it's possible the assassins landed in a different spot from us because they used a different portal?" She felt her stomach fall. "Then they might be on the island, already hunting the Slayer."

Giles regarded her with a grim expression. "Yes."

"Except that they'd have to find cover until dark, no matter how overcast it is," Willow added.

"Good point," Giles said, still wobbly.

Xander eyed the waterway. "It's not that far. Can't we just borrow a boat from someone?"

"I'm afraid it won't be that easy. You see those ruined trees there?" He pointed at the cut forest. "That's a sure sign of Roman occupation. The cuts look fresh, too, meaning they're likely still nearby."

"Like sitting around that fire?" Buffy asked, gesturing at the column of smoke.

"Oh, dear."

Xander lifted his eyebrows. "So? We just ask them if we can borrow a boat, right?"

"Not unless we want to be decorated in our own entrails or set on fire."

"What?" Xander cried.

"The Romans wouldn't take kindly to us being here. We made a choice to dress like British common folk instead of Roman soldiers because we'd be talking to the Druidic Slayer. The Romans would just as soon cut us down as help us."

"Oh, boy," Xander said, then squatted down.

Willow glanced around, then sat down herself. "I don't like this. I feel so out in the open."

"Yes," Giles said. "We should get some cover. Perhaps we can find a boat along the shore. I suggest we move along what's left of the trees, searching the waterline."

"Sounds good," Buffy said, already moving toward the oaks. Her head felt less woolly, more cotton candy now.

In a silent row, they slunk along the trees, keeping watch for any sign of Roman soldiers. The beach lay deserted. No fishermen. No boats. Just lots of sand and some bleached white driftwood. Buffy hoped Xander was right about the timing of the incantation, that if they repeated the same words the assassins had, they'd be deposited at the same instant in time. That meant the vamps didn't have a head start on them. If anything, since they landed in the middle of the day, Buffy and the others had the head start. The assassins, if they survived the daylight at all—which Buffy thought was probable under the heavily overcast sky—would have had to seek shelter. That gave the Scoobies the advantage for now.

The rain, though slight, began to accumulate on

Buffy's woolen cape and tunic. A chill set in, and her teeth chattered. Frequently, she glanced back to be sure the others were okay. Willow was shivering more and more. Her fingernails were blue. Buffy wanted to find shelter, but she knew the vamps wouldn't be slowed down by wet or cold. The sky darkened in the east, and it grew increasingly difficult to make out the shoreline in the gloom. Still no boats. No people. The coastline was utterly deserted.

A half hour later, her leather shoes soaked completely through and her toes so cold she could barely feel them, Buffy stopped. Her wool clothes, utterly drenched now, felt five times their original weight, pulling down on her shoulders. Her back and shoulders ached. She turned to watch the others catch up with her. It was completely dark. Now that night had fallen, the vampires would resume their search for the Druidic Slayer. If they had landed on the island, they had a significant head start. Willow's lips looked dangerously blue, and she walked as if in a daze. She was the last to reach them.

"We need to make a fire and get warm," Buffy told Giles. "The more night sets in, the colder it's going to get."

"We can't! The Romans will spot any flame," Giles reminded her.

Buffy gestured at Willow. "Look at her, Giles! She's freezing."

Giles studied Willow's face. She was no longer shivering, a dangerous sign of the onset of hypothermia.

"What about that fire?" Xander asked, pointing through the trees.

Ahead the shoreline angled inward, and firelight flickered in the tree branches there.

Willow suddenly shucked off her cape, then tried to strip off her tunic.

"What are you doing?" Xander asked her.

She didn't answer, just flung the cloak down on the wet ground, baring her teeth.

Giles picked it up, stilling her hands. "Keep it on. It's wet, but it'll still keep you warm." He draped the cloak over her shoulders.

"Follow me," Buffy said quietly, and they crept forward. Giles fell back, making sure Willow continued to walk.

"It was stupid not to wear modern clothes," he cursed, putting an arm around Willow. She remained silent.

Slowly they crept closer and closer to the fire, pausing often and stepping on pockets of sodden leaves to muffle their approach. Now the shoreline came into view, and Buffy's eyes filled with Roman legionnaires. Five bonfires blazed, embers floating up into the night sky. Dozens of battle horses paced and whinnied. More than fifty boats bobbed on the water, tied to other boats that had been dragged up onto shore. The men paced, talked, checked weaponry, and gazed across at the island. It was clearly a massive military operation.

"Oh, dear," Giles gasped.

"Not 'oh, dear' again, Giles. Stop it with the 'oh dear.' What is it?"

"It seems we've landed at a most inopportune time," he whispered, drawing up next to her.

"These guys?" she asked, hooking her thumb at the soldiers.

"Yes. These guys. They must be the troops of Suetonius Paulinus."

"Sweet on us what?" Xander asked.

"Suetonius Paulinus," Giles corrected. "We've arrived on the same day that the Romans launched their largest, most destructive campaign against the Isle of Anglesey. Thousands of Druids were butchered or burned alive with their own torches."

Buffy stood speechless, gazing at the soldiers, then at the dark shape of the island across the strait.

"It looks like they're ready to launch the invasion within the hour," Giles went on. "They'd attack at night, of course."

Buffy narrowed her eyes at the shadowy island and could now see the faint flicker of firelight among the distant trees there.

"Wait, wait," Xander whispered. "So you're saying that we have to get over to that island while the Druids are made into crispy hash browns by the Romans?"

"It's highly likely," Giles told him. "We will have to steal a boat and arrive there at the same time as the invasion force. It's just the kind of chaotic cover we need."

Xander lifted his hand in protest. "Hold on, hold on. I am not going to steal a boat from a bunch of pumped-up Roman centurions."

"You don't have to," Buffy said. "I will." She eyed the bank, selecting the most shadowed part at the edge of the fires. Three boats floated away from the rest, tied to wooden posts in the ground.

"From what I remember reading about the invasion, some of the Roman soldiers forded the strait by swimming," said Giles.

Buffy looked poignantly at Willow, who still said nothing, staring down mutely at the ground. "But we can't do that, Giles. Willow can't get any wetter. We need to find her a fire. And those Druid fires across the way are going to have to suffice."

"We'll need to make them understand that we're here to help," Giles reminded her. "That may prove difficult."

"I'll leave that up to you, Mr. Linguist," Buffy said. "Now I'm boat bound. Wait here." She turned around a moment later. "Any chance my stealing these boats will mess up the future time line?" she whispered back.

Giles shrugged.

Not the usual Watcher prowess. She looked at Willow and realized that she had little choice. They couldn't swim, and every moment they spent dawdling here gave the vampires an advantage. With some soldiers swimming the strait, Buffy hoped the loss of one boat wouldn't alter the future too much.

She slunk off into the shadows, angling to emerge on the shore right next to the three boats. The men talked and laughed with one another, sometimes gesturing toward the island and exclaiming with upraised fists. Buffy couldn't understand a word of what they said. Giles would know, though. She crept forward slowly, a step or two at a time, pausing frequently to check the men, making sure none of them had turned her way or reacted to any noise she made.

Her shoulders and legs ached as she crouched and moved along. She thought of ditching the cloak, but wondered if she'd need it later. She kept it on just in case. Now she was only fifty or so feet from the boats and had to leave the quiet of the destroyed forest floor. The sandy beach stretched out before her, and she was grateful that the sand would absorb most sound from her movement. With the assistance of the din of Roman chatter and crackling from the bonfires, she stepped out onto the beach undetected, keeping just outside the edge of the firelight. Ahead lay the boats, now only thirty feet away. She moved more quickly now, glancing down the beach for an escape route in case they saw her. She'd lead them away from the others, down the beach, then cut into the forest again and hopefully ditch them.

But they hadn't spotted her yet, and now she was only ten feet from the boats. She eyed the stake and rope that lashed them to the shore. Buffy paused, glancing at the soldiers again. They continued to talk, poke at the fire, and check on their horses. They milled around restlessly, obviously awaiting orders to move.

Buffy reached the stake and silently untied the rope that lashed together the three boats. She walked a few feet to her left, pulling on the boats, hoping they floated free in the water and would be easy to tow. But they resisted, and she knew at least one of them was securely pulled up onto the shore. She turned to creep toward them, rope in hand, then stopped and pulled the wooden stake out of the ground and pocketed it. Could come in handy, and the Romans would be more likely to notice an unused stake.

Glancing at the soldiers again, she made sure they still took no notice of her. Then she reached the boats. Only one lay beached. The other two floated freely, bound to the first. She placed her hands on the cold, wet wood of the first and began to push it out into the water. It moved easily, and relief swept over her.

But just as it hit the water, it screeched on a rock and splashed loudly into the strait. Instantly the group of soldiers turned to her location, peering intently into the darkness. Then three of them took off toward her, shouting.

She had only seconds before they reached her. She leaped into the boat, teetered, and almost went overboard. Ducking down abruptly, she felt around in the bottom of the boat for an oar. Her hands closed around wet wood and she brought the paddle up just as the first soldier reached her. As he plunged into the water to stop her, she hit him hard across the face with the oar, knocking him flat onto his back. His friends reached him then, pulling his unconscious form out of the water.

Buffy thrust the paddle into the water and pushed off the bottom. Then she stroked with all her strength as the two other soldiers splashed out into the water in pursuit. One of them grabbed the edge of the boat just as she swung it around, and she stood up and slammed the hard edge of the paddle down onto his hand. He withdrew his fingers sharply, crying out in pain.

She began to paddle again frantically, gaining distance as the third soldier made a grab for one of the two boats she towed. She paddled farther out into the strait, alarmed to see a growing group of soldiers running to the assistance of the first three.

Now the third soldier grabbed solidly onto one of the towed boats. He threw one dripping leg over the side, then the other one, and he was inside the boat. Buffy continued to paddle, more interested in gaining distance between her and the growing mass of soldiers. She rowed hard, throwing her Slayer strength into it. She glanced over her shoulder. The Roman soldier in the other boat was reeling himself into her boat with the tow cable. He was only a few feet away. Buffy turned in her seat, raised the paddle, and sideswiped him over the edge.

He landed with a loud splash, and she returned to rowing. Now she looked back to the firelit shore and saw two soldiers getting into boats to pursue her. If more followed, she didn't know how she'd fight them all at once. She glanced along the beach in the direction where Giles and the others were and realized she'd lost her place. How far had she rowed? Was she past their location?

She turned and scanned the shore, then the banks of the island, looking for something familiar, something she had seen earlier and could use as a landmark. But the island was just a dark mass, with no detail at all except for the brief flickers of distant firelight.

She stopped rowing momentarily to check the progress of the pursuing Roman soldiers, a moment she dreaded. But they hadn't left the shore. They stood riveted to a spot on the beach. A man in gleaming armor stood before them, a red cape slung over one shoulder. He shouted at them angrily, then waved dismissively in Buffy's direction. The two soldiers climbed out of the boats and returned to the shore obediently.

Buffy turned and rowed a little farther, angling back toward the shore. She untied the other two boats, setting them adrift.

As she neared the shore, she heard Giles's voice whispering her name.

She rowed up onto the beach and stepped out of the boat to pull it onto the sand. "Over here!" she called, careful to keep her voice low.

Slowly three shapes materialized out of the gloom.

Giles walked with his arm around Willow, who stared at the ground.

"I got us a boat."

"I see that. Great work."

"Who was that guy on the beach in the cloak?" she asked.

"I believe it was Suetonius Paulinus himself, though I don't really know what he looked like."

"What did he say to them?"

"He told them not to waste their energy avenging a petty theft. They had to concentrate on the invasion."

"So this is the night," Xander said nervously.

"And here I was hoping to make it to eighteen."

"You will," Buffy assured him. She studied Willow. "Will?"

No response.

"We tried already. She's going into hypothermic shock," Giles told her.

"Then we need to leave now and get to a fire," Buffy said, taking Willow by the hand.

Together they moved toward the lapping water, steeling themselves for the boat trip. They were about to enter the stronghold of Druidism on the eve of invasion.

Chapter Eight

The boat glided silently toward the island, with Buffy's paddle making the only noise as it dipped into the water with each stroke. Xander found another paddle in the bottom of the boat and helped her make progress across the strait. She fought back the feeling of desperation struggling to rise inside her. Even now, the vampires could be killing the Druidic Slayer. They had to get across to the island fast.

The tide was moving out, making their progress easier, bringing them closer and closer to Anglesey. No doubt the Romans had the same plan. Buffy didn't know how long they had before Suetonius Paulinus attacked.

"Druids," Xander said thoughtfully. "Druids." He looked up at Giles as he rowed. "They're the ones who like trees."

"Yes, Xander, they like trees," Giles answered.

"And they built Stonehenge?"

"Well, actually, no, though they likely used it as a place of worship."

Xander's eyes widened. "Worship, yeah! Aren't they also the ones who commit ritual human sacrifice? I knew they were on my list of people I never wanted to meet."

Giles shook his head slightly. "Many ancient cultures practiced human sacrifice. The Maya, the Aztec—it was considered of vital importance. Besides, archaeological finds have produced many animal bones, but evidence for human sacrifice is far more scant on Anglesey."

"Scant? What about that guy they found a few years back? The one in the bog?" He dipped his oar in the water, propelling them forward.

"Lindow Man?" Giles offered.

Xander pointed his finger at him adamantly. "Yes. Lindow Man. Those bogs are bristling with bodies like that. Wasn't that guy ritually murdered in more than one way?"

"Three, to be exact. Bludgeoned, strangled, and throat cut. Plus, he was thrown into the bog, so that could count as four. Though he was likely already dead at the point, so you might not want to count drowning. Three was a sacred number to the Celtic peoples."

"Four different ways! Four! And he was one of their own, wasn't he? A priest? I'd hate to see how they treat people they don't like." He realized he'd stopped rowing and resumed.

"Many religious groups throughout antiquity believed self-sacrifice to be quite noble," Giles explained.

"Maybe, but I seriously doubt the guy killed himself four different ways. That would be a bit challenging." Xander's voice rose. "What if they don't take kindly to us just barging in?"

"Lindow Man was found in England," Giles told him. "This is Wales."

"Oh, and you think they're kinder, gentler human sacrificers over here? You don't think Mr. English Druid and Mr. Welsh Druid get together for tea and chat about the latest guy they killed four times?"

"Well, I hardly think—," Giles started, but he was cut off.

"When was this guy killed?" Xander pressed.

Giles hedged a bit. Took off his glasses. "Well, archaeologists estimate that he was killed around 60 C.E."

"60 C.E.! That year sounds familiar."

"Well, yes. But as I said before, Lindow Man was killed in England."

Xander paused, getting more and more worked up. "What if *I'm* Lindow Man?" he said at last.

"What on earth?" Giles asked, exasperated.

"What if the guy who was *supposed* to be Lindow Man changed places with me, and I am the one destined to be sacrificed. They could drag me over to England and *bang*."

"*Bang*?" Giles repeated. "Yes, I see. Well, that's hardly the case, because you're here now, aren't you?"

"Well . . . ," Xander assented, "I guess so. But time travel is wrought with paradox, my friend. Wrought." He watched a dark vortex whirl in the wake of his paddle.

"Boys," Buffy hissed through clenched teeth, "being quiet is an important part of sneaking."

"Oh, sorry," Xander said, reducing his voice to a whisper.

"Besides, ritual sacrifice is a religious rite," Giles went on quietly. "They wouldn't sacrifice just anyone at random. It's far more likely they'd suspect you of being a Roman spy scouting for the invasion and just outright kill you."

"Oh, great! Great! Way to be encouraging, Giles. And I suppose you'll just watch that happen, in your Watchery way."

"Shhhh!" Buffy told them again. "We're getting closer."

Scanning along the shore, she saw one section that lay relatively dark. No fires flickered between the branches. She pointed silently toward the area, nodding at Xander. He nodded back and helped her steer the boat in that direction. As they glided through the dark waters, the smell of salty sea air filling her nose, Buffy felt the blood thrumming in her ears. She didn't know what to expect once she was over there.

She hoped they'd be friendly, and that the few phrases Giles had learned would get their point across.

In the center of the boat, Giles sat with Willow, vigorously rubbing her arms in an effort to warm her up. Buffy put more strength into paddling, eager to get to a fire and to reach the Druidic Slayer before the vampires did—if she wasn't too late already. Images of the Slayer lying bleeding on the shore came unbidden into her head. She pushed the negative thoughts away.

As the shore came into view, Buffy saw a thick, dark grouping of trees—an excellent place to land in stealth. They were almost to the beach when Willow suddenly stood up, rocking the boat violently. For a second Buffy thought they were all going over, and she dug her paddle down, hoping to touch bottom. She did, and stilled the boat's motion.

"Will?" Buffy asked, turning in her seat to look at her friend.

Willow stared down at her with absolute hatred. "Shut up!" she yelled. "I don't want to hear a word from you!" Her voice thundered in the quiet of the night. Buffy didn't know her friend could yell so loudly, or sound so full of venom. Willow shrugged off her cloak as Giles tugged gently on it, urging her to sit back down. She reeled on him. "And you!" she shouted. "You thought I wouldn't figure out what you've been planning? You lured me out here to kill me!"

Xander leaned forward, pulling his oar up out of the water. "Will," he urged. "Please keep your voice down." He peered nervously at the shore.

"I will not!" she shouted. "You're all trying to kill me! Well, I won't let you!"

Before Buffy could lunge forward, Willow leaped overboard, landing with a splash in the dark water. Though it was shallow, she tumbled forward, and was completely submerged. She struggled, emerged, then managed to stand up. Without a glance back at the boat, she started splashing toward the shore.

"Giles?" Buffy asked, bewildered and scared that the Druids would suddenly learn of their presence.

"Hypothermia. It's one of the stages—delirium."

Buffy instantly began to row again, closing the last few feet to shore. Xander got into a crouching position, then jumped out and pulled the boat up on the beach.

As Buffy climbed out, she caught the briefest glimpse of Willow disappearing into the trees. Buffy moved forward silently, trying to follow, but a tree branch snagged on her cloak. She disentangled herself and moved forward again. She tripped on a root and went down hard on her hands, plunging into the cold mud and scratching her palm on a sharp rock.

She stood up, searching for a hint of Willow in the trees, but saw nothing but darkness up ahead. She crept forward again, this time checking her footing as she went. Behind her Giles and Xander cursed and crashed through the underbrush, making too much noise.

She turned to shush them but discovered they weren't there. Alarmed, she scanned the trees nervously. Where had they gone? And what had been making the crashing noise, then? Behind her lay only forest. She couldn't even see the shore, though she was sure she'd only progressed twenty or so feet.

"Giles!" she whispered.

No response.

"Xander, where are you guys?"

The wind sighed in the branches above.

She turned and pushed forward again, determined to find Willow and then plead with the Druids for a fire, even if she had to use English or draw stick figures in the mud of a shivering person and a warming fire.

Anything could happen to Willow out there in her delirious state.

Another root tripped her, and she pitched forward, barely keeping her balance. When she stood up, a branch tangled painfully in her hair, stopping her progress. She reached up, pulling strands free of the tree's hold. Then she continued on. Behind her the forest creaked and shuffled. Twigs snapped. Leaves rustled.

She spun around only to find an empty, shadowed forest behind her.

As she watched, the shadows shifted, moving from tree to tree. She whirled around. Dark forms beneath the trees darted away, out of sight, sliding along the forest floor and winding up the trunks of trees like shadow snakes.

Buffy steeled herself. This place was not going to spook her out. She was going to find Willow and the others. Then she was going to kick some vampire butt and be home before the Sunnydale Mall closed.

She pushed forward, moving tree limbs out of the way, shifting her eyes between the ground and the distance, searching for Willow. The wind in the boughs sighed more loudly, whispering over her head. Just as she looked up again to scan for Willow, she ran into a low tree limb, which struck her in the thigh. The branches caught in the wool of her cloak. She paused to yank the cloak free, and watched as shadows spilled down the sides of the trees around her, then advanced alarmingly fast, spreading over her.

Coldness hit her skin, and she backed away in a moment of unthinking fear. Then she wrenched the cloak free and started running. The trees bent and swayed, branches swinging down on top of her, catching under her arms, in her hair, snagging at her back. Root after root tripped her, and finally she went down hard, in a mossy patch. Darkness swept up over her and she flipped over, ready to kick her attackers.

Hands emerged from the ferns, arms from the undergrowth, lifting her up, up, until she stood, spitting dirt out of her mouth. And then the shadows stepped closer, dissolving into human form. Eight cloaked figures stood in a circle around her. They all wore medallions with the symbol of a tree.

"Look," she said. "I don't mean to hurt you. Unless you're evil," she added. "Then I probably do." She thought they might be Druids, though. Where was Giles?

They whispered to one another in a language she could not understand, pointing at her clothes.

Some decision made, they drew in closer, taking her arms, and pulled her toward the firelit section of the island.

"Wait!" she said, wondering if she should beat all of them up to escape. But then she decided that wouldn't go over well later, especially not while Giles tried to convince them she was there to help. "I had three friends with me! One of them is sick."

They regarded her with unmoving faces, clearly members of the Stoic-Villains-of-the-Month Club. Why did cloaked people always have to look so grim? Would it kill them to smile, or laugh at a good pun once in a while? Of course, Buffy herself rarely laughed at a pun, usually preferring to groan, especially if Xander was the perpetrator. Where was he?

As they dragged her toward the bonfires, Buffy craned her neck around, searching the woods for any sign of her friends. "Too bad I don't speak Druid!" she shouted for Giles's benefit, in case he lurked nearby. "Having a translator sure would be helpful in the land of cloaks over here!" When there was no response, not even a rustling of shrubbery, she added, "Well, off I go to the ritual sacrifice!"

Images of a wicker man on fire and her inside it flickered into her head. She forced them out and let the strangers lead her onward.

They meandered through the trees, which were quite well behaved compared to earlier. No branches snagging her clothes, no limbs in her hair. She imagined an eerie picture—the obfuscating Druids standing alongside her path, lowering twigs and branches into her way. Had they been there all along, hidden in shadow?

The flickering of a fire grew brighter and brighter, casting light on the trees around it. As they grew closer, the fire dissolved into four separate bonfires. Figures surrounded the fires, at least fifty people in robes, tunics, and cloaks.

And in front of the fire, with new dry clothes, sat

Willow. She shivered now, a good sign, Buffy knew. It meant her body was warming up.

Standing up behind her were Giles and Xander, listening to the woman who appeared to be in charge of the group. Giles nodded, and then Buffy was within earshot. Everyone looked up as she and the druids approached.

"Ah, Buffy," Giles said, walking over to her. "Are you all right?"

"Am I all right? How long have you been here?"

"Since we first landed. These people were kind enough to escort us over here."

"And the trees didn't . . ." Buffy could feel the immense oaks towering over her, weighing down on her.

"The trees didn't what?" Giles asked.

Buffy's voice felt tiny in the shadow of those ancient sentinels. "Nothing."

"Buffy! Hey!" Xander called as she approached. He gave her a little wave, grinning. Grinning a little too much. He was stuck in perma-grin, that expression he got when terrified on the inside and pretending to be brave on the outside.

"What's wrong?" she asked when she drew nearer.

"Nothing. Nothing," Xander said through clenched teeth. "Just keep smiling. Let's just hope that Giles here is getting through to them." He gave a little nod in the direction of a grouping of gray stones at the edge of the firelight. Something thick and red gleamed there, pooling in a small recess in the rock and spilling down the side of the forest floor.

Buffy did her best *probably nothing* shrug. "It may not be human."

"It's the 'may' part that bothers me," Xander said, still grinning like mad and nodding at the gathered Druids.

Giles resumed his conversation with the woman, who nodded and pointed down to the shore, where still more bonfires gleamed in the darkness. Buffy didn't know what they were speaking. It didn't sound like Latin. She didn't know what Druids spoke.

Giles gave her a slight bow, then joined them. "Fascinating!" he said. "Just fascinating!"

"What is?" Xander asked. "How long we've got before we're gutted as a sacred sign of worship?"

Giles shook his head. "No, Xander. Remember what I said about there being no archaeological proof whatsoever that the Druids practiced ritual human sacrifice on Anglesey."

"No proof? Before you said 'scant' proof."

Giles went on. "All we have supporting it is the Roman writing, and that could just be propaganda to make the Druids look even more the fearsome foes that they undoubtedly were. Besides," he added, taking off his glasses and cleaning the left lens, "even if they did, they wouldn't sacrifice just anyone. It would have to mean something."

"Oh," Xander said, his voice momentarily cracking into a falsetto. "That's no more reassuring now than it was the first time I heard that gem of Giles knowledge."

"So what else did you learn?" Buffy asked. She regarded her Watcher in the flickering light. He looked tired.

"Well, the language is quite difficult. I tried several, wanting to avoid Latin, of course. I'm sure they speak it, but under the circumstances, I don't think they'd react well at all to strangers showing up using the tongue of the Roman army. I spoke a bit of a Goidelic ancestor of modern Gaelic. I think they understood. They seem to be quite multilingual. Then I tried a variant of Old Welsh I know a little of, and that seemed to do the trick. At least I think they understood me best when I used the more proto-British dialects . . . ancestors of Welsh, Cornish, and Breton——"

"Giles," Buffy said firmly. "Point."

"Ah, yes. I asked them about a powerful girl who lived on the island, someone who fought——"

Xander interrupted, holding up a protesting finger. "Hey, I thought Slayers were supposed to keep their vocation secret."

"Well, yes. They are. If someone found out the identity of a Slayer, the vampires would hunt her tirelessly. That's why I kept it vague."

Buffy narrowed her eyes at him. "You? Vague?"

He ignored her barb and continued. "I asked her about a girl who fought unusually strongly, perhaps with almost supernatural strength."

To their left, four men and a woman began chanting, holding thin branches. "And?" Buffy prompted him when he grew distracted.

"Oh, yes. She said the girl lived farther down the shore this way, and a bit inland."

"Can one of them show us? We need to get to her

now. Every moment we waste here . . ." She let her sentence trail off.

"I could certainly ask."

"Tell them she's in danger and that you need to get there quickly."

"I will," Giles told her. "But they have their hands rather full with the upcoming Roman invasion."

"They know?" Xander asked.

"Indeed. They have spies on the mainland watching the Romans even now."

Xander nodded in appreciation. "Neat. Intrigue."

While Giles returned to the woman to talk, Buffy knelt down beside Willow, wondering if they should leave her by the fire. "Willow?" she asked.

Her friend looked up sheepishly. "I'm really sorry, Buffy," she said quietly. "I don't know what got into me. I could hear and see myself, and it all made sense at the time."

Buffy stroked her back reassuringly. "Giles said it was the hypothermia."

She pointed at the nearest Druids with her chin. "It's a good thing they found me. I was streaking through the trees, screaming. It was really weird."

"Did the trees . . ." Again she felt the weight of the dark forest at her back.

Willow raised her eyebrows. "Did they what?"

"Never mind."

Giles returned, and Buffy stood up. "They have a man who can lead us to the girl's cabin. She lives there with an older woman. Perhaps it's her Watcher."

Buffy turned to the woman and gave a little

bow in thanks. The woman nodded. "Let's go."

Xander hesitated. "But what about Will?"

Buffy turned to her friend, deciding. "Stay here with her, Xander. I don't like the thought of splitting up, but Willow doesn't look good. I don't want her getting worse."

Xander's eyes filled with fear. "Are you crazy? I'm not staying here." He grasped Willow's shoulder. "*We're* not staying here. I don't want to be a large order of Xander Fillet with fries on the side!"

Willow touched his hand. "They're okay, Xander. I know it. We'll be safe." Then she turned her head toward Buffy. "But won't you need us?"

"Don't worry. We're going to fight vamps. I've done this a hundred times, and I don't want to worry about you."

The guide joined them, a stately-looking man with a long face, long brown beard, and a braid that hung down to his tailbone. On his arms he carried two dry cloaks, which he handed to Buffy and Giles. They nodded their thanks.

As they turned to go, Xander called, "Don't speak that thingy without me! Don't leave us here. I miss my comic books. I miss central heat. I miss pie."

Buffy readied for the dark forest to swallow her. As she walked away, she turned one last time to see Xander sitting next to the fire, his arm around Willow protectively. Two Druids were staring at him, perched on nearby rocks, and Xander reached out with his free hand and patted the trunk of a nearby tree. "Trees good. Love the trees. Love Druids," he added, pointing at them.

Buffy hoped he didn't get them all killed.

• • •

For what felt like hours, Giles and Buffy followed the guide through the forest, following no visible trail from what she could see. Now and again the guide paused to consult the trees. He stopped at a huge oak, and later at a tremendous pine, staring up into their branches, as if navigating by the trees' location. Each time, he consulted the moss on the trunk, the way the branches hung, then chose a direction.

Buffy felt bad about leaving Xander and Willow behind. Normally, she was relieved when they weren't with her in battle. But in this strange place, nearly two thousand years before their own time, she felt odd and out of place. Anything could happen to them back there by the fire. Though she felt she could trust the Druids, she worried that the Romans would attack now and close in on her friends' location. They could be murdered as collateral damage of the invasion.

As she plodded through the dark and quiet forest, moving more and more inland, her nervousness only grew. What if this whole trek through the woods was for nothing, and the woman they found was not the Slayer at all? Even if she was, what if they were too late? The vamps could have landed on the island and killed her by now. Buffy hoped the Druidic Slayer wasn't caught unaware, or distracted by the imminent invasion of the Roman forces.

As they crept farther and farther into the dark forest, Buffy once again felt the uncanny and eerie sensation that the trees surrounding her were alive. Of course, she knew they were alive in a plantlike kind of way, but this was more of a locomoting kind of way. They groaned and creaked, sighed and bent, their branches waving and lowering, raising and brushing against one another.

Her back burned as if hundreds of eyes dug into it, wooden eyes, ancient eyes. Unconsciously, she moved a little closer to Giles. "You feel it too?" he asked.

Buffy nodded, relieved that her Watcher also sensed it and that it wasn't her overactive imagination. Usually he believed her, even if he didn't sense anything himself. But occasionally, like the last time they had to deal with something creepy and wooden, namely a ventriloquist dummy, he hadn't believed her at first. But that had all turned out okay.

But that was just one creature made of wood.

This was an entire forest, and it moved around them, shifting and moaning.

Soon she smelled burning wood, and a small cabin came into view. Out of a narrow chimney curled a long column of smoke. She didn't think she'd be so cavalier as to burn wood on this island.

The guide moved forward, signaling for them to wait outside. He knocked on the door. A woman in her thirties answered, looking weary. The guide exchanged brief words with her and then nodded, waving them forward.

Inside the small cabin, Buffy finally started to warm up. She stood next to the fireplace, reveling in its heat. Giles spoke with the woman, growing more and more excited as he did. Buffy couldn't understand a word. Was she the Slayer?

Finally Giles looked up to her. "She's a Watcher," he told her. "Her name is Eyra."

"Hi," Buffy said, giving her a little wave. She was younger than Giles, looked a little less stuffy. Buffy wondered what she was like as a Watcher. "So where's Incinii?"

"This will probably sound quite familiar to you," Giles said, "but she's disobeyed her Watcher and moved to the front lines to help ward off the Roman invasion."

"Hey, I hardly *ever* ward off Roman invasions," she countered.

Eyra said something to Giles in what sounded like Latin.

"She says we can catch her if we leave right away. She'll be with the group of warriors on the northern-most part of the resistance front. She has a brother among them." Just as Buffy was finally getting warm, Giles stood up. Eyra explained something at length to the guide, pointing out into the forest. Then the guide made a short bow to Giles. Buffy waited for Giles to explain. "He's going to take us down to Incinii. We don't have much time."

"We never do," Buffy lamented, feeling a little sorry for herself. How many times had she passed up perfectly good shoe sales because she had to avert the apocalypse? How many school dances had she missed because some archvillain or another was ascending to power? Okay, maybe just the one, but still, her dress got totally ruined and she didn't get to dance at all. Now it was back to the creepy forest with no time to sit by the fire. Why couldn't this Slayer have lived in Hawaii? Or hey, maybe Fiji?

Seeming to read her mind, Giles said, "C'mon, Buffy," and waved her toward the door. He shook Eyra's hand warmly. Man, Giles was such a Watcher geek. Always wanting to swap notes with some other Watcher so he could see if Buffy was really as ill-behaved as he thought she was. But she did kick ass. And that was what was important.

And now she had some serious assassin vamp ass to kick.

"Can't she come with us?" Buffy asked.

Giles waved good-bye as he left. "She's waiting for an important communication. Once the beach falls under attack, she must get word to a nearby encampment."

Buffy looked over her shoulder as the door shut. It must be hard to sit home and wait.

They began retracing their steps back through the forest, but as they neared the shore, their guide branched off in a new direction. He turned and said something to Giles, then stooped low. Giles did the same, motioning for Buffy to follow.

"He says that the war party is just over that rise," Giles whispered, motioning to a small hill. "He's going ahead to find the Slayer."

The guide crept stealthily forward.

"Can't we go with him?"

"He says they're using magick up there, and he's not sure how it would react to our presence."

"That sounds ominous."

"Indeed. I suggest we wait here."

Buffy nodded and sat down in the wet, leaf-strewn dirt. She leaned against a tree. She peered up at the branches crowding out the sky. She played with the hem of her cloak. Time passed. The guide did not return.

"Giles, I don't like this." She rose to a crouch.

"Neither do I. Perhaps he had difficulties finding her."

"Or perhaps he ditched us," she offered.

Giles furrowed his brow. "I don't think that's the case. More likely the Romans have attacked, and he felt the need to stave off their advances."

"Or was killed."

Giles peered through the gloom toward the small rise. "Or that."

"I should check it out." She stood up, shaking the pine needles and leaves out of her cloak.

"Let's not separate here," Giles said anxiously. "I imagine getting lost would be enormously easy in this forest."

"Yes," Buffy answered, feeling the trees press in on her. They were listening. She knew it.

Together they crept toward the small rise, seeing the gleaming of firelight on the trunks of nearby trees as they approached. Soon they could hear murmuring, chanting, and then the slow, methodical slosh of paddles in water. As they crested the hill, a startling sight lay before them.

A circle of Druids stood to their left, hands raised

to the heavens. They chanted around a stone altar. Blood pooled in a carved-out recess, glistening black in the weak firelight. They wore rough, brown woolen robes and had blue spirals painted on their faces, arms, and hands. Long beards hung to their chests and navels. At the base of the hill gathered too many Celtic warriors to count, leaning on spears, gripping swords, stringing bows. Men and women alike stood in leather armor and metal plating over their chests and thighs. Buffy took in faces, arms, and legs painted with woad, a blue dye derived from a plant. Through these tense warriors shifted strange and eerie women with long, free-flowing hair and billowing robes. They wove among the fighters like snakes, slithering and passing between groups, touching a shoulder here, a head there.

The sloshing of boats grew louder, and Buffy strained to make out anything on the black water. With the dying storm had come calmer winds, and the surface of the strait lay glossy and black. Suddenly that stillness broke, and a line of turbulence on the surface stretched as far as she could see.

The Romans were crossing.

The strait came alive with a flotilla of flat-bottomed boats like the one Buffy had stolen. Loaded with men, the boats drew closer. She heard more frantic splashing and saw an entire row of horses swimming alongside the boats—the cavalry attempting to bring their mounts into battle. The men swam next to their horses, struggling under heavy armor.

Mere moments had passed since Buffy and Giles crested the hill. As the Romans approached, a rank of archers lined the bank and fired volleys of arrows. These hissed through the air, felling men in boats and splashing into the water when they missed.

Then the Romans gave up their silence and a single, voluminous roar rose up from their masses. Cries of rage and fear masked as bravado filled the silent night.

The Celts answered with a chorus of wild cries, whoops, trills, and shouts. More arrows cut the air, raining down on the Romans. The first boat reached the shore, and armored legionnaires poured from it, thundering across the beach to the Celts.

The battle had begun, and Buffy and Giles stood in the middle of it.

Chapter Nine

At once, the Romans leaped from their boats into the shallows, drawing their swords. Hundreds strong, they streamed onto the shore, shouting. The Celtic warriors rushed forward to meet them.

Buffy's mouth went dry. Raw battle unfolded before her, a cacophonous mass of voices and clashing weapons. To her left she heard the circle of Druids chanting, the sound increasing in volume. They lifted their heads to the sky, calling out, imploring. The trees swayed around them. Wind lifted the branches, sighed, and then roared in the leaves.

And then Buffy realized—it wasn't the wind at all.

The trees themselves moved, lifting earth-covered roots from the soil. Snaking their way forward, the branches bent and swayed, closing in on the Roman invaders. The forest hissed and sighed. She took a step back, taking it all in, her mouth parting in astonishment. Her heel bumped against something solid and cold. She reached back and felt the reassuring solid mass of a granite boulder. Then it, too, shifted beneath her hand. The rough stone rotated and moved forward. She spun around, staring at it. The rock unfolded itself, lifting a stone head and bringing forth two massive stone arms. Leaning forward, the boulder pulled itself from the earth, sending soil and ferns spilling down the sides of the little rise. The stone was an ancient monolith, covered beneath centuries of dirt. The tip she had felt with her tentative hand was merely the very top. It continued to burrow out of the earth until it stood up, towering thirty feet above her. The lower stone parted into two massive legs. With a single step, it moved twenty feet off the rise, the ground shuddering beneath it.

Giles gripped her arm tightly. She turned to him as he pointed to a neighboring small rise. Another tremendous stone winnowed its way out of the earth there, soil raining off it as it emerged. Buffy had witnessed vampires crawling out of the dirt countless times. This sight left them all behind. The rocks broke and split along their masses, forming arms and legs and tremendous stone heads with fearsome eyes that gleamed red in the darkness.

The tree warriors closed in, now batting Romans off the beach as if they were made of straw. As a third stone creature joined the first two, the Romans froze, gazing up in horror.

On the beach, the women with long, flowing hair screamed and ran, cloaks streaming out behind them.

At their passing the Celtic warriors worked themselves up into a frenzy. They rushed forward, stabbing the centurions and legionnaires while they stood in shock.

Buffy watched in awe as Roman after Roman stumbled and fell, not even fighting back. The sheer spectacle of the sight froze them to the spot.

Next to her the Druids chanted louder, their cries growing all the more intense and eerie.

On the beach, the same Roman commander she'd seen earlier stepped from a boat. His long red cape billowed behind him. He shouted at his men in Latin, shoved them and forced them into action. Some stumbled beneath his blows, others shook their heads slightly, then raised their swords once more. He strode through the ranks, yelling and berating his men. At once the invasion force came to life. Screaming, the Romans ran inland, clashing with the Celtic warriors.

The tree warriors crashed down heavy limbs upon the Romans, while the stone creatures crushed centurions into the soft mud of the shore. Buffy took in the chaos, the clashing warriors, the screaming, the women running with torches and inciting the troops, the forest come to life to protect its human denizens.

"How in the world are we going to find the Slayer in all this?" she shouted to Giles over the din.

"We need to find our guide. He knows what she looks like."

She looked down at the mesh of struggling bodies at the bottom of the rise. "And how do we do that?" she asked helplessly. Even as she said it, though, she caught a glimpse of a dark green cloak below. At the edge of the fighting, closer to the forest, their guide engaged in heated conversation with a young woman dressed in leather armor and coated with woad. He pointed to the top of the rise where Buffy and Giles stood. She followed his gaze, taking them in. Immediately she wheeled back around, shouting again at the guide. Shaking his head adamantly, he gripped her shoulders, and she shoved him away.

"That's got to be her!" Buffy yelled. "Come on!" Grabbing Giles's arm, she took off down the hill in the direction of the Slayer. But before she reached the bottom, two figures emerged from the clashing warriors. Dressed in cloaks and woolen tunics, at first Buffy thought they were other Celts. But then she noticed the footwear of the second. He wore twentieth-century combat boots.

As Buffy raced down the slope, her feet sliding in loose mud, the two figures reached the Slayer. In the din of combat, the girl did not notice them, just continued to argue with the guide. As Buffy shouted for her to turn, the vampires closed the distance.

Buffy slid and stumbled, righted herself, and sloshed desperately through the oozing mud. As it sucked at her feet, pulling one of her boots off completely, the closer vampire rushed forward. He pulled out a dagger and buried it deep in the Celtic Slayer's back.

Chapter Ten

Pulling her feet free, Buffy raced to the other Slayer. Incinii's eyes went wide, and she fell forward into the guide's arms. The two vamps spotted Buffy, astonishment on their faces. One actually shook his head in disbelief. She'd half expected them to run away. They'd murdered the Slayer, and Buffy had failed. Now their expressions changed. They looked at Buffy with hatred and contempt, arrogantly believing they could kill her, too.

But just as she reached the spot, she saw the Celtic Slayer stand up again, wheeling angrily on the two assassins. Quickly the guide readjusted Incinii's leather armor straps across her back. One of them had blocked the blow, Buffy realized. Incinii was far from murdered. The guide pointed to Buffy, shouting at Incinii above the cacophony around them.

Incinii nodded at her and circled the vampires warily to join Buffy at her side. Clasping Buffy's forearm in greeting, she grinned and said something incomprehensible. Then both of them turned to face their enemies.

Now, with two Slayers bearing down on them, the assassin vamps didn't look so bold. They started to back away, eyes darting around to spot possible escape routes. Another stone warrior emerged from the darkness. The vampire in combat boots shuddered slightly as the creature stepped clear over him to reach the beach. His face contorted in fear, and he looked at his partner, eyes wide.

"Don't freak out on me, Jason!" said the other vamp, seeing the look in his cohort's eyes. "Let's just get this done." Then he turned to Buffy, his eyes sharp and keen, his body ready to fight. "I've killed you twice before," he said to her, "and I'm going to do it again."

"Thanks for volunteering," she told him. "I wasn't sure which one of you losers to dust first." She sounded brave, but inside, his words hit hard. What did he mean? Had she herself been one of the Slayers they tried to kill? She swallowed hard. Had they tried to kill her when she was just a kid? What had gone wrong?

"Victor!" Jason cried nervously, interrupting her thoughts. "This isn't the best place to fight!" He leaped back as a group of Celtic warriors crashed into him, struggling with three Roman centurions. A tree limb swung down, connecting with one of the Romans' helmets, opening it with a crack. Buffy saw blood spray over Jason. He blinked it out of his eyes, regaining his balance. "We're going to get squashed!"

"Just kill the Celtic Slayer. Finish our mission. That's all," Victor ordered him, not taking his eyes off Buffy. Jason raced forward to join the other vampire.

"Can't we take this fight somewhere else?" Jason shouted. "I have a bad feeling about this."

In her peripheral vision, Buffy took in the chaos around her. Off to her left, she spotted Giles crouching in the dense foliage. She hoped he wouldn't get himself squished. Beyond them, toward the beach, bloody bodies tangled and clashed. War cries and trills resonated in the air. Arrows whined and hit home. Swords clacked sharply against shields. Men screamed in agony. One boulder creature waded out into the dark waters and drowned the Romans as they tried to land.

It was not the best place for a personal fight. The vamp had a point.

But then Victor raced forward, bending low at the last minute and sweeping his leg out. His foot caught Buffy in the knee and she turned quickly, deflecting much of the blow. He leaped upright, thrusting his palm out and connecting with her chin. She reeled backward, struck a tree. Using it as a brace, she kicked him hard as he closed in again, connecting with his solar plexus. He bent over, gripping his chest. Buffy jumped up, grabbed hold of a branch, and swung, kicking Victor in the face with both feet. He stumbled backward, crashing down into the mud.

Next to her, Incinii struggled with Jason, who despite being scared was doing a damn fine job. Too good a job. He pinned Incinii against a boulder and produced a knife from inside his cloak. As Victor turned and threw a kick, Buffy leaped over his leg, landing next to Incinii. She struck Jason hard on the arm, then grabbed it and wrenched it around, snapping it at the elbow. The knife tumbled to the forest floor.

Incinii kicked him hard in the stomach, then picked up a jagged shard of wood from the ground. Strong arms clenched around Buffy's throat from behind. She slammed her foot down into Victor's instep, grabbed his arms, and flung him harshly over her shoulder. His head cracked against the boulder, leaving a smear of glistening blood behind.

He stood up, feeling the blood seeping from his scalp. "That hurt, Slayer!" he shouted.

"Good!"

Again he pulled out his knife, the one he'd stabbed Incinii with. "Let's end this!"

"I couldn't agree more," she retorted, glancing over at Incinii. She stood on top of Jason, who lay prone in the mud, spitting pine needles out of his mouth. She arced the wooden stake in the air, and then Victor rushed to meet Buffy. She snapped her head back to him, dodging out of the way and tripping him as he passed. He leaped back up, recovering more quickly than she expected, reeling and striking her hard in the kidney. She caught the flash of steel, saw the knife zipping in, and then the earth shuddered and rose up beneath them. They rolled, falling into the dirt.

The boulder with Victor's blood rose upward, two great eyes blinking open, taking them in. As Buffy struggled to stand up, a mouth rose into view, full of sharp stone teeth. Then a pair of massive shoulders, followed by a thick torso. The earth heaved up again, sending Buffy and Victor tumbling down the rising slope.

A few feet away, Jason threw Incinii off him, rolling over on top of her. She kneed him in the chest, flinging him away, and he slid down the loose mud. The stone creature emerged fully from the earth, glaring down at Jason. The vampire did not notice. Instead, he righted himself at the bottom of the slope, found his fallen knife, and marched angrily back toward Incinii.

A tremendous stone foot crashed down on him, pulverizing his bones. When the massive weight lifted, Buffy saw a disgusting tangle of flesh and splintered bone. Incinii jumped up, wiped mud out of her eyes, and drove the stake deeply into the mess. Dust billowed around her as she struck the heart.

Incinii looked up at the stone creature and grinned.

"Damn you!" Victor cursed, suddenly staggering to his feet. "Jason!" he shouted.

He dashed forward to his fallen comrade. Dust settled in the massive footprint, the only sign of his friend. Victor wheeled on Incinii, his eyes enraged. "Now I kill you for myself!" he shouted, rushing toward her.

A shadow fell over him as the tremendous stone creature raised its foot again.

Victor stopped short. He stared up at the massive rock, then back at Incinii. With one long glance at Buffy, he turned and ran full speed into the mass of clashing warriors. Buffy tried to follow, muscling her way through, but she heard Giles calling to her, urging her to return.

She pulled out just as a spear narrowly missed her. It wouldn't be the smartest thing to charge into the battle.

She ran to where Incinii stood, and Giles joined them. "We need to track the assassin on the other side of the struggle," he urged them. "We can't possibly fight our way through that. We'd surely be killed."

They stared at the continuing battle before them. The massive stone warrior stepped out onto the beach, joining its friends. "Let's go!" Buffy shouted, running along the edge of the skirmish. She hoped they could pick up Victor's trail on the other side.

Suddenly another vampire burst out of the bushes, closing in on the fleeing assassin. "Victor!" the emerging figure shouted. "Don't leave without me!" Buffy continued chase. A few minutes later a bright flash of light brought her eyes to the sky. A vortex appeared about a mile away, spiraling and brilliant. "They're going back!" Giles shouted.

"You mean that's it? They're giving up?"

"Apparently. For now."

Incinii stared at the dizzying vortex. She asked Giles a question, which he answered at length. Buffy couldn't understand a word. She didn't like this. Who was the fleeing figure who'd stayed out of the fight altogether? The elusive Lucien? And why would they give up like that? Sure, their fellow assassin had died, but it didn't make sense to come all the way back here and then give up—unless he was planning on coming back at a different time. He was definitely outgunned this time. But they'd made the decision in an instant, and left so quickly. Why not bide their time to kill her in the same visit? It didn't make sense.

Unless, she thought. Unless this was only *one* of his stops.

"He's going to kill another Slayer," Buffy said, turning to Giles. "We've got to follow him!"

Giles stopped, searching her face in the darkness. Incinii stood silently by, glancing back toward the battle.

"You think they've targeted more than one Slayer?" he asked.

"That's got to be it. They must have more options. They have all of time. They can travel anywhere, to any time period. Right now, another Slayer is about to die. We've got to stop them!"

Chapter Eleven

As the portal tugged at their hair and clothes, Victor took a final glance around ancient Britain. Once again, he'd lost his best friend. What was the point of Lucien saving him, only to lose him in the next time jump? Lucien and Victor readied themselves for the trip back to 1998. This wasn't the kind of travel Victor preferred. Too nauseating.

"What do we do now?" Victor asked above the roar of wind.

"We kill the next Slayer."

"What about Buffy?" Victor asked, curious about Lucien's reaction. "She knows about this."

"We can't be certain that she knows about the others. My guess is she stumbled onto our hideout and took the primitive version of the spell for 60 C.E."

"You left that lying around?" Victor asked, incredulous.

"It was a rough draft! It didn't even land us on the island, remember? When we tested it out, it put us on the Welsh mainland. Besides, it's the only spell I left there. She doesn't even know we've targeted more than one Slayer."

"If she knows where the hideout is, she can catch up to us there," Victor pointed out.

"We have no reason to go back. We have the incantations." Lucien patted his jacket. "You've got a copy too, and so does Gorga in case we fail."

"That ought to be rich." Victor thought of the three-hundred-pound slab of meat with the battle-ax.

"We just move on to the next Slayer. There's no sense returning to a time period Buffy has the incantation for. We'd just be fighting her over and over."

"Sounds like fun," Victor growled, eager to fight her again.

The portal gained in intensity, lifting them off their feet. Together the assassins vanished into the future, ready to kill again.

Chapter Twelve

As the vampires' portal faded in the distance, Giles gathered his thoughts, formulating a plan. "Okay. Right now we need to regroup. It's important we not think of time as our enemy. We don't have to rush. We can think this out. No matter when they've targeted another Slayer, we have time to return to 1998 and figure it out."

"But, Giles! They could be killing her right now!"

Giles gripped her shoulder. "No. They are killing her in another time period, just like this one. We will find out when, and arrive at the same time as the assassins, just as we did this time."

"It makes my head hurt, Giles."

He looked at her reassuringly. "Let's go find Willow and Xander and return to 1998."

"Right. Okay. We do a little recon work, find out

where they went, and follow them. How will we find Lucien? We only have the one spell."

"Are you sure there were no others in the cavern room?" Giles asked.

"Positive. I collected every scrap of paper in there."

"Then he must be keeping any other incantations on his person," Giles surmised.

"So how do we find him? Wait in that little room? He'll notice that I've been there, or that someone's been there, anyway," she pointed out. "He might move to another location."

"When we return, we can have Angel put surveillance on the room. If they move, we'll know."

Buffy agreed. It made sense.

Giles turned to Incinii, speaking to her urgently. She shook her head, pointing back toward the battle, then launched into a lengthy monologue, which Giles asked her to repeat twice.

Buffy followed as they turned around, heading back toward the beach. Giles explained as they walked. "I believe I understood most of her response. I told her we needed to rejoin our friends, whom we left back by a bonfire. She responded that if her Slayer duties were finished for tonight, then she must rejoin the battle. She will help us find our guide, and he will lead us back."

They walked a little farther in silence, Incinii turning to smile apologetically at Buffy. She saw something in the Celtic Slayer's eyes—a kind of age, wisdom, and deep sadness. Buffy realized she was lucky in comparison. She definitely had issue with living her teenage years dusting vamps in graveyards and slicing the heads off demons. But while Sunnydale was certainly under continuous attacks by the forces of darkness, at least it was not also under attack by marauding invaders. She briefly imagined what Incinii must feel, torn between defending her home against an invading army and simultaneously fighting off the usual vampires, praying mantis women, and mother Bezor demons. Incinii must get close to no time to shop. And Buffy also imagined she rarely felt safe. Even when she'd spent an evening slaying, Incinii contended with the looming threat of Roman invaders. Plus Giles had told her that Incinii had struggled with the night terror demon for years, a creature Buffy herself had faced. The beast repeatedly took over Incinii's body while she slept. She couldn't rest peacefully. For her, it never ended.

As they hurried back toward the battle, Buffy watched Incinii straighten, then check her armor clasps, her short sword and bow. She was a warrior, made for battle. Unlike Buffy, though, she seemed to be eagerly anticipating the conflict. Even now Buffy caught her smiling, awaiting the fight before her. Buffy didn't enjoy fighting, didn't enjoy killing and destroying things, even when they were evil. The day she did enjoy it would be the day she lost something integral to her soul.

The clashing of swords on metal grew louder, and then Buffy could hear the screams of pure agony and terror. When they crested the rise once again, she sucked in her breath in horror. The Romans had lit the Celtic warriors on fire. Everywhere she looked, figures bathed in flame raced to and fro, shrieking in anguish. The Druids who had been gathered in a circle no longer stood there. Buffy couldn't make them out in the chaos. One of the stone creatures had fallen, lifeless, onto the beach, and Roman archers climbed it to fire arrows from higher ground.

The smell of burning hair and flesh hung heavily in the air, and Buffy felt her gorge rise in her throat. Incinii screamed in anger and lifted her sword high. She rushed down onto the warfield, trilling out a battle cry. She struck down one Roman centurion, then another, driving her sword deep into their bellies and throats. As she waded into the combat, she threw down burning warriors and smothered flames with their fallen cloaks. Wheeling, she dragged a Roman cavalryman from his saddle and viciously slit his throat. When Buffy last caught sight of her, Incinii was mounting the stolen horse and riding into the thick of the battle, striking downward with her sword.

This was a different world. Completely foreign. Buffy couldn't imagine killing other humans and was glad she didn't have to defend her homeland like this. As the firelight flickered on the glinting, bloody armor of the Romans, Buffy stood utterly still. The screaming around her grew so intense it almost felt like it came from inside her own head. Men and women on fire shrieked and panicked. Romans stole torches and lit the forest on fire. Another stone giant toppled, and a tree creature ground to a halt. The Druid magick was not holding together. The Romans broke their circle, and now, with flames licking at the trunks of trees, they desecrated the sacred forest.

"We need to leave," Giles said, "now!"

"But, Giles," Buffy argued, shocked at the horrific scene before her. "We can't just go—these people need help!"

Giles grabbed her shoulders, forcing her to look at him. "Buffy," he said firmly, "this happened a long time ago. I know it feels very immediate right now, but all this happened more than two thousand years ago. These events unfolded just as we see them now."

"But, Giles!" she pressed, watching a woman dive into the dirt, desperately trying to quench the flames engulfing her hair.

"We must go. These events have to occur as they did historically. We can't interfere, or we're no better than Lucien. Besides, if we change the sequence of events, we could even make this worse."

"It doesn't feel right!" Buffy insisted.

"I know it doesn't," Giles agreed, looking around him. "But the two of us couldn't do much good here anyway. The Romans are just too powerful, too many in number. It's why they won."

He turned her away from the scene, forcing her to move off the rise, down the slope. "What about Incinii?" she asked.

"She'll be fine," Giles reassured her. "She's one of the longest-lived Slayers. She lives through this night. She lives a long time."

Feeling hollow and haunted, Buffy allowed Giles

to lead her into the quiet of the forest. "I don't think we're going to find our guide," he said. He peered into the forest. "And I don't know about you, but I don't think I'd be able to make my way back to the bonfire where we left the others."

Buffy stared in that direction too. She thought of the meandering way the guide had led them. "Not a chance."

"We might be able to retrace our footsteps back to the cabin, though," Giles said. "Then Eyra can lead us to the bonfire."

Buffy thought of the trees, alive and sinuous, and dreaded returning to that crawling forest. She swallowed her fear and followed Giles into the darkness.

Chapter Thirteen

After only twenty minutes of stumbling lost through the forest, they spotted the flickering candlelight from Eyra's cabin.

"Oh, what a relief!" Giles sighed, unable to help himself. He didn't want to let Buffy know how nervous the willowy trees made him.

He rapped on the door, and in a few moments Eyra opened it hurriedly. Her expression visibly fell when he saw it was only them. "Did you see her?" she asked Giles in Old Welsh.

"Yes," Giles answered.

"And is she . . . ?" the Watcher's voice trailed off.

"She's fighting. And doing quite well the last time we saw her."

"Thank the gods for that," Eyra responded, letting

out a sigh of relief. "She is so stubborn. I ordered her not to fight, then I begged her."

"I know how you feel," Giles said sympathetically, with a sidelong glance at Buffy.

Eyra frowned. "But then again, I myself am involved. I just sent word to the other encampment. Now I must just wait here, hoping Incinii is all right."

Eyra then remembered her manners and invited them in. But Giles said, "Actually, could you help us get back to our friends? I'm afraid we lost our guide in the ruckus of battle." At least that's what he hoped he said. His Old Welsh wasn't exactly spanking accurate.

Eyra nodded. "I can walk you back there. The guide mentioned you'd been at Fendoch's fire."

"Thank you. It's time we left."

"And where exactly did you hail from?" asked Eyra.

Giles paused, unsure of what to say. Then he told Eyra the truth, that they'd come from a land on the other side of the world. As far as current archaeological evidence held, these people had not yet visited North America. Eyra marveled at his explanation. Giles decided not to mention the time bit." You must tell me about it!" Eyra said curiously, perking up for the first time since they'd met.

Giles agreed, hoping he wouldn't throw off the time continuum by talking vaguely about California. Eyra closed her cabin door, glancing hopefully one last time down the path that led from the beach. No sign of Incinii.

Then, with Giles describing the wonders of Sunnydale, they started off for Fendoch's fire.

Thirty minutes later Buffy and Giles arrived at the roaring bonfire where they'd left Willow and Xander. Eyra bowed, saying her good-byes, and melted away into the shadows. To Buffy's utter relief, her two friends still sat next to the flickering flames. Color shone on Willow's face. Her cheeks stood out, ruddy and healthy. Her lips were pink instead of blue.

"Buffy!" she cried out as they drew near. She leaped up and hugged her friend.

Xander stood up, squashing Buffy at the same time. "I'm so glad to see you! Can we get out of here now?"

Giles regarded the group hug sadly. "I was in mortal jeopardy as well, you know."

"Oh, Giles," Willow said, breaking away and hugging him, too. Xander just extended his Buffy hug until she pulled away. "So did you find the assassins?" Willow asked, turning back to Buffy.

"Yes. And killed one of them. But the other got away. And there was someone else, too, hiding in the shadows. He ran off too."

Xander raised his eyebrows incredulously. "You're kidding."

"Unfortunately not," Giles said. "And Buffy has a theory that this is only the first of a series of attempts on Slayers' lives."

"We have to get back to 1998 and figure out who the next target is," she explained.

"As long as we get off this creepy island," Xander whispered, glancing surreptitiously around at the nearby stones glistening with blood.

Giles motioned for them to follow. "I suggest we move away from witnesses before opening the portal," he suggested.

All four took turns bowing and thanking the Celtic warriors for allowing them the use of their fire. They smiled, grasping the visitors' arms in parting, but Buffy clearly saw the grayness beneath the smiles, the worries of the incoming Roman army. Once again she felt the pang of abandoning people who needed help. But Giles was right, she supposed. This wasn't their fight. It had been waged long ago without her help. Tonight would have to be no different.

Following Giles off into the dark of the forest, Buffy forced herself to go.

They gathered together, and Giles spoke the incantation. In moments the portal expanded into view, brilliant and swirling. A wind kicked up, sucking leaves and pine needles into the vortex. Buffy's hair whipped toward the spiraling light and then she felt drawn toward it, feet sliding in the mud. The force grew in strength, and she fought the urge to grab onto something. Her feet lifted off the ground and she careened headfirst into the vortex. Willow's hand found hers, and they screamed as their velocity increased. Just when she thought they would crash headlong into concrete on the other side, the speed cut down. Her stomach lurched. In the next instant the light dimmed and winked out, and they tumbled out onto asphalt. A car honked and swerved around them, its headlights blinding Buffy. She closed her eyes to the night. Willow landed on top of her, then Giles and Xander smacked onto the ground to their left.

As more cars braked and honked, Buffy forced herself to stand and drag Willow out of the street. They'd landed in downtown Sunnydale, she saw with bleary eyes. She staggered into the street again, grabbed Giles's foot and Xander's wrist, and dragged them out of harm as well. Then she collapsed on the sidewalk, nausea rising in her throat. From a club nearby, she could hear the distant strains of "One Week" by the Barenaked Ladies. They were definitely in 1998. Now they just had to find out who the next targeted Slayer was and dive into the dizzying wormhole once again.

She had to find Lucien.

She struggled to stay on her feet and failed. As she fell to her knees, a second blinding flash of light startled her. She closed her eyes against the brightness and felt another body slam into hers. She fell on her side. Whoever it was weighed a ton.

She rolled the person off her and turned to face him. She didn't recognize the man. He was a vampire. She knew that instinctively. His clothing style dated from at least the early eighteen hundreds, but they were new. His long brown hair was pulled back in a ponytail and affixed with a black ribbon. She grabbed him by the back of his neck, forcing him to his feet.

"Lucien, I presume?" she asked him.

The vampire whimpered. "Oh, damn."

Holding him, she looked up to the sky to see a second portal spinning just to the left of their own. Another vampire flew out of their vortex, landing near Giles.

Lucien twisted in Buffy's grip, and she slammed him against the alley wall. "You leave before us, and we still arrive first. Tough luck." He tried to throw her off. She stood her ground. "Don't make me dust you. You might live a whole extra day if you cooperate."

"How generous," he snarled.

Groggy, the second vamp rose to his feet. "Giles!" Buffy shouted. "Get him!"

Giles lay on the ground, shaking his head lightly. "Get whom?" he mumbled.

"The other assassin!" Briefly she thought of dragging Lucien over to Victor, trying to get them both. But she knew Victor was too good a fighter for her to pull it off. Lucien had stayed out of the action on Anglesey, which meant he thought himself too good to get his hands dirty in combat. Even now he only struggled slightly in her grasp. She could even feel him trembling beneath her grip.

"Xander!" she shouted. "Willow! Get him!" Victor chanced a look over his shoulder at the Slayer, taking in his boss's condition.

"Lucien!" he shouted. "Damn it! I can't always cover your sorry ass!"

"Go on without me," Lucien called back. "Just carry out the plan."

"Shut up," Buffy yelled, slapping her hand over his mouth and punching him in the stomach. He licked her hand, and she involuntarily pulled it away in disgust.

"Enlist help. You remember," Lucien reminded Victor.

"Yeah, yeah," Victor said, and darted away down the alley.

"Get him!" Buffy yelled again to her friends. "Or come guard this guy!"

Stumbling, Giles rushed to her side, pinning Lucien against the brick.

Buffy gave chase on unsteady legs, running through the dark alley. Ahead she heard a garbage can overturn, the crash of glass bottles rolling and shattering on asphalt.

He wasn't far ahead.

She picked up speed, her head swimming with the motion. Dizziness claimed her and she tripped, stumbled on a high crack in the cement, and righted herself. She ran on.

A dog barked, and she turned the corner in that direction. Ahead she saw Victor's fleeing figure. His wool cloak bloomed out behind him as he ran. He, too, staggered, still intoxicated from the vortex's effect.

At an intersection, he headed away from the graveyard, away from the entrance to the underground tunnels. He was trying to mislead her. But it didn't matter. She knew where the hidden room was. In time, Victor would realize that she knew it too.

He darted out of view around a corner, and she reached the spot a few seconds later. The alley was a dead end. She peered up, catching his fleeing shape jumping from rooftop to rooftop above.

Damn. She couldn't catch him now.

She tried anyway, running along the base of the buildings, but ultimately lost him in the maze of the warehouse district.

By now she felt completely putrid, and she stopped to catch her breath.

"Bad trip?" asked a voice behind her.

She spun to see Angel standing there. "Don't do that!" she told him, her heart hammering from the start he'd given her.

"Sorry." He came closer to her, took her in his arms. "You're wet."

"It was raining."

"I think I remember what that is," he said wryly. Buffy was glad she wouldn't experience a drenching like that in Sunnydale.

"Did you get them?" he asked.

She shook her head. "One of them. Caught another."

"That's something."

"Not enough. One got away. The worst one."

He put his arms around her. Kissed her forehead. He brought his hand up under her chin and lifted her head. His lips pressed against her, and Buffy felt the stress and tension of the trip spill out of her, replaced by a pleasant tingling feeling of excitement.

She kissed him back passionately.

Then she pulled away, keeping her arms around him. "How long were we gone?"

"An hour," Angel told her.

An hour? She couldn't believe it.

"I left the others back there with Lucien."

He raised his eyebrows. "He's the one you caught?"

"Yep."

"I'd like to meet the guy."

"I'd like to beat the guy," she retorted. "This way."

She led Angel back to the others, who now stood circled around Lucien, held firmly by Giles.

"Ah, Angel," Giles greeted him. "How long were we gone?"

"An hour," chorused Buffy and Angel.

"Wow, that's all?" Willow asked, amazed.

Xander regarded her knowledgeably. "That's the way it is with time travel. What's an eternity in one time period is a mere blink of an eye in another."

"Yes, Mr. Expert," Giles said blithely as Lucien struggled in his grasp. "Let's get our criminal mastermind here back to the library."

Lucien sneered at them in contempt. "What are you going to do with me?"

"Torture you," Buffy told him, narrowing her eyes on him. "But first . . ." She strode forward and frisked him, immediately finding the folded incantations in his jacket pocket. She opened them, then scanned the page. "Thank you," she said.

"Ooh, may I?" asked Giles, holding his hand out for the pages. She swapped with him, a handful of pages for a stranglehold on Lucien. Together they all marched toward the library.

At the library, Buffy pushed Lucien into the cage and locked it. It mainly held file cabinets, but it doubled as a handy lockup. Over time, they'd captured quite a few

people and left them in that same cage, Xander among
them. Last year he'd been possessed by a hyena
demon, and they'd locked him in there while they figured out how to cure him.

Now Lucien scowled on the other side of the cage
door grating. "This stops nothing," he told Buffy.

"Oh, I think it stops a great deal," she said, waving
the incantations in front of him.

His frown deepened. "If that's all of them."

Buffy bluffed. "Well, I have a feeling it is. Mainly
because you wouldn't reveal to me just now that there
were more if there actually were. You'd just bide your
time, hoping I wouldn't figure that part out. You
wouldn't just give it away. You may not look it, but you
must have a modicum of intelligence to have gotten
this far."

Lucien blanched at the insult, and Buffy knew
immediately that his intellectual ego would be a good
weapon to wield against him.

"I'll watch him if you want to talk," Angel offered.
He crossed his arms, staring in at Lucien threateningly.

"Thanks." Buffy glanced at the clock.

"You know, we have a little bit of time, and it
would be worth it to do things right." Giles told her,
noticing her anxiousness. "Whenever we leave for the
next jump, we'll still arrive at the same time as the
assassins. We can take a little time to eat something
and prepare for the next trip."

"Are you serious?" Xander asked, then turned to
his friend. "Will. Pizza."

"Definitely," she agreed.

"Great," Giles said. "You two bring us back food, pizza if it has to be," he said distastefully. "Buffy and I will plan."

They nodded and left the library, discussing toppings.

Buffy grew excited at the thought of food. She hadn't eaten in over twenty hours, and her stomach growled voraciously. She hoped they'd return soon with cheesy goodness.

"Giles," she said, gesturing with her chin at his office.

He nodded, and they entered the office. "Okay. What do we need to do?"

Giles opened his notebook where he'd translated the three spells. "There are three time periods here. A Civil War Slayer named Agatha Primrose, a Sumerian Slayer named Ejuk, and a Slayer named Marguerite Allard, who lived during the French Revolution."

"Civil War? French Revolution? Why do I have a feeling this is going to be even worse than Anglesey?"

"Because it probably will be," Giles answered. He glanced out of the small window in the door at the cage. "After all, getting caught in the crossfire of a war waged with guns will be far more dangerous. Lucien can survive gunshot wounds. We can't."

"I'd like to give him something pointier than a bullet and see if he survives that." Buffy glared at him.

"We need him alive for now," Giles reminded her.

"I know," Buffy said. "But I just want to stake that smug look off his face." She turned back to the translations. "So which Slayer do we save first?"

Giles leaned back in his chair. "It shouldn't matter, actually. Remember, we'll arrive at the same time as the assassins in all the time periods."

"Ack. I get it. So we just choose whichever one we want?"

"Essentially, though we may want to choose the French Revolution last."

"Why is that?" She sat down on the edge of his desk.

"We'll have to have proper attire for that—long pants, and specifically liberty hats and red, white, and blue cockades."

"Why?"

"So we don't get our heads cut off."

"Good idea. That would put a crimp in the plans."

"Indeed." He stood up. "Let's raid the drama department again."

"Giles! You're such a ruffian!"

He grinned. "I know."

In the costume closet of the drama room, they found some simple shirts, pants, and dresses made of light cotton and polyester. "I'm afraid none of these will do. The styles and material are all wrong," Giles said. He picked up a few headdresses and some earrings from a box of jewelry. "You could wear this, I suppose," he told her, handing her a headdress. Made of cheap, bronze-colored metal, it sported three flowers sprouting from the back of it.

She eyed it dubiously. "Is this authentic?"

"Well, not authentic metal, but the style is pretty

accurate. These come from that talent show act last year—the one where the students recited part of the *Epic of Gilgamesh*."

"The Epic of who?"

"Gilgamesh. He was a Sumerian king. He happens to be *the* Sumerian king in the era we're traveling back to."

She picked up one of the blue cotton dresses. It was made of old T-shirts, she realized. "And you don't think they'd buy this?"

Giles set down a shirt he was holding and regarded her resolutely. "Well, I suppose they'll more likely 'buy' this, as you say, than suspect we're actually time travelers from the future there to thwart an assassination on a secret Slayer of vampires."

Buffy held up the headdress. It was lined with tinfoil on the inside. "I'm not so sure. Isn't there some costume shop we can go to?"

Giles looked at his watch. "That's not a bad idea." Returning armfuls of the clothing to the closet, Giles chattered excitedly. "This really is quite fascinating," he told her over a mound of hastily sewn shirts. Buffy thought she spied some gold lamé peeking out coyly. *That* definitely wasn't authentic.

Back in his office, they thumbed through the phone book and found a costume shop that was still open. Willow and Xander returned with the pizza, which they all devoured with abandon. Even Giles ate a few slices.

Then he left her to brief the others and departed for the costume shop. Buffy dreaded the getup he would rent. Xander stood terrified, convinced his outfit would involve tights.

"They didn't wear tights in any of these places, Xander," Willow assured him. "We're not visiting an eighteenth-century court in Vienna or anything. We're going to look like farmers. Something subtle."

"Except that 'liberty cap' thing. That doesn't sound subtle. What is it?"

Buffy shook her head. "He didn't elaborate. It's for the best."

She frowned.

"What is it?" Angel asked, sensing her preoccupation.

"Something Victor said back there." She looked at them, lowering her voice so Lucien couldn't hear. "He said he'd killed me twice before."

"What does that mean?" Angel asked.

"That's what I wondered." She frowned. "Unless they've already been back in time and killed me."

"But they didn't. You're here," Angel pointed out.

Xander regarded her thoughtfully. "She's only here in this point in the time line. If they'd traveled back in time and killed her, she would have ceased to exist in the future, and she never would have known the difference."

"So what happened?" she asked Xander.

"It must have failed for some reason. They obviously didn't kill you, because you're here."

"But Victor said he *did* kill me."

"Well, maybe he traveled back in time afterward and

unkilled you, restoring the time line," Xander suggested.

"Why would he do that?" Angel asked.

"Maybe killing the Buffster didn't have the effect they were going for. Maybe things got worse."

"Of course things would be worse," Willow agreed. "Sunnydale would be hell on earth."

"Exactly," Xander said. "So they obviously failed, because despite its overly balmy temperatures at times, and its not so stellar nightlife, it is decidedly not hell on earth."

An hour later Giles returned, boxes of costumes in hand. Quickly they rummaged through them, selecting outfits.

Buffy chose a light blue linen dress for the Sumerian trip. Giles said linen would make them appear upper-crusty and educated. They'd have an easier time talking to people that way, he explained. Buffy didn't see how she'd be able to talk to anyone at all in ancient Sumerian. It wasn't exactly a foreign language elective at Sunnydale High.

They'd have to heavily rely on Giles, except during the American Civil War, to communicate their needs. She'd keep careful watch on him during the time jumps. No more hapless knocks on the head for Giles.

He gave them all simple cloth satchels, each filled with a pencil, paper, a bottle of water, and in Buffy's case, stakes. After putting on a brown linen dress with a fancy metalwork belt, Willow sat down at her computer. She called up the Internet, downloading several maps they would need: the Sumerian city of Uruk in 2700

B.C.E., Paris in 1792, and maps of 1862 Tennessee, near Pittsburg Landing, in the vicinity of that Slayer's farmhouse.

Suddenly she grew pale. "Oh, no . . . April sixth, 1862, Pittsburg Landing . . . I thought that name sounded familiar."

"What is it, Will?" Buffy asked.

She looked up. "The Battle of Shiloh. That's the morning of one of the bloodiest battles of the Civil War."

Lucien laughed inside the cage. "Have fun," he told them.

Giles scowled at him. "Be quiet," he ordered. He placed a gentle hand on Willow's shoulder. "Download battle maps. We need to know where the troops are, where the heavy combat occurred. We should be able to avoid the conflict."

"If you could control exactly where you land," Lucien sneered, "which you can't. You'll be instantly cut down by gunfire."

Willow's eyes grew wider.

"Or maybe just have your head blown off by a cannonball," he continued.

Buffy walked over to the cage, placing her hands on her hips. "Well, that would kill off your boys, too, wouldn't it?" she asked.

Lucien shut up.

She turned back to her friends, taking in their Sumerian costumes. Xander wore a handsome brown tunic, tied in the front with a gold thread. Giles wore a similar style, in blue linen with a silver tie.

Willow printed out copies of the maps, and they added them to their satchel contents. Giles studied the Watcher journals, then gathered the others close. "This Slayer is named Ejuk. She lives in the city of Uruk."

Angel walked to Buffy and embraced her. "Don't worry about this loser," he said, hooking his thumb at Lucien. "I'll make sure he doesn't go anywhere."

"Thank you, Angel," she told him, pulling back to meet his eyes. "I wish you could come with us."

"Me too."

Buffy thought again of their daylight arrival in Wales and knew Angel was right to stay behind. Besides, now they needed him here to guard Lucien. She stood on her toes, kissing him softly on the mouth. He returned the kiss, and her stomach erupted in pleasant butterflies.

Then she shouldered her satchel and turned to Giles. "Let's go kick some vampire ass."

Giles nodded and unfolded the incantation for ancient Sumeria. He spoke the words loud and clear, though his voice trembled. As the wormhole opened in the air above them, Buffy didn't know what to expect. She only knew her next stop would take her into the heart of the most ancient civilization on Earth.

Chapter Fourteen

Uruk, 2700 B.C.E.

Buffy braced herself as the wormhole spat her out into a watery trench. Her hands and legs gushed into wet soil, and her nostrils filled with the rich scent of earth and vegetation. She rolled over in time to see Xander hurtling toward her. She tried to leap up on wobbly legs and fell over again. Xander landed with a loud *plop* in a neighboring trench. Then Willow and Giles appeared as silhouettes in the bright vortex.

They tumbled out, crashing into a row of short green plants nearby.

They lay in an irrigated field, Buffy realized. She propped herself up on one elbow and looked out over their surroundings. Squinting, she watched the dazzling light from the portal before it winked out. With her hands sinking into the freshly tilled soil, she stared out in wonder at the scene before her.

In the distance stretched vast fields of crops. Nearby, about a quarter of a mile away, stood an immense wall of clay bricks, elaborately painted and inlaid with images: dragons, creatures that looked to be half goat and half fish, kings and queens before retinues of servants. She'd expected to land in a sweltering desert, but instead they'd arrived in a lush, vegetated area. To her left roared the vast waters of the Euphrates River. Palms lined the shore. Reeds grew thick in the shallows along the banks. With a clear blue sky above them, and a fragrant breeze drifting off the river, it was heavenly. Buffy felt a strange stirring inside, almost of familiarity. *Maybe because the temperature and humidity are similar to Southern California?* she thought.

Giles was the next to sit up. He groaned. "Perhaps we should consider building a small cushioned vehicle of some sort to travel within," he suggested, rubbing his head.

Buffy had to admit, that sounded pretty good. Right now her knee throbbed from hitting a rock in the field.

Willow and Xander struggled up as well. "Wow," Willow said. "This weather! The air feels . . ."

"Fresh," Xander answered. "It's unpolluted." He breathed deeply.

Buffy herself felt a little heady from all the oxygen. She supposed breathing yellow smog every day for the first sixteen years of her life had left her somewhat ill-equipped for fresh air.

The air must have been fresh in Wales, too, but with the thick humidity and pouring rain, she hadn't noticed it. Now, sitting out in the warm sunlight, in spite of wearing soggy clothes, she breathed in the fragrant air and felt the warmth of sunlight on her face.

They stood up, appraising one another in the bright sun. They weren't too muddy, just a splotch here and there. Giles checked his satchel, making sure all the books were still inside. After pulling out a map and studying it for a few minutes, he pointed to the wall and said, "That's the north gate of Uruk. We need to pass through to the city."

Over the wall rose a dazzling array of buildings—immense ziggurats, a tremendous bell tower, and a variety of temples and columned buildings. Nervousness bloomed in Buffy's stomach. While they were nearly three thousand years earlier than their last time jump, this civilization towered before her, monumental and staggeringly real. Their visit to the Druids, mainly spent in forests, could almost have been in any century. With the exception of the people—armored Romans and woad-streaked Celts—the land itself was so untouched that Buffy imagined it might look the same today. But this was not the case with Uruk. Before her stood a vast and ancient city, vibrantly new and fresh. In her own time, this area, now lush and green, was present-day Iraq, a desert full of dust and ruins. Yet here lay the start of civilization itself, the first great cities. She'd read of them in Western Civilization, been bored into daydreaming during her teacher's lectures. But here Uruk was, real and inviting, and Buffy found herself speechless at its gates.

"We must make our way to the city," Giles said.

Buffy dislodged her feet from the mud of the fields and glanced around. Once again, they'd arrived in the day. It was a good thing they hadn't brought Angel with them, though his help would have come in handy on Anglesey.

If the vamps had landed near them, they would be toast. The only way they could have survived would have been to land in the city itself and dodge into a nearby doorway or shadowed house. No heavily clouded sky to protect them now.

Briefly she looked down at the soil, wondering if the vampires would be able to bury themselves in the dirt before they exploded into ash. She didn't know if this was possible—it didn't seem like it would be. Nevertheless, she began to picture them writhing about in the soil beneath her feet, a hideous crop of the undead.

Giles moved forward, walking down a narrow line of growing barley. Buffy did the same, following close behind.

"Will we be able to get in through the gate?" Willow asked. "Will they have guards?" Her voice sounded small and frightened.

Xander stopped. "Guards? Like guards-with-spears guards?"

"No, Xander," Giles told him. "More likely guards-with-arrows guards."

When he saw Xander's expression of horror, he relented. "Actually, during this time, Sumeria was at peace. I expect we'll be able to walk right in through the city gates without any incident whatsoever. Uruk traded extensively with other Sumerian city states, and I imagine we will look like travelers to them."

Buffy looked down at her blue embroidered robe. At least it was linen, and not scratchy like the wool she'd worn on Anglesey. She hoped Giles was right about their financial stature. If people saw them in linen, they might be treated with greater respect and be able to ask questions without arousing too much suspicion.

As the four drew nearer, the city wall loomed up before them. Soon Buffy saw a great opening, a doorway that she could have slid her entire high school through, if she were in the mood to drag huge buildings around. No bars or metal blocked their way. As they got even closer, Buffy saw that the gates had the ability to close—two massive doors inlaid with copper stood on either side. But right now they hung wide open. On either side, above the doors, rose two matching towers. And pacing in those towers, staring down at them, were frowning guards. Buffy gave a little wave before Giles stilled her hand. "That might not be the best idea," he counseled her.

"I thought you said we'd look just like traders."

"Well, I certainly hope that's how we'll look," he muttered, passing through the massive doors. When no arrows rained down on him, Buffy and the others followed.

On the other side of the doorway, Buffy stopped in her tracks, bending her head back to take it all in. All around her stood tremendous buildings of golden mud bricks, elaborately painted and glistening with copper inlay. In the center of the city, some distance away, loomed a massive ziggurat. Greenery and blossoms draped down the sides of the pyramid-shaped structure, creating one of the most striking scenes she'd ever taken in.

"Are those the Hanging Gardens?" Xander asked, staring as well.

"No, those were built later. But these are clearly a striking predecessor. Fascinating!"

Entire orchards stretched out between buildings, the city fragrant and green and teeming with inviting fruit.

As they passed under the thick shadow of the gate, Buffy heard a voice calling out to them. She didn't recognize the language, but that didn't surprise her. As long as Giles could talk to the locals and not get them killed, she was cool with that.

Just inside the gate stood a young man, probably not much older than Buffy. He was lean, tanned, and muscular, wearing a linen tunic decorated with silver thread around the cuffs. He was no commoner.

Giles told them, "I'm going to try to have a conversation."

"Good luck," Xander said without much conviction.

The young man spoke to them again, repeating what he'd said before in a practiced tone. He wore a satchel over one shoulder and clutched a wooden stylus in his hand. He spoke the same line again, and Buffy realized he was some sort of vendor, like a guy selling popcorn at a baseball game. Giles smiled, waved, and approached him. Buffy looked out over the vast city, which stretched far to the horizon, a maze of mud-brick houses, temples, lush greenery, and narrow passageways. Maybe the guy was selling a map. They needed one.

Giles exchanged halting words with the young man, then shook his head. Her Watcher returned, grinning.

"Well?" Buffy asked. "What was he selling?"

Giles chuckled, then stopped. "It's really rather ironic," he said, laughing again. "He thought we were illiterates who needed his help in recording any transactions we undertook while trading in the city. He's a scribe for hire."

"And he thought you were illiterate?" Xander asked, now laughing too. "Did you show him how it's done?"

Giles, clearly amused, pursed his lips. "I resisted. He's just gotten out of school, and selling his ability is one way young scribes earn a reputation for themselves. His satchel," Giles went on, pointing politely in the scribe's direction, "is full of wet clay tablets that he can write on with that stylus. Then he fires the tablets and returns to collect his fee before we depart the city."

"Wow!" Willow said, looking at the scribe with new interest. The young man smiled at her, and she blushed in return. Buffy smirked. It figured that her friend would find him more attractive after learning he was a third-millennium-B.C.E. bookworm.

"Did you ask him about the Slayer?" Xander asked.

"I did indeed," Giles said, "though I didn't call her that. I asked about warriors in the city. He regarded me blankly." He turned his eyes to the numerous avenues and houses before them. "The population of this city must be staggering. Locating the Sumerian Slayer will not prove as easy as it was on Anglesey."

The four friends stepped away from the gate, moving toward the interior of the city.

"I want to go to that huge ziggurat!" Willow said, pointing toward the tremendous step pyramid rising in the center of the city.

"We're not here to sightsee," Giles reminded her mirthlessly.

"Oh, come on, Giles!" she argued. "After we save the Slayer, we've got to walk around here. This place is amazing! Just think—right now, someone is writing the *Epic of Gilgamesh*. Think of the parallel of flood stories. We could see that in action! Right now Gilgamesh himself is somewhere here in this city. Imagine all the amazing archaeological finds housed in the British Museum. We could see them now, in their original condition!"

Giles began to crack. As beautiful as this place was, Buffy would have been happier to lounge in the temple gardens than traipse around seeing museumy things. She remembered the last time she'd gone to a museum, dragging herself along from exhibit to exhibit, reading countless placards that faded out of her memory mere seconds after reading them. Things had picked up after one of the Incan mummies she saw came to life and tried to kill her friends. But the museum itself was utter dullsville. Buffy didn't relish the thought of seeing an endless stream of "fascinating Sumerian artifacts in their original form."

"We really should go find the Slayer," she said. "It may take us longer than we expected. The population of the city is, as Giles just said, staggering." There. She'd cast her vote. Give her some vamps to fight. A few bruises. A knock on the head. Anything was better than museums.

They nodded assent and continued forward, discussing where to begin. "Oh, I hadn't thought of this before," Giles said, "but what if the Sumerians themselves have museums? Ancient, puzzling artifacts that are long lost or destroyed by our time?" He slapped his hand to his forehead, stopping abruptly. "We could finally understand the gap between nomadic culture and civilization. It's always puzzled archaeologists why humanity jumped from living in scattered villages to full-blown avenues, temples, pyramids, and multitiered societies. Perhaps these Sumerian museums would have evidence of cultures that directly preceded the Sumerians."

"We've got to find out!" Willow said enthusiastically, obligingly becoming Giles's confederate. The betrayal stung deeply. So much for having a best friend. Buffy was going to have to stare at mud bricks until her brain dribbled out of her ear.

Buffy gently took Giles's arm and steered him down the wide avenue. He emerged from his reverie. "This must be the main thoroughfare. Sumerian cities usually contained one main street where a bazaar was held and people hawked their wares. This must be it!"

"So what's the plan?" Buffy asked him. "Do we seek out the Slayer or the vamps?"

Giles stuck his chin out slightly in thought. "In a city of warriors, the Slayer may not stand out as easily. And finding the vamps will prove difficult. I imagine they'll take measures to blend in again. Perhaps finding the Watcher is the way to go in this instance."

"The Watcher?" Buffy asked. "Is this just another chance for you to geek out?"

"I will not 'geek out,' as you put it. At times it is useful to confer with another Watcher. Usually I must do this after a Slayer has died, and they aren't as willing to discuss their experiences. The chance to speak with another active Watcher could prove quite helpful, and I'm considerably more well-versed in Sumerian than I am in Old Welsh."

Xander moved alongside them, listening. "Okay. How do we go about finding the Watcher? Ask around for a stuffy, overeducated person who hangs out with a mouthy, smart-ass, butt-kicking girl?"

"Hey!" Giles and Buffy chorused in protest.

Giles added, "Not all Slayers are like Buffy. In fact, most of them have been quite well-behaved."

"Not appreciated!" Buffy said, pulling ahead of them. Willow caught up to her, still staring around in wonder.

"So we're going the Watcher route?" she asked.

"Apparently so."

"At least we'll have a head start on those vamps with the sun still up."

"Let's hope," Buffy said.

They walked the wide avenue for several more blocks and began to hear a gaggle of voices rising in volume as they continued. Buffy saw a cluster of people in bright and earthy tones milling around one another. Awnings and huge umbrellas shielded tables full of wares, from fruit to cloth to musical instruments. People haggled and examined merchandise, and sellers barked out a litany of phrases, enticing buyers to their stands.

"It's the bazaar," Willow said. "This is where most of the socialization goes on."

"Like the Bronze?" Buffy asked. A lyre player on one corner belted out a lively tune. The music wasn't that bad, but it wasn't Dingoes Ate My Baby.

"This would be an excellent place to ask about the Watcher," Giles suggested. As they entered the sea of buyers and sellers, mingling families, young people, and old men walking with canes, they scanned the tables. Buffy couldn't believe how vibrant the whole place was. She imagined much of the ancient world as dusty relics in museums, or as stagnant images in history textbooks. But this place was so *real*. Something about seeing it in the bright daylight hit her more powerfully than Anglesey. On Anglesey they'd arrived on the island in the heart of darkness. Firelight was the only source of illumination, which made it hard to see faces clearly. But here, swarming in the daylight, the Sumerian culture was alive: ruddy faces wreathed in copper and lapis lazuli headdresses, elaborate beaded necklaces hanging from tanned necks—these millennia-old people were living beings. It hit her hard, and she stopped, staring around at the scene before her. In their costumes, they blended in completely, and people took little notice of them. Only the sellers directed attention their way, as they did to everyone who passed by. Buffy watched one woman in a blue linen dress stroll by. Her black hair was pulled back and fixed in place by an elaborate silver headdress with three large metal flowers protruding from the back. She wore makeup. She'd painted her eyelids robin's-egg blue and highlighted her cheekbones subtly with rouge. She was beautiful, Buffy thought. Not some two-dimensional stone carving she'd seen in a textbook photo. Suddenly all the people around her, some hurrying, some strolling, became nearly overwhelming. She stepped off to the side, next to a peddler's cart.

He asked her something she didn't understand.

Giles turned to search for her, spotted her there and said, "Oh, Buffy! Good show!" He came to her quickly. Turning, she realized she'd stopped at a scribe's cart. Tablets of fresh wet clay, a number of wooden styluses, and baked tablets filled the attractive young man's table.

Giles spoke to him at length, and the young man pointed in the distance to the northeast. He talked further, gesturing with his hands, presumably describing a dwelling.

Willow listened with rapt attention. "If I had anything to trade, I'd get one of these tablets and a stylus. Can you imagine what a cool souvenir that would be of our trip?" she asked.

Buffy looked around at the neighboring carts full

of gold and silver beadwork, elaborate necklaces, and earrings. "Yeah. A clay tablet. What more could you want?"

Buffy realized Xander wasn't with them, and she scanned the nearby crowd for him. At last she found him, engrossed in listening to a gorgeous woman reading from a stone tablet. Somehow, even though he didn't speak the language, Xander found the recitation fascinating.

Giles pulled the girls aside. "The scribe knows a man who is well versed in tales of the gods and history. And he has a young woman as a ward who is an unparalleled warrior."

Buffy nodded her thanks to the scribe. "Sounds like our guy."

"Where in the dickens is Xander?" Giles asked, noticing his absence. Willow pointed dejectedly out into the street, where Xander still listened in rapture.

"Ah," Giles said, catching a few words. "She's a poet."

"Great," Willow murmured, glancing that way. "Looks and talent. Who wants to listen to some crummy poet? She probably has Mesopotamian cooties." She'd had a crush on Xander since time immemorial, but he didn't seem to notice. Willow was too shy to tell him, and Buffy suspected Xander didn't see her like that. In fact, he made more passes at Buffy herself than anyone else, though he occasionally branched out to fall in love with killer praying mantises and homicidal Incan mummies come to life. The Incan mummy had actually seemed quite sweet, until they realized she looked so pretty due to sucking the life out of hapless victims. That kind of ruined her image.

"Xander!" Giles called. "We need to go."

Willow turned around sulkily.

When Xander didn't pull away, Giles strode to him and tapped him on the shoulder. Now Xander turned away sulkily.

They met up again in the center of the wide avenue. "The Watcher lives in a mud-brick house to the northeast of here. We'll have to take back streets to get there."

As they veered off the main path toward a narrow alleyway, a bell rang loudly four times.

"What does that mean? They're calling for the sacrifices of the day?"

"Xander, you have sacrificing on the brain," Buffy said accusingly.

"Only because I've almost been one more times than I can count."

"Touché," she conceded.

"No, Xander," Giles said. "It's four o'clock."

Relief spread across Xander's face.

Willow spoke up, pointing to the bell tower, which they could see rising above the shorter buildings around them. "The Sumerians were the first ones to chime the bells on the hour and half hour. They divided the hour and minute into sixty segments. We adopted that from them."

"Indeed," Giles said, appraising Willow with a smile. "Their entire math system was based on sixty because it was divisible by so many numbers. Of course, our math system is based on ten, and—"

Buffy zoned out, staring at the buildings around her. Like the walls of the city, many of them sported colored brickwork depicting scenes. Bulls, the strange goat-fish creatures, and what looked like a hybrid of a snake, dragon, and wolf filled the murals, as did kings and hordes of people carrying a vast assortment of bushels, boxes, and plants.

While Giles lectured, they covered more distance. The sun dipped below the horizon. The shadowed light of gloaming filled the alleyways. Now in the residential section, they passed more modest domiciles, though many of them were still two stories and bigger than her house in Sunnydale. All of them opened to courtyards in the back, where fruit trees grew plentifully and provided shade. If she lived in the ancient world, this place might not be so bad.

"Here it is!" Giles said excitedly, pointing up. It was now completely dark. Buffy followed his gaze to a two-story mud-brick house. A painted banner hung down, emblazoned with a bull, two stars, and what looked like a vase full of dried flowers. "It's the seal he described."

Giles walked to the entrance of the house, a graceful archway leading inside. He peered in. No one sat in the front rooms. "I'm quite unsure as to Sumerian etiquette at this point," he admitted.

Willow leaned forward. "Hello?" she called, then realized that the word meant nothing here.

Giles followed suit, calling out in Sumerian. No

one answered. Tentatively he stepped inside, glancing around the domicile.

Elaborately furnished, the house was rich with color. Several wooden chairs sat around a table draped with deep red fabric. A reclining couch lay in one corner, clumped with blue and purple pillows. Buffy looked up the stairs. Precipitously narrow, they rose to a loft above, presumably for sleeping. A small light glimmered up there.

"Could he be napping?" Willow asked, voicing Buffy's thoughts.

Giles called out again, but got no response. "Normally I would not be one to enter a house so rudely. But time is of the essence."

"I'll see if anyone's up there," Buffy offered. She climbed the stairs carefully, somewhat worried they'd topple over under her weight. Somehow the word "mud-brick," despite appearing quite sturdy, didn't sound that strong.

At the top of the stairs, she glanced around. A bed stood in the loft, with a small oil lamp burning next to it. And on the bed lay a man in his forties. His open eyes stared up at the ceiling. His jaw hung slack.

He was dead.

Chapter Fifteen

"**G**iles!" Buffy called. "You need to come up here!"

In a few seconds, all four Scoobies gathered at the top of the stairs. Giles moved to the dead Watcher, taking his pulse. He pulled aside part of the man's garb. Two bloody puncture holes bit deeply into his neck. Vamps had killed him but had not shared their own blood. At least Buffy hoped they hadn't.

"He hasn't been dead long," Giles told them.

"Is he going to come back?" Xander asked worriedly.

"One way to be sure," Buffy said. Against one wall leaned a gleaming sword. The edge glinted in the light, clearly sharp. She picked it up, strode to the body, and got ready to bring the blade down hard across the neck.

"Wait!" Giles called out, grabbing her arm. "We

can't interfere with the time line. If this man ultimately became a vampire, then we must let him become one again."

Buffy didn't like this. "What if he was killed by the assassin vamps?"

Giles paused. "We need to find out for sure before we take any action."

"I don't see signs of a struggle," Xander said. "They must have killed him while he was sleeping." After a pause, he added nervously, "Do you think they could still be here?"

Buffy slowly turned around. Near where she'd grabbed the sword stood a curtain covering the entrance to another room. Deeper darkness gathered beneath the fabric. While the open doors and courtyard still let in the dying rays of dusk, that room clearly had no windows. She crept to it quietly, signaling for the others to keep up the chit-chat.

While they bantered on about who could have killed the Watcher, Buffy moved to the curtain and whipped it to the side suddenly. Beyond lay a storeroom containing nuts and fruits. Noticeably cooler than the rest of the house, the storeroom offered little additional space to hide. Disappointed, she replaced the curtain.

"But where is the Slayer?" Willow asked. "If the vamps came here looking for her and killed her Watcher instead . . ."

"We need to search for the vamps!" Buffy said. "They could still be nearby. They could be fighting the Slayer right now!" Quickly she moved to the stairs, but stopped abruptly when she saw that they were no longer alone in the house. They'd been making so much noise talking and searching that they hadn't heard the intruders creep in.

A dozen soldiers lined the steps. The lead one, a shrewd-looking man with a scar on his left cheek, glanced toward the bed. He took in the dead man, then his eyes traveled to the sword in Buffy's hand. His eyes narrowed accusingly. Buffy shook her head in protest, but the men poured onto the upper loft, surrounding them.

The lead soldier shouted at her in Sumerian, and Giles answered him pleadingly. Whatever he said didn't wash. With spears pointed at their backs, they were forced from the house, then marched toward the monstrous palace in the center of the city.

"They're accusing us of murder," Giles explained unnecessarily.

"Where are they taking us?" Buffy asked.

"To be sacrificed," Xander put in.

"Now look," Giles said, being nudged forward by one of the guards. "There's nothing to be afraid of. The Sumerians had a complex legal system, with the rights of civilians very highly honored."

"But we're not civilians," Xander muttered pathetically.

"The Sumerians weren't into sacrifice," Willow told him encouragingly.

"Well, that's something," he muttered.

As they marched toward an uncertain future, Buffy gazed out into the darkness of the city streets. Somewhere out there, the Slayer could be fighting the assassins. Her Watcher was dead. She was probably filled with grief and rage. It might cause her to make mistakes. Buffy needed to break away, to find her and help. But right now, she knew that would only get her killed.

For now, all she could do was wait for a chance to escape, and hope the Sumerian Slayer could hold on a little longer.

Chapter Sixteen

"**W**here are they taking us, Giles?" Buffy asked, glancing once again at the armored guards. How could she catch them unawares?

"Presumably before the king," he answered. "Most grievances are heard by a king and a council of people who come to a decision together."

"Like a judge and jury?" Willow asked.

"And executioner?" Xander added.

Giles nodded.

"You're not supposed to nod, man!" Xander cried, regarding Giles with exasperation.

"Who is the king right now?" Buffy asked.

Giles thought a minute. Counted something out on his right hand. Dust motes billowed up around his feet as he plodded along. "Gilgamesh."

At the mention of this name, three of the armored

guards turned around, two with upraised eyebrows and the third with a scowl. Of course they would have recognized this one word in a sea of unfamiliar ones. Since English wasn't to be invented for nearly three thousand years, Buffy guessed the men had no idea what they were talking about. She realized the advantage.

"I'm thinking of breaking away to go find the Slayer," she said.

Xander sucked in a breath and then released it. "Hey!" he said, catching on. "I think these guards are a bunch of big, smelly, nose-flute-playing funky-duddies."

Willow laughed. "And I think they wouldn't know algebra if it bit them on the patootie."

Xander stifled a laugh. "Good one. Way to be brutal, Will."

Giles regarded Buffy over his shoulder. "I wouldn't advise it, Buffy. They'd search everywhere for you, and you can't exactly dust them. You'd be putting yourself and this mission in grave danger."

"And you don't think that rotting in a prison or being put to death would jeopardize this mission?" she retorted.

Giles thought.

One guard spoke to him brusquely, then pushed him slightly on the shoulder.

"He doesn't want us talking," Giles explained.

"I'm going to take my chances, then," Buffy said. "I've got to find the Slayer. We don't have time for this."

"What about us?" Willow asked.

"No offense, but I'll be faster without you. Go on and hear what King Gorgonzola-Mess has to say. I'll join up with you at the palace."

"I don't like this," Giles said.

"Neither do I. But we can't take the chance that we'll get locked up while the assassins run free."

"Okay," Giles said. "You're sure you can find the palace?"

Buffy sighed, rolled her eyes. "You mean big, pointy building in the middle of town?"

Giles looked in the direction of the tremendous step pyramid. "Ah, yes. Right."

"Okay, guys," she said. "See you later."

And with that, Buffy fell out of line. The two guards behind her turned to stop her with their staffs, which they brought together to block her. With a leap she kicked them aside. Momentarily the guards stood stunned, and then they cried out for help. She kicked one in the head, punched the other one in the stomach, then ran into an alley.

Reluctant to leave the rest of the prisoners unguarded, only three guards pursued her into the narrow corridor.

Quickly outpacing them, she turned one corner, then another. The men separated, covering more ground. In one particularly narrow alleyway, Buffy chimney-crawled up twenty feet, then planted both boots firmly on opposite walls. One of the guards passed beneath her, then a second one. If they were vamps, she'd have pivoted down and staked them. But now she let the men run beneath her and remained silent.

Their shouts echoed up and down the streets around her. The first guard passed beneath her again, going back the way he came.

She waited patiently.

The other guard ran beneath her.

The soldiers waiting in the main corridor called out to their comrades. Five minutes passed. Then ten. Buffy's legs began to ache, and she eyed a balcony just a few feet above her.

But then the main retinue called out once more. Below, the three soldiers met up again and walked out to the main street.

A minute later, she saw the group of soldiers pass by her alleyway, Willow, Xander, and Giles marching along with them.

She'd escaped. For now.

Now she just had to find the Slayer, and then rescue the Scoobies from a Sumerian prison. She didn't know what the Slayer looked like, had no idea where the assassin vamps were hiding, and couldn't imagine what awaited her in a Sumerian jail break.

Better odds than usual.

Chapter Seventeen

Giles watched Buffy disappear down a darkened alley and hoped for the best. His Slayer was not the most patient girl in the world. In fact, she was downright impetuous. Of course, he himself had been rather impetuous when he was younger, in his Ripper days, but that scarcely bore thinking about. At least Buffy didn't resort to the black arts and inadvertently kill one of her friends, as he had done.

He trudged on in the dust, sneaking surreptitious looks at the guards. At any inattentive moment, perhaps the rest of them could slip away as well.

But as the palace loomed nearer and nearer, Giles abandoned this thought. The guards ushered them through the main entrance. Two more soldiers guarded the doorway at spearpoint. They scowled at the prisoners as they passed.

Giles hoped Gilgamesh would be a little more friendly than these fellows were turning out to be. Downright surly they were, and clearly of a mind to think one guilty before proven innocent.

The guards led them down a wide, high-ceilinged corridor lit by wall-mounted torches. The smell of burning oil crept into Giles's nostrils, and he stifled a cough. Thin, acrid smoke hung in a layer near the ceiling of the corridor.

Giles expected to be locked up for the night, but instead the guards marched them to the center of the palace.

They paused at a pair of double doors embedded with detailed copper, lapis lazuli, and gold and adorned with scenes of rams, sheep, goat-fish, kings, chariots, and barley.

Guards posted on both sides of the entryway narrowed their eyes at the new arrivals. One bowed to the commander of the retinue, and then reached up high over his head to grab the door handle. He heaved it outward, revealing the opulent throne room. A long, narrow strip of cloth led up to a throne made of gold and copper. Sitting on the throne was a man, presumably the king, with an impressive beard hanging down to his navel. He wore a large crown, akin to a pope hat but made of precious metals hammered into delicate designs.

In front of him three women, a child, and a lone man were speaking. He listened patiently, then conferred with a group of people Giles couldn't quite see past the doorway.

Then the king turned back to the group of people, smiled, and waved his hand amicably. They bowed and thanked him, backing out of the chamber. Giles could catch only a few words. They spoke far too fast for him to understand everything. But he heard enough to understand that the king had listened to their case— something about them buying their freedom.

Giles had read of this; people could sell themselves into slavery in Sumeria. They could also buy their freedom. Slaves could own land and run businesses. These people had probably sold themselves into slavery, then saved up enough money to buy back their freedom, with the king's blessing.

Giles waited expectantly. Should they enter? Plead their case before King Gilgamesh? He looked anxiously at the guards around him. They did not motion for him to proceed through the door, so Giles just stood. He looked to Willow and Xander, who craned their necks to see through the door.

Then a young man was pushed forward into view. He stood before the king, pleading desperately. Giles caught a few remarks—something about theft, and selling an item illegally. The king conferred with the unseen group of people, then pointed a finger accusingly at the young man.

Giles heard "three months' labor" and "until debt is repaid," and then guards grabbed the young man, who protested beseechingly. The king would have none of it. He pointed angrily toward the door, and Giles felt his heart sink. This was one tough monarch. He hoped that the stories he'd read of his fairness were true. If not, they were going to the gallows.

Chapter Eighteen

Out in the crowded city street, Buffy blended in with the throng of people walking to and fro. She'd lost the guards. She was certain of it. Within minutes she had retraced her path back to the Watcher's house. Inside, men labored on the second floor by lamplight, throwing their shadows into the courtyard. After a few minutes, they emerged from the front door, bearing the dead body on a stretcher. A thin sheet covered the Watcher. People stopped and stared, murmuring questions. None of them fit the profile of a Slayer. Many were men, and most of the women were old enough to be her mother, too old for a Slayer to have stayed alive. Two little girls watched. Too young.

As the men carried the body away, Buffy watched them go. The Slayer was not here.

Was she already murdered?

Buffy regretted not being able to speak the language. She needed Giles. Maybe she'd been wrong to leave them. But if they'd all been locked up, she could have done nothing to save the Slayer, and the Master would rise.

Slipping into the shadows, Buffy began her search for the assassins.

Chapter Nineteen

The guards pushed Giles and the others before the king. Giles walked uncertainly down the long center rug toward the monarch. King Gilgamesh's dark eyes glittered beneath a furrowed brow. He gripped an intimidating spear in his left hand. Giles wished for the comforting presence of Buffy and hoped that she was out there right now, finding the other Slayer.

The guards spoke quickly to the king, again too fast for Giles to catch every word, but he did hear "murder." Lovely. Oh, what a fantastic place to meet one's end. They'd be put to death, the assassins would kill the Sumerian Slayer, and the Master would open the Hellmouth. Chaos would reign on earth.

Giles took a deep breath and tried to recall all he could about the laws of Gilgamesh's time. He'd read the Code of Hammurabi several times, the famous set of ancient laws translated in the early 1900s. But he knew that came later in history. He struggled to recall what laws would have been different in 2700 B.C.E. He hoped it wasn't laws involving suspected murderers. That they would be torn asunder by lions to prove their innocence, for example. Or that they would be hung above a pit of vipers and slowly lowered down, down to a death by poisonous biting.

No. Giles had watched too many Indiana Jones films. He was getting as bad as Xander. He was thinking doom, and he should be thinking triumph.

The king turned to him and spoke. Giles did his best to translate.

"They say you killed the city's royal scribe."

Royal scribe? Gulp. Giles cleared his throat. "We only discovered the body, Your Majesty," he replied. At least that's what he hoped he said. It may have also been "I'll gladly wash your socks, given the right incentive." This time jump was his first shot at actually speaking ancient Sumerian in a conversational context, after all. "He was dead when we arrived."

"And who are you?" asked the king.

Here Giles froze. *Time travelers? Watcher, Slayer, and Scoobies? Futuristic vigilantes bent on destroying a team of assassins?* Giles plunged in. They had limited time. He needed to get them out of there fast. "We came on a mission of protection. We learned that the scribe's ward was in grave danger."

"But you didn't see fit to save the scribe himself?"

Gulp. Giles needed a glass of water. "We did not know he was in danger." Here he turned and looked at Xander and Willow. Their eyebrows were raised, faces worried.

Willow whispered, "Ask him where she is!"

"It would greatly help us if you could tell us where the scribe's ward is," Giles said. "She is in terrible danger."

The king's eyes softened a bit. Giles hoped it wasn't his imagination. He turned to the lead guard. "Did you see Ejuk?" he asked. The guard shook his head. "What threatens her?" he asked Giles. This time the king spoke slower, using fewer words. He knew Giles was obviously a foreigner.

"Assassins," Giles answered, opting to leave out the fangs and undead part.

"Vampires?" asked the king.

Giles's mouth fell open. "Yes," he answered, haltingly.

The King nodded, then turned to his guards. "Sounds like something special is going on. Something worse than usual for our Ejuk."

Giles turned around, whispering the translation to Xander and Willow.

"They know about vampires?" Xander said in disbelief.

Giles grinned in spite of himself. "It makes sense. People in the ancient world didn't believe in different things from what we do now, they just believed in *more*."

"Wow," Willow breathed. "So their Slayer gets to fight out in the open? No secret identity?"

"Her identity as the Slayer must still be secret. Otherwise she'd be too much of a target among the undead. But it's likely she's not the *only* known fighter of evil supernatural forces here. The king probably knows that she kills vampires, but not that she's the Slayer."

"Whew," Xander said. "No secret identity would have been a bummer. I've always wanted one myself. Like a secret spy who infiltrates the strongholds of supervillains on small island countries in the Pacific and—"

The king stopped conferring with the guards and spoke. One left the room. Moments later, four young women entered the room. They wore billowing white linen gowns, and wreaths of gold flowers adorned their heads. Strings of lapis lazuli beads hung from their necks and ears. Each held a small bowl of clear water. Giles was terribly thirsty and welcomed the offering.

One of the women, dark haired and in her early twenties, approached Giles, holding out the bowl. He reached one hand out for it, and then she flung the bowl upward, drenching him in the water. He blinked in surprise, wiping water out of his eyes. The other three women threw water on Xander and Willow, then again on him for good measure.

The king laughed. "You look so funny," he told Giles.

Giles turned to him in disbelief. "Glad to oblige," he muttered in English.

The king cleared his throat and resumed his somber composure. "These are the temple priestesses of the water god, Enki. The water they carry is blessed by the god himself. If you were vampires, you would have been badly burned."

"Sumerian holy water," Willow said, wiping water off her face with one sleeve.

To Giles's horror, Xander winked at the nearest temple priestess, casually pulling his dripping hair out of his eyes.

"I am glad to see you are not vampires your-selves," said the king.

Giles felt a little better. Maybe now they could get somewhere. He glanced at his watch, hidden under his heavy sleeve. They'd been separated from Buffy for an hour now. They had no more time to waste.

"What do you propose we do to help?" asked the king.

Help? This was unexpected. Giles felt a little relief and happiness creeping into him. With the king's help, the guards could search for Ejuk, and where she was, the vamps would be. "Can you help us find Ejuk?" he asked.

The king conferred again with the guards. Starting to grin, Giles turned to Willow and Xander. "Do you realize how exciting this is? We are standing in the court of King Gilgamesh himself! The most famous of all Sumerian monarchs! He quested for eternal life and even found the fruit of immortality, which a snake ate, but that's okay. He still found it. He survived the great flood that killed most of humanity. He killed the great giant of the forest, Humbaba. It was during his reign that cuneiform came into regular use to record every-thing from tales to business receipts."

Willow looked up at the king. "Uh, Giles?"

Giles slowly turned around. The king had overheard

him, and with a frown, demanded to know what he'd said about him. Giles obliged, repeating what he'd said in Sumerian.

"You know that much of my deeds?" asked the king.

"Of course!" Giles said excitedly.

The king turned to three of the guards. "Help these three find Ejuk and stop the assassins. Make sure they have plenty to eat and drink and a place to sleep if you do not succeed tonight."

"Looks like you stroked the right ego," Xander said. "Can I have a temple priestess for my room?" He winked again at the nearest one. She turned away in disdain.

"No, you may not have a temple priestess," Giles snapped.

Willow kicked Xander in the back of the leg.

"Hey!" he said in defense. "There could be gorgeous temple priests out there too."

"They're probably bald, forty, and sacrifice virgins to snake pits," she said.

"Wait a minute!" Giles protested. "What's so bad about being forty?"

"It's ancient!" she answered, then caught herself. "But ancient is good. When it comes to you, anyway, Giles."

"Oh, thank you so very much," he muttered, turning away in mock contempt.

The king finished speaking with the guards. "My men will assist you in finding Ejuk. Please report back to me when you have succeeded."

"We will," Giles said. "And thank you."

"Anything for a fan," answered Gilgamesh.

Chapter Twenty

Outside, in the streets to the east of the palace, Buffy hunted vampires. She slunk through the shadows, keeping out of sight. She pulled out her map of Uruk and tried to place herself. To her left rose the immense ziggurat in the center of town. Its vast steps, now silhouetted against the sky, loomed in the darkness. Behind her lay the Temple of Inanna, the goddess of love. The sanctuary around it formed an entire district, called the Eanna district. Giles had gone on and on till her ears bled about how famous it was. Before her stood another sanctuary, with the White Temple, built almost a thousand years before, just visible beyond it. Past these temples, she could make out the dark, low shadow of the city walls, which extended for more than six miles around the perimeter of Uruk.

She closed her eyes, picturing where she stood in

relation to the ziggurat, where the Scoobies languished in prison, and where the Watcher had died. If she were the Sumerian Slayer, and vampires had killed her Watcher, where would she go? After royally kicking their asses, she'd go to her friends. Or, depending on the competition, maybe her friends first. She might need some research first. But who were the Sumerian Slayer's friends?

Buffy ducked into the deeper darkness under a balcony as a retinue of soldiers marched by. She was getting pretty sick of hiding from the military. First Wales and now this. She wasn't sure where to go now. Unless the same vamp had been sent again, she didn't know what her prey looked like. And he'd probably brought friends.

Her worried mind turned now to Giles and the others. They could be being tortured. They could be catching gods-knew-what in filthy Sumerian prison cells. She should go to them. Break them out.

Buffy turned in the shadows, waited for the soldiers to pass, then headed for the great ziggurat.

Chapter Twenty-one

Inside the ziggurat, Giles was having an excellent time. How thrilling to meet King Gilgamesh! To see the fascinating architecture and cuneiform so vividly detailed and in its original condition! He knew he probably shouldn't be so excited.

They were here to fight vampires, after all, not go on an archeological holiday. But still, he couldn't help feeling a little tempted now and again to stop at a pillar or stele and read the inscriptions. Consequently, it was taking them nearly five minutes for each step.

The three soldiers Gilgamesh had offered marched ahead of them along the corridor, gaining more and more distance. As long as they could recognize Ejuk, though, they would be useful.

Willow hooked her arm in his and hurried Giles along. As he craned his neck, trying to take in all he was missing, a young woman rushed past them. Tears streaked her dirty face, and her jaw jutted out in angry defiance.

"That's her!" Willow whispered.

"That's who?" Giles asked.

"The Slayer!"

"How can you possibly know that?"

Willow shrugged, turning to watch her go. "I just know."

Xander retraced his steps back to them. "Looks like she's going in to see the king. Let's go back and listen at the door."

The three soldiers had now reached the main entrance of the ziggurat and turned to look at Giles. He motioned for them to wait.

Together they crept to the door of the throne room and waited. The young woman bowed before the king, then rose. Giles listened in, catching the gist of what she told him. The royal scribe, Sarkassan, had been killed by ruffians. She vowed to bring them to justice. For now, she requested a burial detail. She began to tremble, then straightened, fighting back her emotions.

The king told her that his men had already recovered the body. He spoke to her quietly and soothingly, saddened by her loss.

"Sarkassan was an unparalleled scribe," the king said, "and generous to all who knew him." He paused, regarding her compassionately. "And you have three strange visitors who have come to help you. They fear for your life." He turned to the soldier nearest him and gave an order Giles couldn't quite make out. "My guard will take you to them." He motioned for them to depart.

At once they turned, heading in Giles's direction. He, Willow, and Xander turned away from the door and hurried to a respectful distance in the great hall. When she emerged, she instantly saw them. Giles recognized now what Willow had seen—the glittering, determined eyes. The age beyond physical age. The sadness, the wisdom, the knowledge that she would never lead a normal life like other girls. The knowledge that she would in all likelihood die prematurely.

As Giles saw her, her tear-streaked face now dry but edged with pain, he knew he would not let that happen.

Chapter Twenty-two

Willow rushed to meet her and opened her mouth to say something, but fell silent. She couldn't talk to her at all. She wanted to comfort her; she felt an immediate kinship with her. Then Willow realized why— she imagined Buffy losing Giles, imagined herself losing Giles. How would they survive that? Willow admired Ejuk for searching the city for the killers, and now marching before the king to request a burial detail.

Willow wasn't sure if she'd be able to respond that way. She'd probably curl up, consumed with grief. But then, maybe not. She had discovered more reserves of strength in the last year than she knew she had.

Now she stood before the Sumerian Slayer, unable to speak. Giles quickly joined them, followed by Xander.

He introduced them all, speaking with more agility now. Willow was pretty impressed by his amount of knowledge. She hoped one day she'd have as much. Only she wouldn't wear as much tweed. At least she hoped she wouldn't.

Giles explained that a team of vampires had targeted her, and that it was likely they who had killed her Watcher. Willow saw two tears leak out of the Slayer's right eye, but she did not openly emote. She held it together, her jaw trembling slightly. Only a couple of years older than Willow herself, Ejuk stood almost six feet tall, her skin nearly bronze. Her green eyes glittered with anger, blinking back another tear, and she wore leather armor on her arms, torso, and legs. Over her right shoulder she'd slung a bow, and a quiver of arrows hung on her back. Willow knew the prey she hunted was exceptionally susceptive to wood.

Giles then described Buffy and asked if Ejuk had seen her. The Slayer shook her head. She hadn't seen the vampires who killed Sarkassan, either.

Willow glanced nervously around the hall, expecting to see vampires lurking behind the massive pillars, or creeping up in the shadows.

Now they just needed Buffy. But where was she?

Chapter Twenty-three

Outside the ziggurat, Buffy crept to the entrance and saw three guards standing in the doorway. She recognized them from before—they had chased her during her escape. She couldn't risk being seen.

Just past them, down a long, elaborate hallway of pillars and intricate carvings, she saw Giles, Xander, and Willow talking to a young woman.

She sized up the situation. Another guard stood behind the woman. Was she the Slayer? Could Buffy take out the three guards and get them all out?

Leaping out of the darkness, she struck.

The guards, standing around talking, didn't see her approach. She was on them in two seconds, banging two of their heads together and kicking the third in the chest. He crashed down and she jumped on top of him, ripping off his helmet and clanking his head against the stone floor. He grunted and fell unconscious. Behind her, the other guards lay still but breathing.

She stormed down the hallway, fixing the last guard in her gaze.

"Buffy! Wait! No!" Giles cried, stepping in front of her. "It's all been ironed out. The guards are going to help us!"

She stopped, turning slowly away from them to see the pile of soldiers in the entryway. "Ooops."

When she turned back around, still full of adrenaline, the guard standing behind Ejuk slunk away back into the throne room.

"Has she seen the vamps?" Buffy asked after he left.

Giles shook his head.

She studied the hallway, all the pillars and recesses, places where assassins could easily hide. "This is a bad area. We need to move."

Ejuk spoke, and Giles translated. He explained that they had come to protect her against vampire assassins. She studied them all warily, then relented, grateful for their help. She was exhausted, she explained, from searching the city for her Watcher's killers. She glanced around the room, then told Giles, "We need an open place. The assassins will come to us." Giles translated.

Buffy nodded. "My thoughts exactly." This Slayer was with it. Strong. Both times now, meeting another Slayer had left her stunned. Here was a woman living the same life as she—dedicated to fighting the forces of darkness, plucked out of the innocence of youth and thrown into a maelstrom of battle tactics, sparring bruises, and ruined dating lives. Great dresses got torn. Dates got killed. Moms got lied to.

But then Buffy realized that this Slayer didn't have a mom to lie to. She'd been orphaned at six, Giles had told her. Raised by her Watcher. Briefly, Buffy missed her parents and then imagined growing up with Giles. He would have dressed her in plaid jumpers. Corduroys. Tweed slacks and sweater-vests. She just knew it.

She smiled at Ejuk, imagining instead what it must be like to grow up in this ancient civilization, with massive stone pyramids and cities filled with fragrant orchards and gardens. When gods and goddesses, monsters and beasts had temples, shrines, and festivals. When magick, divination, and spells were accepted by everyone as a fact of life. In some ways, being a vampire slayer would have been easier at this time. And in other ways, life must have been much harder. Like how often did people take baths here? They had irrigation. Surely they had baths, right? She looked at Ejuk's dirty face, the streaks of tears cutting clean swaths through the filth.

Maybe it was just an off day for her. Buffy had those sometimes. Thinking of the assassins, she hoped today wouldn't be one of them.

• • •

Standing in the grandeur of the long hallway, Xander felt elated. He wandered slightly away from the others, taking it all in. What a cool place this was! What amazing architecture! What delightful temple priestesses. He smiled as one hurried by him, carrying a goblet of dark liquid and a small cake in one hand. She turned away. But he thought she didn't turn away as abruptly as before. Oh, yeah. She was warming up to him. No doubt about it. He glanced around the corridor. There must be something to do here while they yammered on about strategies. As long as he didn't have to do much staking or punching or getting punched or bleeding, he was okay with whatever they decided.

He strolled down the long hallway, taking in the pillars. Some of them depicted everyday scenes of harvesting barley. Others showed glorious battle or the strange beasts with the heads of goats and tails of fish. His feet fell silently on the thick woven carpet. Full of lustrous reds, blues, and golds, the rug extended from the entrance to the throne room. He couldn't believe the craftsmanship that went into all this stuff. Architecture in his time was pretty boring. He didn't pay much attention to it. One mall looked like another, and tracts of houses formed a sea of monotony stretching into the Sunnydale horizon. But this was amazing. Every pillar was different. The walls were etched with symbols, stories, and pictures. Someone had really *thought* about how to make this place awe-inspiring, and they'd succeeded.

He imagined living in a palace like this, lounging on pillows and eating grapes and sipping fruity, refreshing drinks. Manly fruity, refreshing drinks, of course. Another temple priestess walked by, and he winked. She actually smiled back. Not a *hey* smile, but more like a friendly *hey, how's it going* smile. It was nice. And she didn't look like she was a praying mantis at all.

He reached the end of the hall. Lining the wall on that side were a series of immense statues, stretching up forty feet to the ceiling. All of women and men, some figures sat down, while others stood, holding spears or swords or handfuls of grain. At once Xander was struck by their strange eyes. They were huge. Huger than huge. They took up half the statues' heads, bigger than owls' eyes. They stared off into space, looking dazed or spaced out.

Xander stared more closely. They all had mouths on hinges, he saw. Some statues stood with open mouths, others with closed. Some had bits of food hanging out. Willow had told him that the Sumerians fed the statues of their gods and even had huge beds for them to lay down in. But to actually see them was something else.

One statue near the middle had particularly large eyes. In one hand he held what looked like a scythe, and his other hand stretched out, palm up. His lips curled back from stone teeth, and stuck between the front two incisors was a big green glob of what looked like spinach. Xander muffled a laugh. Then he couldn't help it. He burst out into a cackle. As he took in the ridiculous expression on the statue's face, he laughed harder. He listed slightly to one side, and stepped back to regain his balance. The floor shifted under his foot. He stumbled. The stones beneath his feet moved and ground together.

Earthquake! He stepped farther back, looking for a doorway to stand in. And then the shaking stopped. A resonant crack exploded into the hallway. At Xander's eye level, the foot of the statue crumbled and fell away, revealing tremendous, gray, wriggling toes inside. Then the legs of the statue exploded outward, raining stones and dust over Xander. He flung up an arm to shield himself. His eyes followed the statue up, up, to the eyes. With a thunderous peal, the painted stone over the eyes cracked and fell away, revealing two yellow eyes beneath. They swiveled downward, fixing on Xander, an ant at the feet of a god.

The arms shattered. The chest blew apart. And from the crumbling mass of ruined statuary stepped a horrific figure. Forty feet tall, gray, rotted, and clad in maggots and festering sores, the god of the plague rose to his feet, glaring down at Xander. His mouth opened, a dark hole in rotted flesh, and from between the two blistered lips erupted thousands of flies, darkening the air around Xander. They buzzed into Xander's ears, mouth, and eyes. Involuntarily he sucked them in as he tried to get a breath.

Xander went down, crashing to the carpet as a hundred sores opened on his skin, weeping thick yellow liquid. He screamed in agony.

This was not how he wanted to die.

Chapter Twenty-four

One of the priestesses ran by, stopping in horror at the sight. She shouted, and the others ran toward Xander.

"He's awakened Namtar, god of the plague," the priestess told Giles. "And from the looks of it, insulted him somehow."

"Jeez, Xander! We leave you alone for two minutes!" Willow cried out as she ran to him. Then they all saw him lying prone on the floor, his body a mass of roiling insects, no part of his flesh or hair visible beneath the squirming army of flies.

The god stared down at them, anger flaring in his yellow eyes. Buffy gazed up. Namtar recognized them as Xandar's friends. And he looked ripe for some anger spillover.

"Namtar will kill you all!" one of the priestesses

shouted. Giles was quick on the translation, though with one look at her fallen friend, Buffy didn't need it. "We must submit to his will!" And with that, the priestesses abandoned them, fleeing from the palace.

"Thanks for your help!" Willow shouted after them.

The angry god lifted one foot, bringing it down hard over Buffy. She leaped and rolled away, the sandal barely missing her. The temple shuddered. Buffy hoped this summoning wouldn't forever change the time line. What if the god rampaged through the palace, killing some priest or priestess who figured prominently in history? What if the god unleashed a deadly plague on all of Sumeria, crushing civilization just as it was getting started? They had to take care of this, and fast.

Giles rushed to Xander's side, kneeling down next to him. Immediately the roiling mass of flies transferred onto Giles, swarming over his skin. He cried out in agony, and in an instant Buffy watched festering boils erupt over his face and neck. He doubled over, vomiting, and then the flies covered him completely.

Xander staggered to his feet, his eyes haunted and yellow, jaundiced. He rasped at Buffy through blistered lips ruptured with sores. "Help . . . ," he whispered.

On the ground, Giles writhed in pain, crawling to his knees to vomit again, and then collapsing. Buffy backed up, Willow at her side. The god slammed another foot down, knocking them apart. Willow stumbled and crawled to safety next to a pillar.

"What are we going to do?" she called to Buffy.

Buffy jumped into the air, dodging another blow from the god, who smashed his fist down onto the floor beside her. "Where was that spellbook Giles had?"

"He still has it," Willow shouted back, diving out of the way as the other fist screamed down next to her head. It shattered the floor beneath, a spiderweb of cracks spiraling outward from the epicenter.

"We need to get it!" Buffy yelled, leaping over an incoming kick. Namtar's tremendous foot crashed into a pillar, eliciting a yelp of pain from the god. "That was hopeful! At least he can get hurt!"

"Though we aren't doing any of the hurting," Willow pointed out.

Buffy looked to where Giles lay, roiling with flies. She didn't want to fester with boils. If all of them got the plague, there'd be no stopping Namtar, no stopping the assassins, and then the Master would rise. But there was no other option. And she'd need Willow to cast any spells to send this thing back to god oblivion, or god Palm Springs, or whatever hell dimension it had come from.

Sprinting between the god's feet, Ejuk joined Buffy. She made the universal gesture for "What in the world are we going to do?" by raising her hands up next to her head and looking utterly bewildered.

Buffy pointed to Giles, to his satchel, which looked more like a swelling mound of flies than a pouch full of books. Then she pointed to herself, gesturing that she was going to retrieve the satchel. Then she pointed at Ejuk and then to the god, hoping the

Sumerian Slayer would distract him while she got the book. Ejuk nodded and headed off in that direction. A sandaled foot landed where she had been crouching.

With Ejuk distracting Namtar by leaping and jumping around his feet like an espresso-jittered rabbit, Buffy made a break for the book. As soon as she knelt beside Giles and grabbed the satchel, the flies swarmed over her. Darkness filled her vision, and hundreds of squirming insect bodies crawled over her face and into her eyes. She swatted them, trying to shake them off, then rolled as if on fire. Enough buzzed away from her that she was able to get her bearings. Spotting Willow a few yards away, she grabbed the satchel, staggered to her feet, spun around and around, and then let go, launching the bag through the air.

It thumped solidly on the floor next to Willow, and she grabbed it.

Then the flies moved in again. Buffy felt a million points of agony erupt over her body as boils and sores wept open. Bile rose in her throat and she turned to vomit, feeling the aching weight and pain of a high fever sweeping over her body. As she staggered to rise and then fell, coughing and gagging on the roiling mass of flies, she saw that Giles was now insect free.

But seeing his unrecognizable face was almost worse. Infected sores covered his swollen face, spreading painfully down his neck and chest. Maggots crawled on his arms and in his ears. He scraped them away, flinging them to the ground.

Xander looked even worse, his skin yellow and gray, mottled and riddled with lesions.

And then the pain took over her mind. She screamed, squeezing her eyes shut, as her body erupted in sickness, every plague known to humanity sweeping through her simultaneously. She doubled over in agony, then rolled into a fetal position. She could feel her body shutting down, dying.

She couldn't fight like this.

The Master had won.

Chapter Twenty-five

Willow grabbed the satchel. As her Slayer friend fell into unconsciousness, Willow rummaged through its contents. Her fingers found the familiar rough binding of *Lord Echinal's Compendium of Sumerian Oaths, Spells, and Summonses*. It was the most current, comprehensive work on Sumerian magick out there. Of course, it was copyrighted in 1857, but you couldn't have everything. She pulled it out. Giles had placed a worn bookmark near the center denoting the area of special interest to this particular time jump. The bookmark had fallen out.

Willow turned to the table of contents and scanned entries. To her left, Ejuk dodged a blow from a mighty fist, then rolled to the side and kicked Namtar in the little toe. He didn't notice.

And Willow hoped he didn't notice her squeezed

against the pillar, flipping through the book.

At last she passed up "Curses Et Cetera Having to Do with Things Borne of Illness" for "Waking Up a Decidedly Unfriendly God." She flipped to that page, glancing up just in time to see a flying chunk of masonry loosed by Namtar's fist. She ducked, clutching the book. The stone hit the pillar above her and crumbled to dust. Ejuk was really working it now, firing arrows into Namtar's toe and jabbing at his Achilles' heel. Too bad he wasn't a Greek god, or that might have worked. Namtar roared and stomped, squatting down sometimes to try to grab her in his fist. He wasn't having any luck. Ejuk grinned, her lightning agility too fast for the god, and Willow liked her more and more.

Balancing the heavy book on her knee, Willow thumbed to the page in question, glad that at least Lord Echinal had written in English, and not a primitive dialect of Coptic script or some other typical Gilesian language.

She studied the spell, read over its words. Luckily, it was an incantation, something she wouldn't need an elaborate list of ingredients to pull off—if she could pull it off.

She pivoted on her heels, facing Namtar, where he clashed with Ejuk in the center of the grand hallway. She cleared her throat, then swallowed, getting ready to speak the incantation to banish the god. Lord Echinal had written the spells themselves out phonetically beneath the cuneiform symbols. She hoped his transcription was accurate.

She spoke the sounds aloud, not sure where to place emphasis, the words unfamiliar to her. She'd dabbled in magick a few times, but mostly with Giles to guide her. Casting something as serious as a god-banishing terrified her. What if she said something incorrectly and sentenced herself and the others to eternal torment in a hell dimension?

At the sound of the words, Namtar stopped fighting, and his eyes fixed on Willow. A puzzled expression swept over his face. As the incantation came to a close, a thundering *boom* resonated through the long hall. The air shimmered to the left of Namtar, quavering like heat rising off a desert floor, then pulsed outward, bathing Willow in a blast of heat. Ejuk dodged away, taking refuge behind a nearby pillar.

Namtar turned to face the shimmering section of air, alarm spreading on his face. *Aha!* thought Willow. *He knows we have him now!*

The god backed away, nearly stepping on Xander, who lay slumped against one wall, struggling to breathe.

As Willow watched expectantly for the shimmering air to overtake the god and make him vanish, she was astonished by what actually happened.

Instead of the disturbed air becoming a vortex to suck the god back to its regular place of dwelling, something dark appeared in its depths.

Willow caught the flash of glittering scales, then a hint of a lashing tail. Another *boom* thundered around her, her chest reverberating with the cacophony. Then a red eye and a mouth full of fangs flashed into sight.

The air glimmered, a thousand sparks of light, and exploded outward in a maelstrom of hot wind.

The air pressure changed in the room, and Willow swallowed hard to make her ears pop. The wind dissipated. She peered out through watering eyes.

And she saw a monster wink into view, licking its enormous jaws and fixing her with intelligent, gleaming eyes.

She hadn't gotten rid of the god. She'd summoned a creature from hell itself.

Chapter Twenty-six

Ejuk rushed to Willow's side as the creature advanced. She shouted *"Mushussu!"* and pulled Willow out of the way.

Willow didn't know what a *mushussu* was, but with it bearing down on her, snapping its jaws, she wasn't overly eager to find out.

As they dove out of the way, Willow caught a glimpse of Buffy lying prone on the floor, thousands of flies crawling over her body. She had to get to her friend, but she knew that the flies would consume her, too, and then no one would be left to help Ejuk.

Crouching behind a pillar, she showed the book to Ejuk. Pointing at the incantation, she looked questioningly at the Slayer. Ejuk glanced at the cuneiform, running fingers over the smooth page. Willow pointed to the symbols, then to her own mouth. Ejuk's eyes widened and she nodded. She could read it aloud. Get the words right. But that still didn't solve the problem of the *mushussu,* which was about to mushussu them into stains on the carpet.

Ejuk silently read over the symbols, while Willow turned to the snake-dragon, which winnowed its way toward them through the pillars, weaving and growling as it came.

What did it have against them? They hadn't done anything except summon it into being. What, had Willow called it away from a really great snake-dragon tea party, or lured it from a poker game it was winning? Ruined a *mushussu* date?

Namtar stood against one of the walls, clearly nonplussed at the appearance of the snake-dragon. Perhaps they'd tangled before in some mythological epic, Willow thought.

She pointed again to the god and then to the incantation. Ejuk spoke the first line, and Willow realized just how wrong old Echinal had the pronunciation.

The dragon reached them, rearing its tail up to smash them.

They were so intent on banishing the god and avoiding the lashing tail of the tremendous beast that they didn't see the assassins emerge from the shadows behind them. Willow spun at the last minute as a knife plunged deeply into Ejuk's back. The Slayer slumped forward, bracing herself against a pillar. The book fell from Willow's hand and crashed to the floor, speckled with blood.

As Ejuk slid to the floor, Willow stood up to face the vampires, a lone would-be witch against two brutal assassins.

Chapter Twenty-seven

Victor sneered at Willow, recognizing her instantly as one of the Scoobies, Buffy's interminably cheery, stalwart companions. Beyond her, the tremendous snake-dragon caught sight of the rampaging god and spun to confront him.

Victor seized this moment of distraction to close in on Willow. He signaled for his latest crony, Justin, to follow him. Justin, a three-hundred-year-old mohawked vampire with as much experience killing for political reasons as for a croquet set, grinned vacantly. Justin was sloppy and impetuous—everything Jason hadn't been. Lucien had really rounded up the worst people for him to work with. And now that Lucien was locked up, his recruits were limited. Maybe before the next jump, he'd take time to find some people himself.

Victor didn't know how this guy had survived for

three hundred years, and he suspected that Justin traveled with a pack that did most of his kills for him. Lucien had dug him up in some vampire dive in the bad part of town, and Justin was cheap enough to hire. Most vamps were too lazy to join the fight to resurrect the Master without a little monetary incentive. Of course there were a few diehards, like Lucien, and most of them were just as crazy as the French-Canadian vampire himself. Victor had never had to work with such a motley mix of incompetence and sheer psychopathic reasoning skills since he joined in this whole venture.

As the snake-dragon backed the angry god into a small recess, Victor gripped his favorite knife. The blade dripped with the blood of the Slayer, and he licked along the edge. Now he just had to finish the job.

Willow watched them defiantly, balling her hands into fists. She blinked away tears, and Victor could smell her beautiful terror. Her shoulders and legs trembled, and he relished the thought of bringing her down and drinking that innocent blood.

Ejuk started crawling away, and Victor shoved Willow out of the way, bringing up the knife again. But the young witch surprised him. A violent kick to his hand sent the knife flying. Ejuk continued to crawl, and Victor turned back to Willow. He would deal with her first, killing her where she stood.

Chapter Twenty-eight

Willow made a decision quickly. She needed the book. She needed to protect Ejuk. As the Slayer dragged herself across the carpet, moving away from the assassins, Willow brought the book up suddenly under Victor's chin, snapping his head back painfully.

Ejuk stood up on shaky legs, and Willow could hear her labored breathing. The Slayer coughed, spattering the marble floor with blood. She managed to stagger a short distance away, heading straight for Buffy. Victor looked from Willow to the Slayer and opted to follow Ejuk.

Clutching the book, Willow pursued him, resolving to fight him with everything she was worth.

Ejuk reached Buffy's writhing form. She fell on top of her, the flies instantly swarming over her body.

Victor caught up to her, saw the boils and sores on Buffy as the insects cleared away.

Her body teeming with roiling insects, Ejuk had mere seconds. Before the plague could drop her, she ran straight for Victor, throwing her arms around him and embracing him.

Once again the flies transferred to a new home. Nestling inside Victor's ears and eyes, they buzzed and burrowed. The black, wriggling insects covered the assassin's body and he screamed, falling backward. Ejuk released him and crawled away to safety.

Willow caught a movement out of the corner of her eye. The second assassin closed in on Ejuk, producing a long knife from his jacket pocket.

Willow had to act fast. She ran straight for Namtar. The god stood still in one corner, hovering out of view of the *mushussu* in a small recess. The snake-dragon turned now, watching Willow move, its interest rekindled. It slunk low to intercept her. Behind it, the god emerged from his recess, his eyes flashing in anger. The creature moved with more subtlety than the god, who preferred smashing to sneaking. She didn't want to deal with both adversaries at the same time, but had no choice.

Running up to Namtar, she kicked him in the toe. He glared down at her, mouth a grim slit. The snake-dragon was nearly upon them. When she could smell its foul breath close by, she shouted, jumping up and down.

The *mushussu* leaped out from behind a pillar, bringing a clawed hand down on top of her. As the nails crashed into the stone floor, pulverizing it on contact, Willow wriggled out from between two fingers.

The snake-dragon looked up, locked eyes with Namtar.

And then all chaos erupted.

Chapter Twenty-nine

Namtar stepped out from the recess by the wall as the snake-dragon slammed its tail into his side. He stumbled, knocking over a pillar. The temple shook. That couldn't be good. Which columns were support pillars? Willow didn't know, but she suspected they were all important.

With the god and creature fighting above her, Willow dodged and leaped, avoiding their feet. This was not what she'd had in mind.

"Hey!" she shouted at the god. "You're pathetic! You're the lamest excuse for a plague god I've ever seen!"

Namtar didn't even glance down. He reached out one meaty hand and gripped the snake-dragon around the throat. The creature whipped its long neck around, flinging off the god's grip and snapping its jaws down hard on his forearm.

Namtar cried out in fury and pounded a fist into the creature's side. The *mushussu* fell over, rolling to a stop in the center of the hall.

Willow looked to Ejuk. She stood, listing, blood pouring from her back and chest, dodging blows from the second assassin.

On the floor, Victor screamed in agony, rolling back and forth frantically in an effort to squash the flies. It wasn't working.

How could Willow piss off Namtar without using words? Her English was about as useless as a wet sock in a fight.

The book weighed heavily in her hands as she watched the supernatural beings clash. The book! Quickly she ducked out of the way, crouching again. She flipped to the table of contents. There was a section on insults! She flipped to it, then scanned through the translations and the transliterated sounds beneath the cuneiform symbols. She hoped Echinal got some of the words right this time.

Peering up at the god, she shouted out, "You extravagant monkey rump!" in ancient Sumerian.

The god stopped. He held one hand out, keeping the *mushussu* at bay, and glared down at her. Then anger and indignation flushed through his face. Heat radiated off him like the sudden ignition of a bonfire.

Behind her, the assassin struck Ejuk to the ground, raising a knife. The Slayer struggled to kick the blade away, but it descended fast.

Namtar roared. Willow stepped back. It worked.

Namtar all but forgot about the snake-dragon and came after her. She ran straight to the assassin, then stopped, jumping up and down and taunting the god. Man, was she destined for a hell dimension now.

He lowered a fist hard, and she jumped away just in time. Unfortunately, so did the vampire.

Ejuk crawled out of range, leaving an alarming trail of blood on the stone floor. She was losing life fast.

Near her, Buffy groaned and came to, blinking open swollen eyes. One had gone white, unseeing. Her muscles had wasted away, leaving a mere skin-covered skeleton. She tried to rise, but immediately fell again, her haunted face gaunt and gray. Willow realized then that the flies had been on her for too long. Her situation was even more precarious than Ejuk's. The Slayer who had been her dear friend for two years was about to die.

A *whoosh* of wind nearly knocked Willow over. Pain erupted in her back as a massive tail crashed into her, sweeping her out of the way. The snake-dragon crawled onto Namtar's back, digging its claws in deeply. Wounds tore open, leaking blood onto the stone below. The powerful tail wrapped around the god's body, crushing the air from his lungs.

Namtar staggered and swayed. Willow ran as he crashed down, the echoing thud raining plaster and tiles down from the ceiling. She covered her head, then saw Buffy lying exposed and vulnerable. Willow ran to the Slayer's side and shielded her with her body.

"Will?" Buffy breathed. "I can't get up."

"I know," Willow said, fighting back tears. Even if she banished the god and the snake-dragon, how would she heal Buffy and the others? She looked to where Xander lay, now unconscious, viscous drool spilling down his chin. Giles lay some distance away, not moving at all. She studied his back for any sign of movement, a hint of a breath. None came.

While she clutched her friend tightly, the tiles striking her in the back and legs, Willow peered out at the fight. Namtar struggled on all fours, shrugging and swaying, attempting to throw off the *mushussu*. But the creature would not relent. It clung tightly to his back, digging the vicious claws in deeper and deeper.

In a minute he would succeed in throwing off the snake-dragon and would crush Buffy and Willow both if she stayed there. Loath to leave her friend, Willow stood up as the rain of masonry slowed. Still clutching the book, she sprinted away. Namtar struggled to his knees, grasping the snake-dragon around the neck and throwing it violently to one side.

The mohawked assassin took advantage of the distraction and moved again toward Ejuk. Willow selected another insult from the page and shouted, "You have all the intelligence of festering pig stool!" in her best Sumerian yet.

Namtar's head snapped down to meet her gaze, fire raging in his eyes. She was so dead.

She ran to where the assassin vamp crouched over Ejuk. Namtar leaped up to stomp on Willow with both feet. She dove to the side. The god landed solidly, crushing one of the vamp's legs, pulverizing the bone instantly. He cried out in agony, and then the snake-dragon lunged for Namtar. It grabbed him around the throat with both forelegs, digging claws into his flesh. The tail swept around to stabilize its balance and connected with the vampire's head.

In one clean swipe, the head was knocked right off. Dust erupted from where the assassin stood. Ejuk glanced over her shoulder at Willow.

With Namtar once again distracted by the snake-dragon, Willow rushed to Ejuk's side, pointing to the inscription. Ejuk read it over once, then spoke it, loudly and clearly. In an instant Namtar vanished and the snake-dragon crashed to the floor, looking rather surprised and confused.

Willow flipped through the book again, found a creature-banishing spell, and pointed it out to Ejuk. She spoke this one aloud. The shimmering air returned, and Willow gave a short little bow to the *mushussu* as it disappeared into the glimmering haze.

Ejuk collapsed, and Willow stood up in the ruined space. A low moan snapped her attention to where Buffy lay. Where moments before the Slayer lay dying, wasted away to nothing but bones, she now knelt, healthy, pink, and boil free. Xander came to, standing up groggily. Giles rolled over, hoisted himself up, and glanced around, confused.

And to Willow's left, Victor groaned and blinked, propping himself up on one elbow. She walked to him, standing over him. Giles joined her, then Xander. Buffy stood and approached purposefully. She placed a boot on Victor's chest and pulled out a stake.

Lightning fast, Victor produced his knife and slashed Buffy across the ankle, biting through her boot. She cried out and staggered backward.

He leaped up, shouting out an incantation and sprinting away from them. Full of adrenaline, Willow gave chase. The portal winked into view, dazzling her, forcing her to shield her eyes. Victor jumped into it and vanished.

Willow had half a mind to leap in, then decided just to curse. But she didn't. Instead she turned, taking in the Sumerian Slayer, now lying unconscious on the ziggurat floor. The plague had been healed miraculously, but her wounds were not supernatural.

She had no Watcher and no family to look after her.

As Willow glanced around the ruins of the ziggurat's great hall, movement caught her eyes. Three temple priestesses and then Gilgamesh himself appeared. He looked sleepy, rubbing his eyes and yawning. Instead of regal robes, he wore a simple sleeping shirt. He'd slept through the battle. She couldn't believe it.

When the priestesses saw Ejuk, they rushed to her side, examining the wound.

Gilgamesh stepped forward, exchanging words with Giles, who also studied the wound closely. While Willow and the others stood by helplessly, the priestesses fetched a stretcher and carefully placed the Slayer on top.

Ejuk's eyes fluttered as they lifted her. Her gaze found Willow's, and she winked, a faint smile curling her lips. Willow smiled back.

Giles squeezed her shoulder. "She'll be okay. And

when we get back, we can check to see how long she lived. And you," he said to her as the others drew near. "I am stunned. We simply could not have pulled that off without you. You showed unparalleled courage and ingenuity."

Willow looked down, bashful. She wasn't used to overt praise. Her mother made a hobby of ignoring her for the most part. The words meant a lot, and she blushed.

Gilgamesh clasped arms with Giles and then left, following the others to attend to Ejuk.

Alone in the crumbling great hall, Buffy said, "Let's go home."

They all nodded. "Remind me not to laugh at any gods in the future," Xander said.

"Count on it," Buffy retorted. "Or if you do, have it be the god of facials or gift certificates. No more plague gods. Got it?"

"Got it."

The four drew close together, and Giles spoke the incantation. In a moment the portal returned and they dove into it, bracing themselves for the sickening journey home.

Chapter Thirty

Sunnydale, 1998

Buffy wasn't centered in the portal. She spun wildly, head over hips, feet and arms flailing in the gusting wind. When the velocity slowed and the vortex spat her out, she sailed through the air, arms reaching for something to slow her fall. She opened her eyes, saw the ground rushing up beneath her at a painful angle, and then landed with a soft *splash*. Hesitantly, she lifted her spinning head, hearing a familiar sound sweep into her world. A gentle hush, a sigh, then the hush again. Waves. Her hands wriggled in the ground. Soft sand. For one frightening second she thought Giles had made a mistake, sending them to Anglesey instead. Then she peered out onto the beach. The Sunnydale beach. She knew it well. The sun had long since set, and the horizon over the sea sparkled with stars. White caps glowed as the waves pulsed in and out.

Struggling to sit up in the shifting sand, Buffy squinted up at the portal, which immediately dimmed out. She glanced around her. This time she was the last to arrive. Willow's feet stuck out of a sand dune a few feet away. Giles lay on the beach, the waves washing over him. He struggled to remove an errant strand of kelp from his face. She got to her hands and knees, crawling toward Willow, searching for Xander.

Then she spotted him, hanging from the lifeguard station a dozen yards away. His fingers slipped and he fell into the sand below, giving a soft grunt as he landed. "I hate this mode of travel!" he shouted, lying still on the beach.

"I can't say I disagree," Giles said, spitting out slimy bits of green vegetation. He staggered to Buffy, and together they pulled Willow out of the sandbank. Bits of broken seashells and a dried, washed-up jellyfish clung to her hair.

Xander reached them, unsteady on his feet. A car alarm sounded a few blocks away. They were definitely home.

"What's next?" Buffy asked Giles.

"Sleep," said Xander.

"A bath," chimed Willow.

"English breakfast tea, for the love of Pete," moaned Giles.

Buffy shook her head at them. "You guys are no fun."

• • •

On the walk to the library, Buffy stopped to read the date on a newspaper. "It's still Saturday." A wall clock inside a cafe told them it was an hour and a half after they'd left. Buffy felt exhausted. A bath and some sleep did sound good. But she was pretty wound up. Even though she knew they'd arrive at the same time as the assassins on the next time jump, illogically she still felt terrible about taking the time to eat and sleep.

They checked on Angel and Lucien, who cursed when he saw them enter the library. "Killed some more of your boys," Buffy told him.

Lucien's eyes widened. "And Victor?"

"Next time," she assured him, "he'll be dust."

Lucien laughed. "That's unlikely."

Buffy walked closer to the cage. "I seriously doubt it'll be a problem. If he wasn't so concerned with running away all the time, I'd have killed him by now. Where did you dig these guys up? Incompetence 'R' Us?" In truth, she knew at least Victor would be difficult to face down, but she kept that out of her tone and expression.

Lucien scowled, and Buffy turned to hug Angel. Her face pressed against the cool skin of his chest. "Missed you back there," she whispered.

"Missed you back here."

"This guy give you any trouble?" She pulled away.

"No, unfortunately. It would be a real shame to have to rough him up."

Buffy glowered at Lucien over her shoulder. "Yeah. A real shame."

"Well," Giles said, picking up a fresh set of books on the center table. "It's time we got some rest. These next two jumps may be our most difficult yet."

"I guarantee it," Lucien growled.

They ignored him. Giles looked at his watch. "Let's meet back here tomorrow morning at six a.m."

"Six a.m.!" Xander cried. "I know that's a number on my clock, but I've never actually been awake to personally witness it!"

"Well, this will be a new experience for you, then," Giles retorted. "I want us to leave as early as possible. Every time we return, we do so an hour or more later. If we need sleep again, we draw inexorably toward the school week. And I don't think Principal Snyder would take kindly to having a vampire locked in the library storage cage."

Xander crossed his arms. "Fine."

Giles turned to Angel. "I have some additional research to do here, if you want to go eat."

"Thanks," Angel told him.

Buffy looked up at him. "You going to be okay watching this guy for two more time jumps?"

Angel regarded Lucien menacingly. Their eyes met. "Wouldn't have it any other way." He turned back and touched Buffy's shoulder. "Want me to walk you home?"

She smiled. "That sounds nice." She hefted the satchel off her aching shoulder. "Would you carry my books?"

"Of course."

Xander turned to Willow. "Will. Me. You. Pizza?"

"Sounds good. But after I go home and shower. I still have dried kelp in my hair."

They all said good-bye and parted. Buffy couldn't wait to lie down and shut her eyes. They burned with exhaustion. Having the plague could really tire a person out.

The next morning everyone met in the library on time. Giles laid out plain cotton shirts, wool pants, vests, and thick brown jackets for them to wear. "We're jumping into the Civil War," he told them. "We're going as farmers. The clothes are neutral. No blue. No gray. Many of these battles were fought in fields that neighbor farms and plantations, so we should quite easily pass as civilians. I thought all of us should dress as men. Fighting in hoop skirts and a corset might prove difficult."

"I'll say," Buffy agreed, glad that her time period afforded her comfortable halter tops, jeans, and short skirts.

"The Slayer we're saving is Agatha Primrose, who lives in Tennessee. Unfortunately, she doesn't live much further into the future. But if she dies even a week before her natural death, a different Slayer could be activated."

Buffy nodded, feeling sad. She wondered how much further into the future her own life would last.

While they changed, Giles checked all of their satchels, making sure they had maps, paper, pencils, and water. To his own satchel, he added another spell book, and a book on the history of Civil War battles and troop movements. He hoped they wouldn't need it.

Buffy rummaged through the satchel contents, pulling out at least three different maps. "Will we really need all this?" she asked, glancing at a map showing the North and South's battle tactics.

"I hope not," he told her.

Buffy hugged Angel good-bye and gathered with the others while Giles unfolded the incantation. Inside, his stomach gurgled with nervousness. It had been bad enough to jump into the middle of a Roman confrontation. But this would be worse. Over the millennia, warfare had grown more and more efficient. Cannon, gunfire, flying shrapnel. They'd have to tread carefully.

Holding up the incantation, he spoke the words and the portal appeared, its brilliance bathing the library in pulsing light.

Then, holding his breath, he jumped into the vortex, pushing thoughts of errant bullets and the thunder of cannon out of his mind.

Chapter Thirty-one

Tennessee, 1862

The blinding light narrowed to a pinpoint, and Buffy braced herself to tumble out into unknown territory. She felt a hand brush her arm and turned, squinting, to see Willow spinning through the air next to her. The velocity ended abruptly as the portal ejected them into a frigid river, where they landed with a loud splash. Instantly her head went underwater. She struggled, trying to get her bearings as she tumbled uncontrollably through swift-moving water.

She found the surface, came up for air, and stretched out her hands to find something solid. Her fingers slipped over a slimy log, then grasped a rough rock. She gripped its jagged edges, pulling her upper body out of the water. Blinking cold wetness from her eyes, she stared out into a dim night. She clung to the rock in the center of the rain-swollen river. A few feet behind her, Willow flailed in the water. As she streaked by, Buffy grabbed her under the arm, hauling her over the rock and to safety. She didn't see Giles or Xander. The rain poured down over her, though she was so thoroughly soaked she couldn't get any wetter. She shivered in the chilly spring air.

The water drained from her ears as she caught her breath, sucking it in deeply. Splashing and a cry of surprise snapped her attention upstream. Giles and Xander bobbed along in the current. Xander was too limp to be swimming. Giles gripped him under the chin, and blood streamed down Xander's face.

A strong swimmer, Giles made it to their rock, and Buffy took Xander from him. "He hit his head on a submerged rock," Giles said. "I don't think he's conscious."

Buffy looked down at her bleeding friend. "We need to get out of the water. We don't want another repeat of Anglesey." She frowned. "I thought we would be arriving in the middle of a battle. I don't hear anything."

"I don't believe it's started yet," Giles whispered. "But when it does, we must all be exceedingly careful. These old rifles weren't always terribly accurate. One stray ball could fell any of us."

While Giles and Willow pulled their unconscious friend from the river, Buffy darted quickly into the trees along the bank. A tiny fire burned in the distance. For now, this particular area looked relatively clear. Of course, skirmishers or scouts could be hiding in the trees, and she wouldn't see them until they gunned her down. Their neutral farmer costumes might help for now, but they would still be targets for robbery or worse. Soldiers, desperate and hungry, who hadn't seen their families in months, pushed to the limit by endlessly firing on fellow countrymen, could be driven to desperate actions.

Buffy scanned their surroundings. Trees lined the riverbank. The countryside beyond was a patchwork of clearings and clusters of trees, with some denser sections of forest here and there. She watched silently for any sign of the assassins. This time they'd landed in the dark. The vampires wouldn't have to waste any time hiding out until night. Even now they could be on their way to the Slayer. The farmhouse where she lived lay somewhere nearby, but Buffy needed Giles's map to pinpoint the direction. Not seeing any sign of the vampires, she crept back to her friends.

On the riverbank Xander groaned, his eyes fluttering open. "You okay?" Buffy asked him when she reached them. He nodded.

Willow's brow creased with concern as she bent over her friend. "That's pretty nasty. How many fingers am I holding up?" She held up two.

"Six," he answered, groaning and rolling over onto his side. "I feel sick." He vomited into the sand, then wiped his mouth on his sleeve. "Can't I have a time jump where I don't vomit? This is two times in a row."

"Yeah, you had it lucky in Anglesey," Willow said.

"Yep. Nothing to worry about but ritual sacrifice," he muttered.

"Sounds like you might have a concussion. We should probably stash you somewhere until we find the Slayer's house," Buffy said.

Xander raised his eyebrows. "*Stash* me somewhere? I'm not a pile of dirty laundry over here."

"Yeah, but you're about as useful with that knock on your head," she retorted.

"Thanks a lot," he groaned. "At least in Sunnydale I'm good for fetching doughnuts."

"I don't think you'll be finding any jelly doughnuts around here," Willow whispered nervously.

"We're okay for now," Giles said quietly. "Most of the fighting will take place during the day. If we can make it to the Slayer's house before dawn, we can skirt around much of the fighting."

"We don't have much time," Buffy said, looking to the sky. A dim light glowed above the eastern horizon.

"What about stashing me?" Xander asked.

"We'll find a place." Buffy stood up, scanning the shore for a good area to hide him. What seemed dark and shadowed now might not be at all come daybreak. The best place to leave him would be in the Slayer's farmhouse, if they could get to it easily. She reached into her satchel and pulled out the maps.

Giles flicked a match, and they studied the lines and drawings. "Here's the Tennessee River," Giles said, pointing to a thin blue squiggle running diagonally across.

Buffy laid a fingertip on a small square. "And here's the farmhouse."

"So we just need to figure out where along this squiggle we are," Willow murmured, scanning the shore.

Few landmarks marked the map. Pittsburg Landing, the spot currently occupied by General Ulysses S. Grant, lay just to the west of the Tennessee River. Shiloh Church stood farther to the west. The farmhouse lay on the eastern side of the river, away from the area of battle. Buffy took the map and walked again to the thick of the trees. Giles followed her.

"Those fires," he said, pointing to the flames in the darkness on their side of the river, "are likely Union camps. The Confederates wouldn't risk starting fires if they wanted to surprise the enemy. That means we are clearly on the wrong side of the bank. We need to ford the river."

Buffy nodded. The farmhouse lay south of the road to Savannah, on a small, unnamed road that wound through the countryside. If they crossed the river now, the house could be to the north or south. They needed to start from a landmark. If they could make it to the Savannah road, they should spot the smaller farmhouse road.

She glanced back at the map, squinting in the darkness. She located where Grant had positioned his men, and where Generals Johnston and Beauregard of the Confederate Army waited. If the fires were Grant's, they were close to the road, just to the south. A different Union encampment would mean they might have to head north a bit.

"The map was a good idea, Giles," Buffy admitted.

"I thought you'd feel that way once you got here." He grinned. "History still too dusty for you?"

"Right now history's too dark for me," she said, struggling to make out features on the map. She couldn't get her bearings. The road could lie in either direction. If they waited until light, on the first day of one of the bloodiest battles of the Civil War, they'd all be in danger.

Her best chance was to do a little scouting now. The road to Savannah met the river almost directly across from Pittsburg Landing. She just needed to find Grant's encampment at Pittsburg Landing and go from there. Who knew all that orienteering in sixth-grade camp would actually pay off? Maybe one day she'd find a lifesaving reason for making a macrame owl.

She and Giles returned to the others. "You all need to cross the river, and I need to do a little scouting," she told them.

Giles immediately shook his head. "It's not safe."

"None of this is safe, Giles," she argued. "It's better I go out there now than have us all traipsing about with no idea which direction to go." She gripped his arm affectionately. "I'll be careful. They won't even know I'm there."

"Buffy, I don't like this," Willow said, her eyes wide in the dark.

"I know, Will, but I'll be okay. It's the best chance we've got."

"What about me?" Xander said. "I still need to be stashed."

"The others can carry you. Cross the river at this point and wait for me. Stay out of sight if I'm not back before dawn."

"You don't have to tell us that," Xander said. "I'll be burying myself in leaves and dirt, thank you very much."

Buffy watched as her friends lifted Xander and helped him into a shadowed copse. "I'll be back soon," she whispered, and crept away from her friends, toward a nation at war.

Chapter Thirty-two

Stealthily Buffy kept to the trees, slinking closer to the flickering fires. She hoped they were Grant's, as his men held the most northern position. If more fires glimmered beyond those, then she would keep heading north until she located Pittsburg Landing.

She scanned the ground for landmarks on the map. She didn't see any. But once she found Pittsburg Landing, she'd swim the river, and walk down the opposite bank until she found the others. That way they wouldn't have to cross dangerous ground and risk a bullet.

On the horizon, the glow of dawn grew in intensity. The crack of a rifle sounded to her left, startlingly close. She ducked low beneath the branches, squatting. Peering out, she watched for any hint of movement. Through the trees a hundred yards off emerged two Confederate soldiers, their rifles and pistols gripped tightly in both hands. She sat still, watching them. Fortunately, they hadn't seen her. Quickly they ran across an open space and found shelter again in a nearby copse of trees. They moved furtively, glancing in every direction. Perhaps they were scouts, getting a bead on the Union position.

The rifle sounded again, still from her left, and Buffy watched in horror as one of the men went down, screaming in pain. His friend crouched low beside him, peering backward into the trees. While the wounded soldier cried out, thrashing in the grass, the other held him down and cocked his pistol, aiming it into the nearby forest.

A cloud of smoke billowed up from the edge of the trees as the rifle fired again, much closer. The second soldier cried out, falling dead, sprawling over his companion. From out of the trees stepped a Union soldier, wearing the green uniform of a sharpshooter. Grime streaked his face, and his uniform was torn in a dozen places. He gripped his rifle in one hand and jogged to the two soldiers, his pistol drawn and aimed. When he reached the men, he stood over them for a long minute, checking to see if they were alive. Then he holstered his pistol and wiped sweat from his brow. They all looked about the same age, early twenties, maybe just teenagers. It hit Buffy hard. They were only a bit older than she was. Fighting each other, killing each other. Some states were even split down the middle, with some families fighting for the North and others for the South. Neighbors fighting neighbors. It would be as if she picked up a rifle and gunned down people from her own state or even town, sneaking around in the forests of the United States, shooting other Americans.

She waited for him to go. When he had slunk away across another clearing and entered the trees some distance away, she stood up. Glancing in all directions, she chanced a run across the field.

Up ahead lay another cluster of trees, then a small clearing, then more trees. A gentle hill rose up before her, dotted with oak and hickory trees. Just a few more feet, and she'd be safely undercover.

With a deafening report, a bullet whizzed by her head. She had been spotted.

Chapter Thirty-three

"Stop!" a man shouted.

Buffy ran.

From the trees behind her emerged a Confederate scout, his pistol drawn. She fled the small clearing, racing up the little hill. Reaching the small grouping of trees, she flung her body flat against one of the trunks and chanced a look back.

The scout charged across the field, heading directly for her.

Her stomach went sour at the thought of being spotted. On top of the shaking fear she felt at being in a war zone, what if this changed the scout's original path? What if he got killed now, when originally he had survived the Civil War? Then all of his descendents would never be born. She had to ditch him.

She left the safety of the trunk and ran farther up the

hill, toward a denser part of the forest. The faint dawn light was absent in these thick trees. She stumbled over a fallen log, then turned and looked back at it. It was immense, a centuries-old tree that had toppled years before. Partially hollow, its thick trunk sported dozens of ferns and lush green moss.

"Stop!" the scout yelled again, alarmingly close.

Buffy ran back to the fallen log and lay down next to it. Quickly she wriggled her body inside the hollow cavity, heaping earth onto herself. The smell of dirt crept into her nostrils. With a thud the scout landed on top of the log. He jumped down on the other side, and for a second that lasted far too long, he paused, scanning the trees for her.

"Stop, I say!"

Buffy held her breath. He hadn't seen her hide.

Picking a direction, the soldier rushed away, cocking his pistol and carelessly tripping over fallen branches in his haste.

When she was certain he'd gone, Buffy crawled out of the log, brushing the dirt from her woolen trousers and jacket. She stood up. By now the world was almost light. She could see farther than she'd been able to before. Through the thick trunks, she could make out another clearing, with objects and people moving silently in it.

Hurriedly she crept to the edge of the trees. She stood at the top of the rise. The hill sloped away beneath her, opening out into a vast meadow. A sea of gray uniforms, thousands of soldiers strong, filled the clearing. Lines of cannon brought up the rear. For a second she thought she'd grown deaf, for she couldn't hear them at all. Then one man coughed, and she realized they were poised for an attack, hoping to surprise Grant. She looked out into the distance, hoping to spot the Union camp and therefore Pittsburg Landing.

But instead she saw something else, completely unexpected. A huge river, wending its way through the countryside, vast and swift.

They hadn't landed in the Tennessee River.

For there it was, clearly, a massive, coursing body of water ten times bigger than what they'd tumbled into. They must have landed in some tributary, or in an unconnected stream, which meant she didn't know where she was after all.

Quietly she pulled out the map, gently unfolding it to make as little noise as possible. In the dim light, she tried to make out the squiggles and blocks and arrows. She scanned the brief battle description written down by Giles. With this many soldiers present, this gathering must be the main attack force of Johnston, which surprised Grant by attacking at six a.m.

She wouldn't be able to stick to the shores of the Tennessee River to find the road like she'd thought. For even though she could see it twinkling in the distance, the Tennessee River still lay miles to the northeast. She had to plunge forward, into the heart of the occupied territory. Behind her amassed more and more soldiers from Johnston's stronghold in Corinth, Mississippi. And ahead of her waited Grant's unsuspecting army, thousands strong.

Right now, instead of standing on the edge of the conflict, she was in the center of it.

Chapter Thirty-four

Buffy waited in silence, and light slowly crept into her world. Now about a quarter mile away, she could see a shadowed log building behind a small group of trees. A cross stood on the roof, at the top of a rough-hewn steeple. Shiloh Chapel. She looked at her map. This was the location of one of the most tenacious parts of the attack, where many soldiers lost their lives. It was one of the most dangerous places for her to go. But she couldn't stay where she was, either. If anyone saw her, as the scout had done, they would likely shoot her on sight for fear she'd give away the surprise attack.

Her neutral farmer outfit might not mean much on a day like this, with soldiers psyched up for battle and everyone tense and terrified.

She studied the map closely. Behind her ran the

stream they'd landed in. To her right, she heard the trickling of another small river. If she stood south of Shiloh Church, with the rising sun to her right, that put her somewhere along the Shiloh Branch or Rhea Springs. To get to Pittsburg Landing as quickly as possible, she would have to skirt slightly south, going around the Southern army. When she could no longer see their numbers, she'd head north. Unfortunately, there were no creeks she could follow. She'd have to use the sun. Looking at the scale bar, she calculated about two miles to the farmhouse if she followed that course, and she'd have to cross the Tennessee River along the way.

She scanned the battle description again. For now, the Scoobies were safe where they were. The Confederates would not pass back that way until evening the next day, when they had faced defeat. They'd march along the Corinth Road, which Buffy still had not come across. She had some time.

She looked ahead at the mass of soldiers, which now began to move forward, marching deliberately and silently through the dense sections of trees and open spaces. The battle was about to begin.

Her best bet was to scout ahead, figure out exactly where the Union army waited, and figure out a way around them. Then she'd go back for the others, and together they'd make their way toward the farmhouse.

An eruption of rifle fire ahead of her forced her to clamp her hands over her ears. The deafening shots echoed over the countryside. Birds chattered and flew away, leaving feathers behind. Confederate soldiers whooped and uttered war cries, and another simultaneous boom of a thousand rifles reported and echoed around her.

Screams rose up. Then an answering cry of rifle fire. The boom of a cannon.

Buffy turned and ran, heading south, down the small rise.

She skirted along the side of the battle, choosing her way carefully. Every time she had to run from one thicket of trees to another, her heart pounded heavily in her chest. Soldiers could be anywhere, clustered in any group of trees. But she managed to remain unseen.

Finally she began to head north again. She crossed two meandering streams and placed herself roughly on the map. The crack and report of rifle fire was unending. How many bullets were used? How many soldiers fallen? She tried not to think about that. Instead, she mentally recorded the path she took, so that she could retrace it later with the others.

She ran up another small rise, hid in a cluster of trees, and peered out. Ahead lay some kind of small dirt road, rambling through an orchard. At first she thought snow clung to the branches. She crept closer, moving down from the rise. No soldiers in sight. Now closer, she realized the snow was white peach blossoms. To see such beauty in the middle of a violent battle struck her powerfully.

The fruit trees were thick enough to offer plentiful cover, and she reached them in a few seconds. She studied the road, trying to place it on the map. Over the centuries, so many wagons, horses, soldiers, and carts had passed along this way that the road had actually sunk into the earth. She took in a quick breath. Sunk into the earth. The Sunken Road. She found it on the map.

Here the Union soldiers held back the Confederate advance until the Southern artillery had all but obliterated them and their position. She heard the nearby shot of a rifle. It was already starting—the Union formation of the "Hornet's Nest," a location the South fought to overtake during the entire battle. Though heavy casualties resulted, the maneuver had bought enough time for Union reinforcements to arrive, leading to their victory. But that time was in the future. For now, the Union soldiers fought for their lives, cries of pain echoing up as one after another was picked off by Confederate snipers.

She started to move off the road, then suddenly realized that she was much farther north than she thought. As she ran down one embankment of the road, crossed it, and ran up the opposite, she caught sight of the Union sharpshooters, a hundred feet away. They used the natural sunken contours of the road to their advantage. The riflemen lay on their bellies in the dirt, partially protected from gunfire by the banks of earth on both sides. Scores of uniformed men covered the sunken, deep path meandering through the oak-hickory forest.

The crack of gunfire and the booming of cannon filled her world. The acrid smell of gunpowder floated low in the air, a layer of smoke visible just above her head. She stood beneath a peach tree, catching her breath, and imagined taking a gun, kissing her mom good-bye, and traveling south to kill Alabamans. Or north to kill Virginians. She shook her head. The idea was crazy.

But it was exactly what these people were doing.

Gunned down by the Hornet's Nest, a Confederate soldier slumped down at the base of an oak, blood blossoming in his chest. She watched, transfixed in horror.

Then she pivoted south, deafened by the roar of gunfire erupting from the Union soldiers. Confederates answered their fire, inviting more, and another thick cloud of smoke rose up through the forest. The acrid stench of gunfire gagged her and made her eyes stream.

Silently she made her way south again, away from the conflict. But as she left the road behind, a solitary shot rang out, a little closer than the others. Buffy ran on. Her leg felt strange and wet, but she didn't stop. She ran farther south but kept getting slower and slower. She didn't understand it. Her leg wouldn't do what she asked it to do. It got sluggish, then locked up. She fell. Forced herself to stand again. Plummeted back to the ground.

Then she looked down at her right leg. Blood soaked her trousers. She'd been hit. Shot. Her body trembled. Her teeth chattered. She forced herself up, gripping the trunk of a tree to steady herself.

Though she needed help, a sudden fear to advance seized her. Breathing in and out, she tried to focus. This was what it had been like. Soldiers scared like this. All the time. They didn't see their families for years at a time, or never again if they fell on the battlefield.

Up ahead, on the far side of a group of trees, she heard a sudden moan of pain, then someone sobbing uncontrollably. She blinked sweat out of her eyes. Tried to think. She was bleeding, and bad. She needed to make a tourniquet. Another crying voice floated by on the wind.

Leaning against the tree, Buffy yanked the belt from around her waist. She wrapped it around her thigh and tightened until it hurt and throbbed. She knew there was a Union field hospital around here, but she had no idea where. And could she go there? She stumbled away from the tree, determined to make it to the farmhouse. She was halfway to it. In either direction, she'd have to walk a mile. Her leg continued to bleed, the tourniquet not yet stanching the flow of blood. Her body began to shake uncontrollably. She wiped her palms, slick with sticky blood, on her pants and staggered forward.

She was thirsty. So thirsty.

Ahead, the moans and cries grew louder. She passed through a clump of trees and fell. Lifting her head, she saw a small pond surrounded by ancient oak trees. Dozens of soldiers, Union and Confederate alike, lay littered around it. Some drank, some bathed their wounds. The water ran red. Groans rose pitifully up from the pond's edges.

The clouds rumbled overhead. A small drizzle began to rain over them, droplets collecting on the branches, glistening in the fallen leaves.

In front of the pond stood one particularly tremendous oak tree, branches the size of its trunk, still bare after the winter. The tree was old, she realized, terribly old. A Union soldier dragged himself over its roots, then propped himself beneath its branches. He breathed his last desperate ragged breaths in its shelter. Then he slumped over, dead.

The unbearable dryness in Buffy's throat compelled her to drag herself forward. Every muscle trembled and shook, rebelling against the movement. But she forced herself. The crying and suffering soldiers took no notice of her as she pulled herself to the edge of the pond, leaving a trail of blood in her wake.

The water tantalizingly close, but out of reach, her body ached for a drink. A Confederate soldier fell over next to her, his sightless eyes staring up at the gray, roiling sky.

She forced herself to focus on the grand trees and shadowed valleys, golden fields in which the deer gathered at dusk. She tried to imagine what this place must have been like before humans arrived, before scores of soldiers died for causes like securing advantageous locations to fire cannon. She imagined the fields and groves of trees without the thousands of bleeding and broken soldiers, but instead full of foraging deer and black bear.

She pushed past the fallen soldier, trying to reach the water. She thought of Giles, of how he'd looked out for her, of her mother telling her to do her homework. How she longed to be back there. How welcome doing her homework sounded right now. As her vision swam,

Buffy tried hard to hold on to consciousness. She would get a drink and then somehow make it to the field hospital. She had to. If she didn't, she would die and the assassins would kill the other Slayer. The Master would reign, and everything she held dear would perish.

Another soldier fell by her side, then another and another. She became just another body piled before Bloody Pond, fighting for a drink, fighting to stay alive just one more precious moment.

Her vision darkened and tunneled, and Buffy cried out in dismay, flailing in her efforts to force herself to stand. Tears streamed down her face. Then her body stopped shaking, and the world went dark.

Chapter Thirty-five

Buffy's eyes fluttered open, feeling impossibly heavy. She lifted her eyelids, and with considerable effort stared up at the night sky above her. Stars filled the skies, more brilliant than she'd ever seen them before. The Milky Way stretched across the heavens. The sky twinkled with a billion distant suns.

An elbow jarred her shoulder. In her right ear, she heard a slurping noise. Slowly she tilted her heavy head to look in that direction. A dark shape bent over the soldier next to her, dipping its head and licking. Then a horrific face leaped into view, a leering face staring down at her, running a pointed tongue over fangs grown long and sharp.

Her mind fought through a haze of pain as the face loomed closer. It was something she knew, something familiar. And somehow she'd always been able to stop it in the past. But now she couldn't remember. She felt so tired. She tried to lift one arm, but it lay at her side, pinned down by the weight of a fallen Confederate soldier.

Buffy blinked, her worldview filling with the terrifying face, the protruding brow ridges, the yellow, feverish eyes. It bore down on her, grinning, and she felt the cold lips against her neck.

Just as the mouth opened against her flesh and she felt the wet fangs meet her skin, the entire creature erupted into dust. Flecks rained down over her face and eyes, and she squeezed them shut.

When she opened them again, mere moments later, the hideous slurping sound had stopped. Above her swam the face of a young woman. Curls of blond hair escaped from a black riding hat. "You don't look like a typical soldier," she said.

Buffy opened her mouth to answer, but found it so dry that her tongue was rough and her lips cracked open painfully.

"Don't try to talk. I've alerted the field hospital to a number of dying here. They should be here shortly." She gripped Buffy's hand. "I can stay with you for a little while, but then I need to get out there again."

Buffy ran her tongue over chapped lips. "Slayer . . . ," she whispered.

The woman's eyebrows rose in surprise.

"Me . . . too . . . ," Buffy managed, her voice gone. "Danger."

"Don't try to talk." She glanced around, scanning the shadows. "Are you telling me you're a Slayer?" she whispered.

Buffy managed a nod.

"Then I think we need to get you out of here."

She grabbed Buffy's arm to pull her up. When the weight hit her leg, a primal shriek of pain erupted from Buffy's lips. The woman looked down at the gunshot. "You're gravely wounded. I can help you back at my farmhouse. It's not too far from here."

She lifted Buffy up carefully under her knees and shoulders and carried her for an interminable distance. Buffy lost consciousness.

When she awoke, jostling around in the back of a horse-drawn carriage, she reached up and gripped the woman's skirts.

"My friends . . . need to save them."

The woman slowed the horse and pivoted in the driver's seat. "Where are they?"

Buffy frowned, trying to fight the haze in her mind to recall the map. "Shiloh Branch . . . or Rhea Spring . . . by the Corinth Road." Pain bloomed suddenly in her leg, and she gritted her teeth, sucking in air.

The woman thought a moment, then wheeled the cart around, riding swiftly back in the direction they'd come. All the jostling hurt Buffy's leg more, but she bit down on the pain, concentrating on the others. At least now they'd found the Slayer, or rather she had found Buffy. All they had to do was wait for the assassin vamps to strike. Of course, Buffy wouldn't be much help when they did.

The carriage bounced along over rolling hills. They forded the two streams Buffy remembered crossing earlier that day. *That day?* she wondered suddenly.

How long had she been out? What if days had passed and Giles and the others had moved on, or worse, been killed?

Soon the burble of a larger body of water met her ears. She tried to sit up in the wagon, tried even to lift her head above the side rails, but couldn't. She just lay. "Giles . . . ," she whispered to the other Slayer.

"Giles!" the woman called softly. They rode on. "Giles!" Bouncing along the shores of the Shiloh Branch, she called his name over and over again, careful not to alert any passing scouts.

"Here!" came Xander's voice.

Buffy had never heard such a welcome sound. She tugged on the Slayer's skirts. The wagon slowed, and Xander emerged from the dense foliage near the riverbank, the blood on his head now dried.

He looked first at the woman, then at Buffy lying in the back of the wagon. "Oh, my God."

She reached for him, and he took her hand. "Will?" she whispered.

"She's here," he told her. "She just went to get us some water. Giles left hours ago, though, trying to find you."

"I found her at the edge of a pond, among a group of wounded soldiers," the Slayer told them. "Who are you all? Is she really a Slayer?"

Xander smiled down at her and squeezed her hand. "The best."

"I need to get you to safety, then you can explain. Who is Giles?"

"Her Watcher."

The woman nodded, her mouth suddenly tight. "Then it's vital we find him. But first, she needs medical attention. We must get to my farmhouse."

Xander nodded, releasing Buffy's hand. He jogged back to the river and returned with Willow. "Oh, Buffy," she cried, "am I glad to see you!" As she neared the wagon, her voice trailed off. She stopped in horror, staring at her fallen friend. Then, biting her lower lip, she climbed into the back. When she saw the tourniquet and the blood, she whispered, "Oh, please no." She gripped Buffy's hand.

The crack of a rifle sounded just a few hundred yards away.

"Get in!" the other Slayer ordered Xander. "We need to go now!"

He climbed up hastily, nearly toppling over, and the woman cracked the reins. Whinnying, the horse took off at a solid clip, tearing them away from the gunfire.

Buffy looked at her two friends, thrown around in the small wagon. She felt her eyes sting and swell. So heavy. She had to shut them, just for a little while. As she faded off, she felt Willow checking the tourniquet. And then the blackness swallowed her.

Chapter Thirty-six

A violent jostle jarred Buffy awake. Night pressed close. Willow gripped her hand in the back of the wagon, her skin warm. Buffy shook, her body trembling uncontrollably. The wagon tossed them together in the back of the carriage, Xander nearly toppled over, then Willow. Buffy felt sick.

Above them the stars still gleamed, a million jewels in the blackness of the sky. She no longer heard the trickling of the river. Now other sounds filled the night. Moans, sobbing, crying. She tried to lift her head to see over the wagon's edge. Willow pressed a hand to her chest, kept her from rising. "Don't," she whispered. "You don't want this image."

Tears streamed down Willow's dirty face. She pivoted her head to look over her shoulder, breathing shallowly.

The battlefield. Buffy knew they crossed it now. Thousands of soldiers lay dying in all directions, their pitiful cries like the eerie ululations of ghosts long lost to the living world.

"Look," said Xander to Willow. He pointed.

Willow gasped. "Oh, no . . ."

Buffy tried to swallow, but her dry throat rebelled. "What?" she rasped.

"Vampires," Xander whispered, his voice haunted and hollow.

"Hundreds of them," Willow added. "Feeding off the dying."

Buffy gripped her hand, a monumental effort that took all her strength. "Stop."

Willow shook her hand. "You can't fight right now, Buffy," she said, the tears in her voice rising to the surface.

"You may not even—," Xander started.

"Xander, don't," Willow told him forcefully.

Buffy arced her eyes toward the woman driving the wagon. "Slayer . . ."

Xander touched Buffy's shoulder compassionately. "She's stopped, Buffy. More times than we can count. She staked the vamps feeding off soldiers who still have a chance, at least once the doctors from the field hospitals get to them." He paused, glancing in the woman's direction. "She stopped too many times," he said, his mouth now just a gray slit. "It may have cost you your—"

"Don't!" Willow said again, nearly shouting.

Her shout was answered by another, crying out

somewhere to the left. The cry was terrified and abandoned, something uttered when there's nothing left to lose, and you are determined to have your last actions on this earth count for something.

It was Giles.

Chapter Thirty-seven

Willow stood up in the carriage, releasing Buffy's hand. "Giles!" she shouted. "Stop the wagon!"

The Slayer slowed the wagon, and Willow jumped out before it came to a halt. She landed hard in the muddy earth. Before her in the dark lay thousands of wounded and dying soldiers, crying out for water, or lost wives, or children.

And somewhere out there was Giles, fighting for his life.

Xander leaped out beside her, then almost fell over with dizziness from his head wound.

"Stay here with Buffy," she told him.

Xander stilled himself on the edge of the wagon. "I can't. The Slayer will protect her."

"I can do this," she told him.

"No, you can't, Will. If he's wounded, it's going to take both of us to carry him back to the wagon."

She looked into his determined gaze and relented. As Giles cried out again, she pinpointed his location, nearly straight ahead, and ran in that direction. As she grew closer, the cries resolved into words. Giles was cursing. And quite the blue streak at that.

Dark shapes slithered and slinked between the dying men in front of them. The littered soldiers of Shiloh were one long smorgasbord for the undead.

The creatures advanced toward a center point. Some of them crawled, drinking from hapless victims along the way. Others crept stealthily forward, bodies braced for a fight. And in the center of those advancing shapes stood Giles. As one reached him, he cried out, thrusting a sharpened stick into the chest of the attacking vampire. The creature exploded into dust. Then Giles pivoted, shouting, driving the stick into the chest of another. Three more came, and he dusted them all.

As Willow grew closer, she heard the rough edges of his accent. Not the genteel Giles she was used to, but guttural, visceral. He cursed again, flipping a vampire over onto its back and driving the stake home. Now only two remained. He egged them on, taunting them, his eyes glittering with hatred. He gripped the first one around the throat, crushing the vampire's larynx, and then drove the stake into his heart.

The last one, now afraid without its brethren, turned and bolted. Giles didn't let it go. Leaping over wounded soldiers, he ran after it, calling it so many names Willow didn't even recognize half of them.

This was Ripper.

This was the essence of Giles's youth emerging in the heat of mortal battle. In his early twenties, he'd left Oxford University and moved to London. He fell in with a thrill-seeking group of friends who tinkered with the dark arts for fun. One of them died because of it. Giles had gone by the name Ripper, and he'd been violent and ruthless in his actions.

And now their gentle librarian and friend was giving them a glimpse of those days. He caught up with the vampire, swinging out a leg to trip him. The vamp fell hard, sprawling into the grass, and Giles brought the stake down, piercing the heart through the back of the rib cage.

As the vamp blossomed into dust, Giles lifted his head to the skies and gave a primal scream of rage.

Willow ran forward. "Giles!" she shouted.

He spun, tensed, ready to stake her.

She stopped. "Giles!"

He paused, his shoulders relaxing. His grip loosened on the stake, and he said, "Willow." Then, glancing around and seeing no more creeping shadows, he added, "There are so many vampires here. I couldn't find Buffy. And I couldn't just stand by and tolerate . . ." His voice trailed off, and Willow rushed to him.

"You were amazing, Giles," Xander said, hurrying forward to join them. "And no little amount of scary."

And even more amazing was that he had no wounds at all, save the smallest scratch on his arm. His sleeve was torn there, revealing the thin red line. Willow ushered him quickly toward the wagon. "We have Buffy and Agatha. We're all together." They reached the wagon, and Agatha turned around in the driver's seat to watch their approach. "But Buffy's wounded," Willow finished.

She climbed into the back of the wagon, followed by Xander.

"You're her Watcher?" the Slayer asked.

"Yes. And you're Agatha?" he asked.

She nodded, then regarded him curiously. "I can't imagine my Watcher doing what you just did. I didn't even need to step in and help."

"Well, yes," Giles said, climbing up into the bed of the wagon. "Dark past."

"I gathered that." She flicked the reins and the horse moved forward again, taking them ever closer to the farmhouse.

Willow watched anxiously while Giles examined Buffy's wound. "The tourniquet may have saved her life. But she needs a doctor," he said at last.

"Giles," Buffy whispered, then shut her eyes again.

Willow watched while her friend fell into unconsciousness once more. She was glad Agatha had stopped to slay opportunistic vamps on the battlefield. She only prayed that by stopping so many times the Slayer hadn't cost Buffy her life.

Chapter Thirty-eight

Buffy awoke, groggy and disoriented, to someone moving her leg. She grunted in pain, then focused on the person. A strange man met her gaze. He was fairly young, perhaps in his late twenties or early thirties, with a full black beard and shoulder-length black hair. He wore the uniform of the Union army, complete with wide belt and tarnished buttons that had been too long in the field. But his eyes were kind, and she relaxed a little.

"I am Dr. Milton Henderson," he told her, "a surgeon with the Thirty-second Regiment of Pennsylvania."

She raised her head, realizing with great relief that she could. Already she felt stronger.

"I've sewn up your wound. Fortunately, the ball passed through cleanly. Your field tourniquet saved your life. You should heal quickly, but you must take proper precautions to ward off infection."

Giles came into view, peering over the surgeon's shoulder. "Buffy? How are you?"

She nodded, managing a small sigh of relief.

"Agatha convinced Dr. Henderson to come from the field hospital across the river."

The doctor smiled. "I was supposed to be getting some sleep. But Agatha can be insistent."

"We're lucky he was here," Giles added.

She didn't need Giles to tell her how lucky. She'd nearly bled to death, and she had no illusions about that. She swallowed, finding her throat still dry. "Water?" she asked, her voice raspy. She sounded like she'd spent her life chain-smoking.

Dr. Henderson picked up a glass of water from the table and tipped it to her lips. She steadied his hand with her own and drank deeply. How sweet the water was, the finest thing she'd ever drunk. She finished the entire glass, then asked for another.

Encouraged, Giles smiled. "It's good to have you back."

She propped herself up on one elbow and drank the next glass on her own. "What about the"—she looked pointedly at the surgeon—"people we were looking for?"

"No sign of them yet. But with all the people we . . . said good-bye to on the battlefield out there, we may never meet up with them."

Buffy nodded. She understood. The thousands of dying soldiers out there would attract hundreds of vampires looking for an easy feast. They'd slain count-less numbers of them, and there was a chance that the assassins were among their numbers. She frowned then, thinking of Victor. He wasn't stupid, and she doubted he would make himself vulnerable on the field like that, feeding carelessly. He would have stuck to the shadows, his objective to kill Agatha more important than an easy meal.

"Let's stay on our guard," she told Giles. "I have a bad feeling."

Dr. Henderson raised his eyebrows, and Buffy added, "About the cheese. I have a bad feeling about the cheese. It may have gone bad."

"Of course," Giles answered. "When you're up to it, we'll discuss it with Agatha."

Buffy sat up. "I'm up to it now."

Dr. Henderson placed his hands on his hips. "I'm afraid I must differ, Miss Summers. You must rest, at least for one more night. You can't walk on that leg yet. In fact, I advise you not to walk on that leg for several weeks. But I can see you're a determined young woman, so I only advise you not to push yourself. You came very close to death, young lady."

Buffy nodded, then shook his hand. "Thank you."

"My pleasure." He packed up the rest of his kit, gauze, needles, and thread, and placed everything into a worn black leather satchel. "And now I must return to the field hospital and see to the new arrivals. Miss Summers." He kissed her hand and made a short bow, then turned and shook hands with Giles.

When he exited the room, Giles shut the door behind him. "It's been close, Buffy. I thought we might lose you."

"Well, here I am. And we need to be ready for those vamps." Not for the first time, Buffy felt grateful that vampires couldn't break into houses. They needed an invitation from the people living there. That meant they didn't have to fortify doors or windows. The vamps would have to wait for them to wander outside, and that gave her time to heal and devise a plan with Agatha.

An hour later Buffy wore a clean pair of trousers and a freshly washed shirt. She sat in the kitchen, sipping tea with cream and sugar from a delicate china cup. Of all the time jumps, this had been the most brutal, and it felt strange to be drinking tea from an elegant tea set.

Agatha's farmhouse stood on one hundred and thirty acres of Tennessee oak-hickory forest, with pastures for her cows, horses, and chickens. Most of the animals had been requisitioned by the Union army, but she still had enough for eggs and milk, and they'd left her two horses. Large glass windows overlooked green fields and trees just getting their spring leaves. In the distance, a ridgeline was dotted white with blooming shadbush and dogwood trees. Several redbud trees bloomed purple-pink just outside the yard.

Agatha sat across from her, wearing a plaid day dress complete with hoop skirts. Her long hair, perfectly coiffed, was swept up and held in place by a silver comb. She wore a cameo pin at the neckline of her dress.

Giles and the others had explained to her where they'd come from and why. At first she hadn't believed them, but eventually she'd grown to trust them. Three days had passed since Buffy was shot, and the Battle of Shiloh was over. Grant had won, driving the Confederate soldiers down south, back to Corinth, Mississippi. For now, the field hospital worked around the clock to help the wounded, but more than twenty thousand soldiers had been injured or killed.

The sun, hanging low on the horizon, gleamed in through the windows, giving the illusion of a normal spring day, in which no war was being fought.

Agatha smiled at her over the rim of her tea cup.

"Do you live here alone?" Buffy asked her.

"My father lives here too. He's fighting right now. Since he left, my Watcher comes by every day. He bought a little place over that ridge." She pointed to the ridge dotted with white trees. "I haven't seen my father for six months, though his name hasn't been on any of the casualty lists. I check frequently at the field hospital." She sipped her tea, looking out over the yard. "I pray for his return every day."

Buffy wasn't sure what to say, so she continued drinking the tea, postponing the need to say something. When she'd drunk the entire cup, she said, "I can't imagine what that must be like."

Agatha put her cup down gently, the china rattling against the saucer. "It's hard. I lost my mother when I was a child. Scarlet fever. Sometimes the pain never seems to end."

"I know," Buffy said, thinking of all the killing and death she'd witnessed firsthand, wrought by both the undead and now human warfare.

"We'll never lead normal lives," Agatha said distantly. "You and I. We'll always be different. While some young women are courted and attend balls, you and I will be fighting vampires in the mud and musty, abandoned barns. It's all we have." The sadness in Agatha's voice pressed in on Buffy.

She set her cup down. "It's not all we have," Buffy told her. "We have people who love us. Our parents. Our Watchers. Our friends." She thought of Angel, of how much she missed him, especially now, separated by more than a hundred and thirty years. It occurred to her that he was alive, even now. He'd be in Europe, but the thought that she could cross the Atlantic at that instant and see him hit her powerfully. Then she remembered that he wouldn't be the sweet man she knew, brave and generous. He'd be Angelus, one of the most feared and evil vampires ever to stalk the earth. In 1898 he'd killed the young gypsy girl, and her family had cursed him forever by returning the human soul to his soulless body. Since then, he'd wandered in self-perpetuating torment, grieving the terrible deeds Angelus had wrought on the innocent. But now, in 1862, that redemption of Angel was more than thirty years away, and she never wanted to meet the evil Angelus.

"That may be, but people talk. I haven't been invited to a party or a ball since I started fighting vampires."

Buffy knew what she meant. While she definitely had her share of nights dancing at the Bronze, boys weren't exactly beating down her door to go out with her. There was Owen, who had almost gotten killed on the first date. And Xander, who'd practically torn her throat out while possessed by a hyena demon. And then Angel, who was all doom and gloom, this omen and that omen, and gee, hope you survive tonight because the Master is rising. But it just wasn't the same as good, old-fashioned romance. Whatever happened to seeing a movie? Or eating in a nice restaurant? With Angel it was always fights in garbage-strewn alleys and smoochies in the graveyard. What was wrong with her life?

She smiled at Agatha. This was what she'd missed about meeting the other Slayers: the commiseration. There they'd been, people who really could have understood how she felt about being a Slayer, and she'd been unable to speak with them. "I'm glad you speak English," she told Agatha.

The Slayer smiled, puzzled. "What?"

Just then Giles, Willow, and Xander entered through the kitchen door. They carried pails of milk and eggs. Xander wore overalls, and his cut looked much better.

"Guys," Buffy told them, "the farmer outfits were just a disguise. You don't actually have to be them."

"Very funny," Xander said. "Laugh all you like. But do you know how hard it is to milk a cow? It doesn't just come out like in the movies. You have to work at it. Tease it out. It's hard."

"Sounds like you have another girlfriend," she told him.

"Ha-ha," Xander retorted mirthlessly.

"And, Will, did you have to coax those eggs from the chickens?" Buffy asked.

"Nope. They just laid them and I picked them up."

"Next time you get the cow," Xander told her.

Giles set the pail of milk on the kitchen table and smiled at Buffy. "It's good to see you up and around."

"Any sign of our friends yet?"

Willow spoke up. "Nope. But I thought I caught the shadow of something creeping around outside last night. Could have been one of them."

Buffy looked over her shoulder, toward the west. The sun continued to dip lower. It would be dark in another two hours, and they'd have to be ready then.

After a dinner of fried eggs, biscuits, and gravy, they sat around next to the fire. The sun sank below the horizon. As Buffy sat in a rocking chair, her injured leg propped up on a footstool, she stared into the flames. Already her wound had vastly improved, compliments of supernatural Slayer healing rate.

The back door squeaked open, and everyone but Agatha spun around in their seats, anticipating an attack. Instead, a brown-haired man in a fancy suit walked through the door and shut it behind himself.

"Evening," he said, his face showing surprise at their presence.

"Niles Hallowell," Agatha said, "I'd like to you to meet four extraordinary people." She introduced all of them, saving Buffy for last. "And this," she said, gesturing at Buffy, "is Buffy Summers. She's a Slayer."

"Impossible!" said Niles.

"Niles is my Watcher," Agatha explained.

Buffy raised her eyebrows. "Your Watcher is named

Niles? Gee, Giles, you have a lot in common already. Niles. Giles."

"Yes, very amusing," he muttered.

"There cannot be more than two living Slayers," Niles went on, unrelenting.

Giles stood up and shook the man's hand. "We aren't from this time period. We've traveled from the future in order stop a team of assassins from murdering Agatha before her natural death."

"Ooo-weeeee-ooooo," Xander said, then did his best rendition of the *Twilight Zone* theme. Agatha and Niles stared at him blankly, as if he'd gone mad. "Oh, right. 1862."

Niles said nothing.

"I don't think I like the sound of all this," said Agatha. "It's frightening. You all know when I'm allotted to die, and it gives me the creeps."

"Hey, you say 'creeps' back here? Cool! Slang is old."

Agatha raised an eyebrow at him.

"I didn't mean you were old, just that slang dates back further than . . ." Xander trailed off before he made things worse.

"We're here to stop you from dying before your natural time," Buffy told her. "What's worse, knowing that we are aware of the year of your natural death, or dying younger than that?"

Agatha turned away, staring into the fire.

Buffy felt bad. She knew that Agatha didn't die that much further into the future. But if she died in the next few days, a different Slayer would be activated instead of the one who should be. Some powerful Slayers came after Agatha's time, including Lucy Hanover, who roamed the Ghost Roads, helping lost souls. Would that be true of Buffy, too? Would the Slayers after her be powerful and heroic?

She thought of Agatha's wishes to attend balls and meet "a handsome gentleman," as she'd put it. She probably wouldn't have the chance. Would Buffy's life be the same too? Were all Slayers destined for short lives and misery? She gritted her teeth. At least Agatha would have all the time coming to her. No two-bit assassins would rob her of that as long as Buffy was alive.

"Just a moment." Niles cut into her thoughts. "I need some time to assimilate this information. I must have details if we're to trust you."

"Of course," Giles told him.

While Niles listened intently, Buffy and the others told him about Lucien and the time magick. They briefed him on the plot to kill Slayers before their natural deaths in order to disrupt the Slayer time line. Niles asked why they would go to these great lengths, and Buffy explained about the Master and his ascension. Frequently Giles shushed her when she gave away more than he thought was needed. He was quite paranoid about messing up the time line. He warned them repeatedly not to talk of historical events, inventions, or persons of future importance, including those related to the outcome of the Civil War. As if Buffy knew all that, anyway. She knew the North won, but aside from Giles's briefing of the Battle of Shiloh, that was about all she knew.

At last Niles understood. "And we have seen no sign of these devils?"

"No," Agatha told him, "though I killed a lot of vampires on the battlefield. They could have been among them."

"I think we've got at least one more to worry about," Buffy said, thinking of Victor. "Maybe more."

"Perhaps I should stay here for tonight," the Watcher offered.

"That would be wise," Giles said. "If they've been watching the house, then by now I'm sure they've learned you are Agatha's Watcher. If you left now, they could take you hostage, demanding that Agatha give herself up."

"That would be unfortunate," Niles conceded, fixing Giles with an annoyed glance.

And here Buffy thought they'd get along famously.

"And now, Agatha, I need to have a word with you in private," Niles said.

Agatha nodded, rising from her chair. "If you will excuse me," she said. She looked pointedly at Xander and Giles, who looked back blankly. Then Giles suddenly stood up, pulling Xander up by the arm. Agatha nodded courteously and left the room with her Watcher. The kitchen door swung shut behind them.

"What was that all about?" Xander said after they'd gone. He rubbed his arm and sat down again.

"We're supposed to rise when a lady stands up," Giles told him, taking his seat as well.

"How quaint," Willow said.

Buffy stood up, and on autopilot, so did Giles and Xander. "You don't have to do that," she told them. "I want to go listen at the door."

"Buffy, don't!" Willow told her. "You should respect their privacy."

"This guy is off, somehow. He's seething with anger. Didn't any of you guys feel that?"

Giles tilted his head to the side thoughtfully. "Well, yes, now that you mention it."

With the help of a cane, Buffy crept to the swinging door that separated the kitchen from the living room. She pushed it open just a crack. In the center of the room stood Watcher and Slayer.

"Did you give thought to what I said earlier?" Niles asked Agatha quietly, merely a whisper in the big house.

"Of course, Niles, but I have to do my part," she answered, just as quietly.

"A Slayer does not have time to be a spy."

"But without my help, the Union would have suffered even heavier losses."

Niles pointed vaguely out the window. "That world out there, that fight, is between two political parties. You fight a greater battle for justice between two worlds, evil and good. That's the war that needs you, Agatha. This human war will wage on tirelessly with or without your help."

Agatha turned away from him, her face full of sorrow. "But where do I draw the line between good and evil? Surely humanity causes its share of evil." She turned back to him. "Beyond that window lie thousands of wounded or dead soldiers. If a spy like me had delivered word of the surprise attack, some of those casualties could have been avoided."

Niles crossed his arms over his chest stubbornly. "I won't have it. It's too risky. If you were found out by Confederate scouts, you would be shot or lynched. You're too important to risk by taking part in this god-awful war."

She pointed an accusing finger at his chest. "This war is ravaging my homeland, Niles. It's easier for you to remain distant to it. You are British, and your home is secure. I can't ignore battles taking place in the very fields surrounding my land."

"I don't expect you to ignore it, Agatha. I merely want you to adhere to your duties as the Slayer."

"And I will!" she said, her voice slightly raised. "I will do both." She crossed her arms too, her chin raised defiantly. "Now don't talk to me again of this matter. You are my Watcher, and I listen to your counsel in all things having to do with the slaying of vampires. But I will not turn my back on my country, even if you request it."

Then Agatha spun on her heels and climbed the stairs to her bedroom.

Niles sighed in exasperation, then flung himself down in a nearby chair. He brought one hand to his face, resting his forehead there. Buffy backed slowly into the kitchen, careful not to trip on her injured leg.

"Did you guys hear all that?" she whispered.

"Only some of it," Willow said. "She's a spy?"

Buffy nodded, making her way back to the chair. She sat down with some difficulty and propped her leg up again on the footstool.

A few moments later Agatha returned to the kitchen. She smoothed her skirts and forced a smile. "I apologize for my rudeness as a hostess," she said. "But we had a matter to attend to."

Agatha had just finished her sentence when a Molotov cocktail sailed through a window, shattering it. The flaming bottle of whiskey skittered across the floor. Instantly the window curtains went up in flames. Then another crashed through a different window. Niles cried out in surprise, bursting through the swinging door. The living room was on fire, the windows there shattered.

Three more flaming bottles crashed through the remaining windows, spreading fire in their wake. Buffy and the others leaped up as a wall of flame sealed off the back door. She leaned on the cane, rushing to the front door. A sideboard full of china roared with fire, flames spreading to the door itself.

One cocktail had landed on the stairs leading to the upper floor, and the dry wood erupted instantly, blocking off the route entirely.

They were trapped, and Buffy's world filled with fire.

Chapter Thirty-nine

"**B**uffy! This way!" Xander's voice cut through the chaos. "There's a basement entrance that's still clear!"

Buffy ran into the front room with the others close behind. Down a narrow hallway stood an open door. Xander waved her forward. She reached him, and he turned and raced down a set of rickety wooden steps into the waiting darkness of the cellar.

Buffy followed closely, the two Watchers, Agatha, and Willow piling up in the doorway above. The smell of dank earth filled Buffy's nose as she hobbled across the dirt floor, following Xander. He reached another, shorter set of steps on the opposite end of the cellar. Flickering light gleamed through the high windows of the basement, shedding some light on the scene. At the top of the short flight of stairs, two double doors tilted at an angle. He went to them and flung them open quickly. The way out was clear. No flames flickered nearby.

As they raced out, Buffy braced herself, ready to fight. She emerged, the heat consuming the house, causing her to turn away from the blaze.

There, standing nearby, were not the two vampires she had expected, but nine.

Victor had found some recruits.

This time, he had to die.

Chapter Forty

Victor watched the Slayer emerge from the cellar doors. They'd just been rounding the house to set fire to those, too. But they'd been too slow. This team he'd assembled left a lot to be desired. All of them had drunk on the battlefield till they were bloated. They moved slowly, and were so overfed that even their coordination was sloppy.

"Set them on fire!" he ordered two vampires closest to the Scoobies. Though they each held two torches, the vamps turned to Victor, blank expressions on their faces.

"Who?" they asked in unison.

"Them!" Victor shouted, pointing at Buffy and the others.

The two moved forward with all the urgency of drunken sloths racing drowsy snails. By the time they'd reached Buffy's position, Giles and the others had run to safety. Buffy kicked the lead vamp with her good leg, stole his torch, and staked him with it. She set the other one on fire. Both erupted into ashes. Agatha joined her side.

Then Buffy pointed the torch at Victor. "This one's mine," she told Agatha.

As three other vampires moved to attack, Victor crept back. Might as well let the other vamps die and tire out the Slayers as much as possible. He didn't relish the thought of fighting both at the same time.

But Buffy made a beeline for him, the torch upraised threateningly. She limped from an injury, obviously biting back pain, but it wasn't stopping her. A cruel determination gleamed in her eyes, and Victor fought the urge to run.

He did move, though, skirting around her, hoping to join the three more vamps who had not yet attacked.

Behind him, Agatha dusted one, then another vampire. He heard the gasp of their bodies turning to dust. Daring a look over at the struggle, he saw her engaged with the third vampire. Another one of Lucien's lame recruits, the third vampire had been undead for about thirty minutes when Lucien recruited him. Literally. He'd waited for the guy to crawl out of the earth in the cemetery and then gave him his first assignment.

And while he'd been only thirty minutes old— three days and thirty minutes old by now—he had been a black belt aikido instructor while living. And while that sounded really tough, the guy's name was Hiram Gigglesworth. Seriously. Victor had even read the tombstone name twice in disbelief. But the guy could kick some serious ass. Victor had to give that to him. Ever since they'd arrived, he'd been kicking everyone's ass—except, that is, of the people he'd been sent there to defeat.

By now the guy was worn out, cut in a dozen places by bayonets, shot, and even had a hatchet driven into his shoulder blade. Plus, he'd joined the vampire glut on the battlefield. He was like a junkie for the soldiers' blood, and Victor had to pull him off them more times than he could count just so they could reach the farmhouse.

Victor had recruited help along the way. Just telling these new vamps that he was out to dust two Slayers made them join up fast. Well, those that didn't run away screaming joined up pretty fast. And those that did join were generally cocky jerks with something to prove, who were actually stupid enough to think they could take out a Slayer.

But as long as it worked to Victor's advantage, that was fine with him.

Now Buffy moved forward, cutting off his path toward the other three vamps. Xander joined Agatha and together they held Hiram down in an attempt to stake him. They weren't doing too well. He threw both of them off, then leaped and kicked, connecting painfully with Xander's jaw. Agatha got the other boot in her stomach.

Victor continued to back away, seeing out of the

corner of his eye that now even the two Watchers and the young slip of a girl, Willow, were busting out the moves. The vamps were so stupid and slow that the Watchers dusted one with a mulberry tree branch.

The Brits moved on to the next vampire. Now only two lackeys survived, in addition to him and Hiram.

Buffy ran at Victor, favoring her injured leg and thrusting the flaming torch before her. Victor dodged to the side, but she reached his sleeve with the flame. The fire spread up to his shoulder, catching his hair on fire. As it spread over his torso, panic set in. Dammit! He hated fire. Ever since he'd nearly burned to death in the London Fire of 1666, he'd been outright paranoid about it. It was fine as a weapon wielded against his enemy, but when it pointed at him, he nearly lost all self-control. Buffy wasn't supposed to escape from that burning house. She was supposed to die inside.

He made a grab for her, hoping to set her aflame, but she ducked and rolled away. He dropped to the ground, desperate to put the flames out. He rolled in the wet grass, the flames hissing. Most of them went out.

To his left, between rolls, he saw Hiram advancing again on Agatha. Xander lay nearby, unmoving.

He rolled again to crush the last flame, and then Buffy was on top of him, suddenly, her weight landing solidly on his back. He heard his bones crack.

She drove the burning end of the torch deeply into his back. He screamed as the wood connected with his heart.

The heat spread throughout his body, and for the briefest second, he could actually feel his molecules separating as he turned to dust.

His final thought was that he couldn't believe Hiram Gigglesworth had lasted longer than he had.

Chapter Forty-one

As Victor turned to ashes beneath her, Buffy reached inside his jacket pocket, pulling out the folded incantations. He vanished beneath her, and she landed with a thump on the ground.

Two vampires came at her sluggishly, a gaunt female and a plump male with long, stringy brown hair. Buffy rose, wincing at the pain in her leg, and whipped the torch around to face them. Flames still licked around the end of the wood, and she rushed forward, impaling and killing the female. When the other vamp grabbed her, she twisted out of his grasp. Niles rushed forward, leaping on the vampire's back. The vampire staggered under the weight and fell. Niles fell clumsily on top of him, so now Buffy couldn't move in for the fatal stake. She waited for the Watcher to get to his feet, then told him to stand back.

Slowly the bloated vampire rose. She spotted a tree behind him with a low hanging branch, sharp and broken off at the end. With a solid kick, Buffy connected with his head, sending him reeling backward into the tree. The protruding branch pierced his heart. She landed from the kick, sweating from the agony of standing on her injured leg.

Now only one vampire remained, a big brute of a guy fighting Agatha.

Buffy limped to the Slayer. "This one isn't cooperating," said Agatha, leaping high in her skirts and delivering a wicked kick to the giant's neck. His head snapped backward violently, and he stumbled, arms windmilling. Buffy ran up behind him, planted the torch firmly on the ground, and let the beast fall backward onto it.

Dust billowed upward.

Teamwork. It was the best.

Agatha stood gasping over the ash-strewn site, catching her breath.

"We did it," Buffy exclaimed.

"That was it?" the Slayer asked. "No more?"

Buffy peered into the gloom surrounding the fire. No other vamps loomed on the periphery. Victor had been their leader, and if any had seen this display of dustage, they probably hadn't hung around.

Now Agatha turned toward the fire. Searing heat radiated from it, causing perspiration to spring up on Buffy's brow. "My home," Agatha said. "It's gone." The southern side of the house collapsed as she said it, fiery timbers raining down in the darkness. "I've lived here since I was born."

Niles joined her, placing an arm around her. "You can stay at my house until your father returns."

She stared into the flames, uncertain. "Will he return?" she asked him at last, meeting his gaze.

"Yes," Niles told her emphatically.

Buffy looked to Giles, who stood nearby, hands on his knees, listening. She raised her eyebrows, and her Watcher nodded. *Yes, her father does return.*

Buffy went to her, putting an arm around her as well. "You're safe now, at least from the assassins." Her leg pulsed with pain, as if it were on fire, but she didn't look at it. Blood trickled down her skin under the pants leg.

"Thank you," Agatha said, but her voice was tiny and hollow, small in the face of such a huge loss. Now her mother was gone, her father away, and her childhood home with everything she had was turning to ash.

Buffy felt a hard, painful lump grow in her throat and turned away. She wanted to stay, to help her rebuild, but nothing could make up for this loss. They needed to get back. If more Slayers had been targeted, every moment counted.

She hoped the loss of Victor would prove grave for Lucien. Victor had been clever and ruthless. But now he was just another demon destroyed.

Buffy and the Scoobies saw Agatha and Niles safely to the Watcher's house, then said their goodbyes.

Buffy felt this parting more than the others, perhaps because she had truly bonded with Agatha. Or perhaps because she knew the Slayer didn't live far into the future. Again she questioned her own mortality, but forced those thoughts away quickly.

After they'd all hugged good-bye, Giles ushered her, Willow, and Xander out to the back field.

He performed the incantations. The sickening spiral of light winked into view, pulling at twigs, grass, and fallen leaves. It tugged at her hair, then her body, and all four leaped into the portal, returning once again to their home.

Chapter Forty-two

Sunnydale, 1998

With a painful thump, Buffy landed in a pile of garbage behind the Sunnydale health food store. Her hand squished into a moldering pile of wheat germ, and her face plopped down into a discarded tub of garlic hummus. She spat it out, trying to lift her head. Rolling over, she watched Xander, then Willow, surge out of the vortex. Light played over the alley walls. Giles groaned somewhere nearby. Xander tumbled downward, and Buffy shifted to the side just before he crashed down next to her.

Willow landed feetfirst on a garbage bag, which split open on impact. Couscous and part of a vegetarian burger spilled out, oozing over her boots.

Buffy's leg throbbed, and she hoped she didn't get any rotting hummus in the wound. She wiped the garlic concoction off her face. Ack. She wouldn't be kissing Angel anytime soon. Sunlight streamed down into the alley, allowing Buffy to see every bit of festering garbage clinging to her in explicit detail.

"First kelp, now seaweed," Giles muttered. "And we're not even near the ocean." He pulled a long strand of green slime off his face.

Wincing with pain, Buffy used the alley wall to rise and steady herself. Willow rushed to her side and supported her. Xander lay still, unmoving in the heap of trash. "I think I have a banana in my ear," he told them. Rising, Giles offered his hand and shakily helped Xander to his feet. "I can't take much more of this," Xander said. "This is the worst way to travel!" He gestured rudely at the vanished portal.

"Hey, I thought you were all 'I'm the time travel expert,'" Willow told him.

"That was before I knew it involved throwing up, trash heaps, and hanging precariously from lifeguard towers."

As the others brushed themselves off, Buffy pulled out the incantations she'd stolen from Victor. They were a duplicate of the ones they'd gotten from Lucien. "No additional time periods. Do we still need to go to the French Revolution?" Buffy asked Giles as they walked out of the alley.

"What do you mean?"

"I killed Victor. The last recurring assassin. Now neither Lucien nor Victor will be able to get new recruits."

Giles looked thoughtful. "They may have a backup plan—other assassins already chosen in the event Victor doesn't return. I think Lucien's reaction to the news of Victor will be quite telling in this instance." He flicked a piece of granola off his sleeve.

Willow followed his thought. "Right. If he insists that we have no reason to go to Paris, then we can be sure he has someone waiting in the wings. If he encourages us to go, then we'll know he has no one and is just hoping we'll get killed by angry mobs."

"Angry mobs?" Xander asked. "Angry mobs?"

"Yes, Xander," Willow told him. "The French Revolution. Angry mobs. Guillotines."

He swallowed. "Guillotines?" He brought a hand to his neck. "Doesn't this guy ever pick sunny Acapulco or a nice beach in the Bahamas?"

"Tell me about it," Buffy said. "He's evil."

"My Little Pony evil," Xander agreed.

Emerging from the alley, they blinked in the sunlight, getting their bearings. Heading off in different directions, they agreed to all meet at the library in an hour.

Buffy burst through the double doors of the library. "Hah!" she said to Lucien.

The vampire looked up sleepily, then raised his eyebrows.

"Hah?" Angel asked, standing up.

"Consider your master plan officially minus one Victor."

Lucien struggled to hide the dismay in his face. Failed. He pursed his lips together angrily, his eyes glowering. "Well, then," he said. "You've won."

"Not quite," Giles said, entering the room. He held up the French Revolution incantation. "How many backup assassins do you have?"

Lucien bared his teeth. "None," he hissed. "You've killed them. Victor was my best." But he averted his eyes nervously as he said it.

Buffy looked at her Watcher. "Well, Giles?"

"Right. I'll get the clothes."

Lucien threaded his thin fingers through the cage door. "What are you doing?"

"Getting ready for the next time jump," Buffy told him.

"But there's no reason for you to make the final one," he said. "You've won." He was a little *too* insistent.

"Then you won't care if we just check on the French Slayer, right?"

He cleared his throat nervously. "Why would I care?"

"Exactly. Why would you care?"

After Willow and Xander arrived, they dressed in the clothes Giles laid out—white cotton shirts, black jackets, long black pants, and strange floppy hats, each with a red, white, and blue rosette made of ribbon.

"They're liberty cockades," Giles informed them, pointing to a rosette. "They signify that we support the Revolution. We're jumping to 1792, a time when we don't want to be confused with aristocrats."

Buffy picked up the shirt and pants.

"Again, dressing as a man will give you maximum mobility."

She nodded, then took her outfit to the women's restroom to change.

When they all met back in the library, dressed in eighteenth-century garb, Giles checked their satchels for the obligatory paper and pencil, water, and maps.

"Giles," Buffy said, "I've been carrying that paper and pencil around this whole time. I haven't used it yet."

"Keep it," he told her. Then he lifted the tiny stub of a pencil. "You could use it as a stake."

She rolled her eyes. "Well, if I run into a vampire that's four inches tall, I'll be prepared."

"Okay," Giles said, ready to brief them. "Let's go to my office." Inside, they closed the door. Angel stood close to Buffy, and she welcomed his presence. "This Slayer is Marguerite Allard. She's an aristocrat in a time of great unrest in Paris. This will be dangerous."

Buffy's leg ached, and she hoped this jump wouldn't be worse than Shiloh.

"I've marked her address on your maps. Should we get separated, let's meet at her house."

They all agreed, and Giles took out the incantation

for 1792. Angel wished them luck, kissing Buffy good-bye. "Be careful there," he whispered to her. He turned then and left the tiny office.

Giles spoke the incantation, and Buffy braced herself to return to a world at war.

Chapter Forty-three

Paris, 1792

Buffy whirled through the portal, landing painfully on one shoulder in a puddle of vile-smelling water. She struggled to her feet, groggy, the shouts from a nearby crowd filling the air.

The darkness of night filled the city streets and dank alleyways. She turned back to the portal to await the others' arrival and saw a second portal, spinning in the air some distance away.

A figure sailed out of it, followed by a second. The assassins! She couldn't believe it! They'd actually arrived in roughly the same place at the same time.

Steadying her legs, she stumbled toward them,

nauseous and dizzy from the portal travel. The cobblestones beneath her feet made the going rough. She twisted her ankles more than once in her haste. Finally the grogginess wore off and Buffy quickened her pace, limping on her wounded leg.

One of the vampires had landed in the center of the street. With the shouts and cries of an angry crowd, still out of sight, he didn't hear her approach.

She reached into her jacket pocket, pulling out a fresh stake. The vampire propped himself up, shaking off the ill effects of the transport. She didn't recognize him, but he was huge. A monster of a guy with a bald head and the physique of a school bus. So Lucien did have backups waiting.

Almost upon him, she leaped. The second vampire lay some distance away, trying to rise to his feet. Buffy landed solidly on the bald vampire, straddling him. As he gazed up, surprised and terrified, she thrust the stake into his heart. Dust plumed upward, and she fell to the street beneath.

Now she stood up quickly. The second vampire stood up, staring at her in horror. The shouting of the mob grew closer and closer. The vampire turned and ran. She sprinted after him. As she rounded a corner in pursuit, she ran full-on into an angry mob scene straight out of *Frankenstein*. Torches blazed; swarthy, dirt-clad people shouted. Spittle sprayed. Pitchforks, guns, and swords were lifted above heads angrily.

The vampire dashed into the midst of the roiling

mass of people. Buffy followed, immediately slowed by the writhing throng of bodies, and she cursed her bum leg. She clawed her way past a woman in a muddy gown, squeezed by a man who apparently hadn't taken a bath in his entire life, shoved past a guy hawking etchings of a recent hanging, and emerged in a small pocket of space.

She whirled in all directions, searching for the vampire. Twenty feet ahead she saw his brown, frizzy head weaving through the crowd. She pushed on in that direction. A hand grabbed her and shoved her as she moved. People shouted at her, asking her brusque questions in French. She ignored them, couldn't understand them anyway.

Then a mass of shouting sprang up, and simultaneously the crowd roared, *"Vive la nation!"* A rotten cabbage sailed by her head, followed by a stream of decaying tomatoes. She jumped up and down, trying to catch sight of the frizzy head. The crowd was too thick, too vast to see over where she was. She spotted a wooden staircase climbing up the side of a nearby building. Thrusting through the crowd, she reached it, finding it clogged with even more people. Why were they all just standing around like this, shouting?

She pushed by a young boy and his mother and climbed a couple of steps, searching the crowd for the assassin's head.

She saw him nowhere. She scanned the crowd for five minutes, searching for his unkempt brown hair. A sea of hats stretched out before her. She didn't see a single bare-headed person. She'd lost him.

A renewed frenzy from among the crowd brought her gaze up. *"Vive la révolution!"* they shouted in unison.

From this vantage point she saw the reason for the gathering. She stood at the edge of the Place de la Révolution. In the center loomed a high platform with a guillotine on top. Four soldiers of the Republic stood on the stairs leading to the execution platform.

A wagon had arrived, carrying a young girl no older than twelve and two adults, who could have been her mother and father. Though they were grimy now, their clothes had at one time been very expensive, the height of Paris fashion. Aristocrats, Buffy realized, going to the guillotine.

Her mind traveled to the *Scarlet Pimpernel* miniseries she'd seen once as a little kid, with Anthony Andrews as the gallant English hero saving aristocrats from the guillotine. For a second she expected him to arrive, swinging into view from a grappling hook slung over a nearby building. But as the soldiers dragged the crying and pleading family from the wagon and forced them up the small stairs to the execution platform, Buffy remembered it was just fiction.

She couldn't believe these people were going to be executed. What crime had they committed? Being rich? Being extravagant? The crowd seethed with hatred, throwing more rotted lettuce heads and melons at them. One putrid tomato hit the mother in the face, and she stood shocked for a moment, the seeds and pulp dripping off her cheek.

Then the guards shoved her forward, and the family piled up on the platform. They grabbed the little girl. She screamed in terror as they shoved her toward the guillotine.

Buffy couldn't just stand there and watch. "What's wrong with you people!" she shouted. "She's just a kid!"

A few people turned to stare at her, but most kept their eyes firmly fixed on the anticipated execution.

Buffy couldn't bear it. She leaped off the stairs, shoving the watching mother and son out of her way, and surged into the crowd. She knew she shouldn't change history. If that little girl lived, she could forever alter the future. But Buffy didn't care. She couldn't just stand by. She pressed forward.

So little space existed between bodies that she'd only pushed forward a few feet before she heard the sickening *snick* of the guillotine blade. The crowd screamed with delight, urging the soldiers to send the next prisoner up.

She continued to fight forward, shoving people, knocking them out of the way, not worried about using her Slayer strength. If they had a few bruises tomorrow, so be it. She shoved a few feet more and heard the second downsweep of the guillotine.

Again the crowd roared with satisfaction, cheering and thrusting their weapons into the air.

Buffy couldn't see the guillotine at all now. She pushed people aside, winnowing her way through the throng. The guillotine blade screamed down for the third time. The crowd jumped and cheered, jostling her violently. An elbow came down on her head, then a knee in her back.

She stopped. The family was dead.

Disgusted and horrified, Buffy pushed her way backward, working toward the alley next to the stairwell she'd used. Someone bumped into her sore leg, and she sucked in a sharp breath, then pressed on.

After ten minutes of struggling past more elbows, arms, and feet in her path, she emerged from the crowd. Locating the alley, she ran to it, wanting to find the others.

They had a huge advantage this time. She had already staked one of the assassins, and she knew what the other one looked like. They could move quickly this time, perhaps staking the other vampire before even finding the Slayer.

Some of her stress dissipated.

She hurried down the narrow alley back toward their entry point. When she arrived, Willow and Giles spotted her. "How far away did you land?" Willow asked her.

"I got one of them!" she told them. "The vampires landed right next to us! I saw them come out of the portal and everything!"

"I thought I saw a strange glimmer in the sky as I landed," Giles said, "but it vanished almost immediately."

Buffy went on. "I staked one right off the bat. The other one got away, but I know what he looks like."

"Remarkable," Giles said.

"That's fantastic!" Willow agreed.

"Where's Xander?"

"He went off searching for you," Willow told her.

Buffy hooked her thumb in the direction of the guillotine-occupied square. "There's a really angry mob over that way. I don't think it's safe."

Just then a breathless Xander ran out of the shadows. "There's a really angry mob over there. This place isn't safe!"

He rested, leaning over, hands on his knees.

"It's okay," Giles told him. "We've landed during the Reign of Terror."

"And that's *okay*?" Xander asked incredulously.

"What's the Reign of Terror?" Buffy asked.

"One of the bloodiest parts of the French Revolution, when unbelievable numbers of people were sent to the guillotine. Most of them had been fingered by Robespierre, the Revolution's public accuser. Eventually they even cut his head off," Willow explained.

"Eeeek," said Xander.

"I guess they didn't want to eat cake," Buffy said.

"It will all be fine," Giles reassured them. "Just be sure to wear your liberty caps and Republic rosettes." He pointed to the red, blue, and white ribbon cockades he'd made them all put on before leaving. Buffy's liberty cap slouched loosely on her head, and the wool itched.

"And be sure not to put on any short pants!" he added.

"Excuse me?" asked Xander.

"Short pants. The nobility and bourgeoisie wear them. One of the strongest groups in the revolution, the Sans-Culottes, wear long pants."

"The French Revolution was fought over knickers?" Xander asked, amazed.

"No, Xander," Willow told him. "It was more what the knickers represented. Wealth and the extravagance of the bourgeoisie and the nobility."

"You're going to fit right in, Will," Buffy said.

"Well, the peasants had a point," Willow pressed. "All those rich aristocrats prancing around in their fancy pants, spending money willy-nilly on chocolates and extravagant carriages and clothes that were the latest fashion. The peasants couldn't afford the latest fashions, and their moms weren't exactly pressing to have them fit in and be popular or anything. And then there were the bourgeoisie, pretending to be so fashion-conscious and self-righteous, insulting the peasants every day and putting them down in front of the drinking fountain, when really the aristocrats were just a bunch of shallow cheerleaders who probably couldn't even memorize their own locker combinations."

"Uh, Will?" Xander asked. "We still talking about the French Revolution here?"

"Yes!" she said defiantly, sticking her chin out. "It was exactly like that."

"Well, okay, then. Just checking," he told her.

"Giles, where does the Slayer live?" Buffy asked.

He reached into his satchel, pulling out a small notebook and a map of Revolution-era Paris. "It's near the intersection of Rue Saint Honoré and Rue de Richelieu, near the Place du Carrousel. But we need to be careful. It's a very wealthy part of town, and tensions will be high there."

"Let's go. I say we stick to our habit of finding the Slayer first and waiting for the assassin to come to her," Buffy said. "Meanwhile, I'll keep my eye out for the guy."

Giles nodded his assent, and with Willow and Xander still discussing the finer points of the French Revolution and its cruel football players, they headed in that direction.

Willow looked on in disbelief. "It's burned down."

Buffy stared at the blackened ruins of the house. A light drizzle rained from the sky, hissing on the burned remains. "This happened recently," she said. She scanned the streets, wondering if the Slayer might still be nearby. The garbage-strewn road before them lay empty. Suddenly hooting and shouting pulled their attention to a grimy side alley. A woman and man emerged, raising a bottle of cheap wine, staggering and leaning on each other. They disappeared down a side street.

"It's not the only house that was burned," Willow said, pointing out several other buildings black with fire scars.

"Power to the people," Giles murmured under his

breath. "We can still try the Watcher's house." He regarded his map. "It's down this street, a little closer to the library, the *bibliothèque*."

"Now how did we guess that?" Buffy said ruefully.

"I'm sure it's a complete coincidence," Giles told her.

"I'm sure."

They covered the remaining distance to the Watcher's house, nervously watching any people who passed them. Shouts resounded. All around, cries pierced the night, and the smell of fires and festering garbage hung heavily in the air.

"This is it," Giles announced when they had reached a rather posh-looking town house, complete with ten chimneys and several balconies.

"And he lives considerably better than you," Xander said.

"She lives, actually," Giles corrected. "She does live considerably better than I."

They walked up the short flight of brick steps to the large wooden double doors and knocked. No one answered. Giles called out to the upper windows, and Buffy tried the doors at the side and in the back of the house. All the windows were dark. No one stirred inside.

"She's out," Willow said at last.

Hastily Giles produced a paper and pencil and scrawled a note in French to the Watcher, warning her of the assassin and stating that he could be recruiting more help. Then he stuck the note between the door frame and the door.

"How will we find the Slayer now?" Willow asked. "She could have fled Paris for all we know, or even the country!"

"We can ask around," Xander offered.

A group of angry-looking ruffians wearing long pants and liberty hats walked by, giving them a nod. Giles nodded back.

Willow gave a little wave, smiling through gritted teeth. "This place makes me nervous. I can feel the tension pressing in on me. It's practically suffocating."

"Yes," Giles agreed. "It is rather like the old cliché about a powder keg."

Buffy could feel it too. She could hear the roar of angry crowds in the distance, and her nostrils filled with the smell of scorched wood. The Slayer and her family had been driven out of their home. Poor people wallowed in the gutter with nothing to eat. Armed soldiers and gangs of thugs roamed the streets. Everyone was looking for someone to blame for their misery. Even the king had been executed.

"I think we need to find the vampire. I know what he looks like, and the sooner we find him, the less time he'll have to get recruits like Victor did."

"Sounds good," Xander said. "I don't like the thought of fighting that many vamps at once again."

Buffy remembered him spending much of that fight slumped in a limp pile on the grass, but she didn't mention it.

"This is an excellent idea," Giles said. "Because you killed his companion, the vampire will almost certainly seek some sort of backup."

"But where do we look?" asked Willow.

"Vampire bars. Eighteenth-century equivalents to Willy's?" Buffy suggested.

"How will we find them?" Xander asked. "Hang out in seedy alleyways and wait for vampires to follow?"

"Good idea," Buffy said. "And I think we should split up."

"What?" Xander cried. "Are you crazy? We can't split up! That's exactly what you're not supposed to do in supernatural situations. As soon as you split up, you're picked off one by one. Maniacs spear you with pitchforks. Masked lunatics come after you with chain saws."

"But we don't have that much time, Xander," Buffy insisted. "The more time he has to get help, the more vampires we'll be fighting when we find the Slayer. Paris is a big city, and who knows how many vampire bars there are? We'll break into two groups and search in a circle radiating out from our point of entry."

"Can I be in your group?" Xander asked.

"Agreed," Buffy said. She turned to Giles. "Watch over Willow."

"I will," he said.

"Where will we all meet up?" Willow asked.

"We'll meet in the center square with the guillotine in two hours. There'll still be a huge crowd there, and it'll be easier for us to blend in. And safer."

Xander raised his index finger. "So you're saying

it'll be safer for us in the middle of a sea of bloodthirsty people instead of hiding in an alley where the blood-thirsty people can find us?"

Buffy nodded. "Exactly."

"Oh, boy."

Together they returned to the city square where Buffy had lost track of the assassin. Then they parted, agreeing to meet there again in two hours.

Xander walked close to Buffy as they navigated the streets. They watched for vampires, and Buffy worried about Giles and Willow. More so about Willow, because she knew Giles was tougher than he seemed, as long as he didn't get knocked on the head. At last they spotted two vampires, one with blood clotted in the corner of her mouth. They had already fed for the evening. Perhaps now they'd be looking to socialize.

Buffy and Xander held to the shadows, trailing the pair in ragged clothes. The male vampire walked with a limp but still managed to swagger with that insuffer-able undead pride.

The pair unwittingly led them down a back alley-way to a grimy little pub teeming with all manner of demons, vampires, and assorted spawn from a variety of hell dimensions.

While the two vampires strolled into the pub, Buffy and Xander crouched down in the shadows next to a reeking pile of garbage. Her leg throbbed from all the walking, and resting it felt heavenly. "How are we going to get in there?" Xander whispered. "We can't just saunter in there and say, 'Gee, anyone seen an assassin?'"

"You're right," Buffy whispered. "They'll immediately sense we're humans." She looked down the alley. A lone vampire approached, staggeringly drunk, weaving in the narrow confines of the alley. "What we need is a distraction."

Xander tensed. "I'm not the distraction, right?"

"No. I won't use you." She pointed behind the teeming stack of garbage. "Quick! Get behind that!"

"Get behind it! I can barely stand the reek from here."

"Then you're volunteering to be the distraction?"

"I'll be behind the garbage." Xander crept over the wet cobblestones, crouching down behind the odoriferous pile of rotting lettuce, coffee grounds, rancid meat scraps, and stained rags reeking of turpentine and urine. "Oh, God." He stifled his gag reflex.

Buffy followed partway, pausing at the edge of the garbage pile, lying in wait for the approaching vamp.

He staggered closer, unaware of them, and just as he turned to step into the pub, she leaped up, grabbing the collar of his shirt. He grunted in surprise as she shoved him into the pub. She ducked back outside as he crashed into a table of horned demons playing cards.

"Hey, what do you think you're doing!" she heard one demon shout in a heavy Scottish accent. "You ruined my hand!"

At the first sound of punching, Buffy ducked her head into the door. The table had erupted into a fight, fists swinging and tails lashing. The next table, jarred by the violence, toppled over. Those patrons, three willowy vampires dressed in elegant clothes, stood up and grabbed the card-playing demons. A horn went through someone's arm, and a table shattered under the weight of a body slam. As a chair sailed overhead, Buffy studied all the faces in the bar. Plenty of vampires, but not the one she was searching for.

She ducked back outside as a bottle shattered against the door frame.

"No luck," she said to the garbage pile. "On to the next bar."

Xander rose, brushing himself off. He sniffed his jacket as he fell in line beside her. "Between this and our last Sunnydale landing, I'm going to smell like a compost heap for a week."

"And that's different how?" she teased him.

"Hey!"

They trawled more neighboring alleys, radiating out from the Place de la Révolution. They found two more vampire hangouts, then four, then six. Each time they used a variation of the same method to scan the crowd within, and each time they came up empty.

"You don't think that guy has already succeeded, do you? Just did it singlehandedly?" Xander warned.

She regarded him gravely. "Let's hope not." A group of Sans-Culottes walked by, glaring at them.

"Man! We're in long pants and they still hate us!" Xander cried.

"It's seems like everyone hates everyone right now," Buffy said, knowing it was more complicated than that. But her gut was sick of the hatred in the air, of the tension and the reek of burning buildings and rotted garbage building up in the streets. This was not how she'd envisioned Paris. She always thought she'd be sitting at some cosmopolitan sidewalk cafe, sipping cappuccino with a fiendishly handsome Parisian poet or painter, bags upon bags of designer clothes piled at her feet.

She made a mental note to return sometime when a Reign of Terror wasn't on.

They worked their way down the next alley, and suddenly Buffy resisted the urge to cry out in relief. There, in front of her, hurried the assassin vampire, his frizzy hair practically glowing in the light from a nearby window.

"There he is!" she whispered loudly to Xander.

He ducked inside a small door halfway down the alley. Loud laughter and the clicking of glasses emanated from within. "Let's go!"

She slunk to the edge of the door, then peered around it. Inside, a raucous bunch of vampires gathered, their feet up on tables. Women in low-cut dresses sat on men's laps sipping mugs full of red, viscous liquid. The assassin headed directly over to a particular table, as if he already knew someone there.

He stopped at the table, joining a man and a woman. The man had long, dark hair, tied in the back with a black ribbon. His back was to Buffy. The woman, also turned away, wore a very elaborate blue velvet gown trimmed with white lace. She laughed at something her companion said, her blond curls bouncing around her shoulders.

The assassin cleared his throat, and the male vampire turned to face him. Buffy sucked in a sharp breath as she saw his face. Ducking out of the door, she pressed flat to the alley wall.

"What is it?" Xander asked, seeing the alarm on her face.

Buffy tried to catch her breath. The assassin wasn't the only one who knew him. Buffy did too.

It was Angel.

Chapter Forty-four

"**A**ngel!" Xander cried, and Buffy clapped a hand over his mouth. In a harsh whisper he said, "You mean Angelus, right? Like in Giles's Watcher journals? Wasn't this when he was the scourge of Europe? Didn't he personally wage his own Reign of Terror on everyone around him? Didn't he kill his own family?"

Buffy said nothing, only nodded. She needed to think.

After a moment, she dared another peek inside. The assassin now sat at the table with Angelus, talking adamantly with him and his companion. She turned slightly to say something to the hired killer, and Buffy recognized her, too. It was Darla, Angelus's sire. This merciless duo had slaughtered unknown masses of people throughout the centuries.

The assassin continued to talk, and Darla and Angelus nodded. Then he showed them something Buffy couldn't quite see. Angelus's body blocked the way. She strained for a look, but to no avail. Darla looked impressed, and the assassin put it away again.

Then he watched them expectantly. Darla and Angelus rose from the table, entering a room behind the bar. Buffy could no longer see them. She ducked out of the way again, wanting to avoid detection.

"What's going on?" Xander asked her.

"I think he's recruiting Darla and Angelus to help," she told him.

"So what do we do now?"

"We need to lure them out somehow, so we can stake them before they find the Slayer."

"Even Angel?"

Buffy didn't answer that question. It made her sick to think about it. She loved Angel. She thought of him back in the future, guarding Lucien for them. She'd make sure she left here without having to do anything like that. "Hold on a second."

She leaned back in and saw Darla and Angelus return. Between them they held a struggling girl, bound and gagged. She'd been bitten several times, and blood streamed down her neck, staining her once white dress deep scarlet.

The assassin's face lit up with excitement as soon as he saw the girl. He nodded to Darla and Angelus.

What was going on? The girl staggered, weak

from loss of blood. The sheer excitement on the assassin's thin face could mean only one thing. This wasn't some snack Darla and Angelus were offering him.

This was the Slayer.

And Buffy was too late.

Chapter Forty-five

Buffy paused outside the pub, getting her thoughts straight. The assassin hadn't arrived at the pub for the first time just now, he'd already struck the bargain with Darla and Angelus sometime earlier.

That probably meant that he knew exactly where to find them from the moment he landed. Which meant it had been the plan all along to enlist two of the deadliest vamps in history.

They'd captured the Slayer for him, and in return . . . in return? How would the duo benefit from such a thing? Why not kill the Slayer themselves? Buffy had to get closer to hear what they were saying over the commotion of the pub. To their right was a small window, only feet away from their table. She signaled for Xander to follow her over there.

They crept silently to a very narrow side alley and

waded through piles of putrid garbage. Their feet slid in raw sewage, and Buffy stifled her urge to gag as the stench blossomed up from her feet.

Behind her Xander did gag, and she turned to shush him. Tears streamed down his face. Removing his liberty cap, he pressed it over his nose and mouth.

She reached the small window. Wooden shutters covered it, but they hung slightly open, and the window-pane had long ago been shattered. She pressed her ear against the wooden shutter and listened.

"So where is she, then?" Angelus asked, his Irish brogue thick. Buffy had never heard it before, though she knew he was originally Irish.

"She can't be far away," said a male voice in a American accent, obviously the assassin.

"And you're sure she'll come to us?" Darla asked in her lilting voice.

"Definitely. She's probably been scouring the city for me. But she's sharp, and she'll find us here sooner or later."

"I'm growing bored with this," said Darla. "It was fun drinking the Slayer, but I have other things I'd like to do with my evening."

Buffy heard Angelus give a soft moan, and she struggled to peer through the tiny slits in the shutter. Darla's fingers combed through his hair, then scratched along his back playfully. "Much better things," she added, her voice growing husky.

Buffy felt a tightness in her stomach. She hated seeing this evil vamp flirting with her boyfriend. Even though he wasn't technically her boyfriend. At least not for another two-hundred-plus years and one soul later. Still. It made her sick.

Darla cooed at him, and he grabbed her harshly behind the neck and brought his mouth to hers, kissing her hungrily and lustily. Buffy looked away. It was too much to bear.

"Who are they talking about?" Xander asked. "I can't quite hear."

"Me," Buffy said.

Darla giggled appreciatively, then said, "You had better produce this second Slayer soon. As I said, I'm starting to lose interest."

"But, Darla," Angelus protested, "think of the power! Drinking two Slayers in one night. It'll be the first time ever that two Slayers were killed at the same time! We'll be infamous!"

"We already are, my darling," she told him, throaty and sensual.

Buffy couldn't take this much longer. Even the garbage didn't make her this nauseous.

A sharp cry brought her attention back to the shutter. She peered through. Darla's teeth clamped down hard on Marguerite's neck, and the young girl swayed in her seat, slumping against the table.

How had she been caught? Buffy couldn't imagine the horror of being the prisoner of ruthless killers. They must have overpowered her, caught her unawares. And now she'd been bitten. But had she drunk their blood as well? Was she forever tainted? Destined to become the very thing she'd dedicated her life to stopping?

Buffy pulled away from the window and looked at Xander in the dark. "The Slayer's weak. I don't think she can last much longer in there. Looks like she's lost a lot of blood."

"What do you suggest?"

"What time is it?"

Xander pushed up his cotton sleeve, reading the Timex hidden beneath. "An hour and ten minutes before we meet the others."

"That's not enough time. They might kill her before that."

"Then what do you suggest? We could start back, look along the route they took—"

"No," Buffy said, holding up her hand. "I've got to face them now."

"But, Buffy! That's not three assassins drunk on soldier blood in there. It's Darla and Angelus! Not to mention the assassin and a whole boatload of drunken vampires just spoiling for a fight!"

"Then I'll have to lure them out here," she said.

"This is a bad idea, Buff. A very bad idea. You can't fight all three."

"I don't have a choice, Xander! That Slayer is about to die, and she's going to continue dying because they're waiting for me. I have to give them what they're waiting for."

She wished now she'd taken a crossbow.

"This is crazy, Buffy. Let's go find the others!" Xander pleaded.

She looked at him gravely, studying his face, the worry there. "Xander, friends are a bonus to a Slayer.

We have to do this gig alone. I've been lucky so far to have you all by my side in a crunch, but in a moment like this, I have to stand on my own."

"I'm going in there with you," Xander said, fear making his voice shake.

"No, you're not."

"Then I'm going to find the others," he finished resolutely.

"Good. Do that." Buffy didn't want to worry about him while she was fighting. She had to preserve the Slayer line.

He began to leave, then turned back. "What are you going to do?"

"I don't know," she said honestly, meeting his eyes in the shadows.

"I'll be back soon," he told her, and took off at a run.

She turned back, peering in through the shutter again, and devised a plan for luring them out. Something low-key. Something that wouldn't attract the attention of the other vampires.

She skirted around the edges of the building, trying to find the best place to fight. At last, a block away, she found a wide alley hidden partially from view from the main street, yet open at both ends. It would allow for her to escape with Marguerite if she needed to.

Reaching into her satchel, she pulled out the small pad of paper and pencil that Giles had insisted they all carry. Finally it would see use.

On a sheet of paper, she wrote, "Outside. One block east. The alley. Bring the Slayer." She tore it off, folded it into a paper airplane, and walked around to the open door again. Taking careful aim, she let it fly. It landed expertly in front of Angelus.

Buffy took off for the alley, pulling a stake out of her satchel as she ran. Once there, she climbed a rickety wooden staircase running down the exterior of one building. Her leg felt stiff as she climbed. Even with her Slayer healing abilities, the wound was doing a number on her agility. With some effort, she ducked down out of view behind two large wooden crates. She wanted to gauge the situation first, make sure it was just the three vampires.

She sat and waited, heart thudding, wondering if Angelus was really the evil monstrosity the Watcher journals made him out to be. She breathed slowly to steady her pulse as she waited. Tonight she might have to stake her love in this lonely alley, or it might see her own death instead.

Chapter Forty-six

Darla, Angelus, and the assassin filed into the alley, dragging the weakly struggling Slayer behind them. They'd blindfolded her. She stumbled, found her footing, and staggered along behind them. Her skin was as pale as porcelain. She'd lost a lot of blood and was close to losing consciousness. Red poured out of the open wound on her neck.

"Come out, come out, wherever you are," Darla sang.

Marguerite twisted suddenly in Angelus's grasp, trying to break loose. He grabbed her around the back of the neck, pulling her close. "And where do you think you're going? What would a trap be without its bait? You're here to bring us the other Slayer. Don't tell me you mean to disappoint."

She shrugged him off, then swayed and fell to the

ground. She delivered a weak kick to his knee, but it was still enough to make him cry out sharply. Angrily he grabbed her hair, wrenching her up to her feet. He pressed his lips close to her ear. "You'd be wise not to do that again,"

Buffy watched as the foursome walked farther into the alley. Then Darla turned to the frizzy-haired assassin. "So? Where is she?"

"She'll be here," he assured her.

It angered Buffy to hear him talking as if he knew her. What did he know? But he was right nonetheless. She wouldn't let them just kill Marguerite, even if they were using the girl as bait to catch her.

She knew it was a trap, but she had to descend anyway.

Waiting for her moment, she sized up the situation. She couldn't fight all three. Perhaps if one of the vamps weren't Angelus, she might pull it off. She'd seen Darla fight before, and she could be ruthless. And she had no idea how well the assassin could fight. He was probably blessed with the same martial arts capacity vamps mysteriously achieved upon rising from their graves. But the other assassins, except Victor, hadn't been that tough.

She'd have to grab the Slayer and run. But Marguerite was in no condition to sprint through the streets of Paris right now. Buffy suddenly wished she'd waited for the others. They could have ushered Marguerite to safety while Buffy held off the vampires.

She hadn't thought this through. She was tired, and her leg still ached from the rifle ball that had passed through it. It still wasn't up to par. She was tired—she'd barely slept lately, constantly worried about the next time jump. At least this was the last. Then she could get some decent sleep. And she wasn't even missing any school, because when they returned, it would still be Sunday. That was hardly fair. At least she should be able to get some good, quality no-school days out of all this.

"Show yourself, or we drain this Slayer," Darla shouted, grabbing Marguerite and pulling her close.

The most she could do would be to fight them while the Slayer ran away.

A group of drunken revelers walked by, shouting. The vampires spun suddenly at the noise.

This was her chance. She leaped down silently, landing on top of Darla. Marguerite sprawled to one side, hitting the alley wall. "Run, Marguerite!" Buffy shouted. The French Slayer rubbed her blindfold against the rough brick of the wall, and soon the dirty cloth fell down around her neck. Understanding Buffy's English, she ran.

Sitting on Darla's stomach, Buffy punched her in the face, then stood up and delivered two kicks to her stomach and kidneys. Standing on her hurt leg, Buffy wondered if the kick hurt her or Darla more. But Darla swore, rolling into a fetal position. Quickly Angelus narrowed in on Buffy. She ducked under a kick, then a series of blows. He'd been a vampire for only thirty-nine years but was still deadly, she discovered. She kicked him hard in the face, and as he staggered backward, she swept his feet out from under him. Arms windmilling, he crashed hard onto the cobbles. Buffy looked toward the Slayer. She hadn't made it out of the alley. The assassin blocked her way, dodging back and forth in front of her, leering and laughing.

Marguerite stumbled.

Buffy made a break for the other Slayer and fell flat on her face as a weight crashed into her back and shoulders. She smelled the familiar scent of Angel, temporarily stunned by the vivid good memories it brought back. Then she elbowed him in the side, flipped on her back, and brought a heel down hard to his groin.

She felt the reassuring weight of the stake in her vest pocket but didn't reach for it. The only vamp she wanted to waste was the assassin. She couldn't mess with the time line, and Darla and Angelus lived far into the future. And she couldn't stake Angelus, anyway. He might be a beast now, but eventually he became her love.

With Angelus groaning and cursing her, Buffy leaped up, reaching the Slayer and the assassin. "Come on!" she shouted to Marguerite, grabbing her by the elbow.

Buffy heard footsteps thundering down the main street, then Willow shouting, "Buffy?"

The assassin turned toward the voices.

"Willow, down here! Get Marguerite to safety!" Buffy yelled. She tackled the assassin from behind, and he fell hard. She straddled him, punching him harshly in the back of the head. She reached inside his jacket, patting him down for incantations. She found the telltale paper and stuck it in her own pocket. Then she produced the stake, raising it to thrust through the assassin's heart.

A hand grabbed her wrist harshly, yanking her up off the ground. For a second she was airborne, surprised at the brute force of the attack. She landed solidly on her feet, twisting her arm out of the grip.

Angelus stood before her, his head dripping blood from a gash above his eye. He blinked the red liquid away to clear his vision.

"Finish her, Angelus! That's my boy!" Darla shouted from down the alley.

Buffy looked at Angelus, at his dark eyes. When she met him, he never would have listened to Darla. He had staked his sire in the Bronze in 1997 to save Buffy. This time, however, there was no chance of enlisting Angel's help. This time he was the enemy.

Chapter Forty-seven

Buffy readied herself to fight Angelus. She tucked the stake back inside her vest pocket, not wanting to use it. At this action, Angelus raised a puzzled eyebrow.

The assassin jumped to his feet, grabbing Marguerite.

"Take your chance now, Franco!" shouted Darla, keeping safely out of the fray, Buffy noticed. No reason to mess up her pretty dress with all the frills. She had minions to do her bidding.

Angelus stood between Buffy and the Slayer now. Franco, as she now knew he was called, stood near Marguerite. So nice to finally learn his name just as she was about to dust him.

"Run to your left!" she told Marguerite. The French Slayer must have definitely understood some

English, because she took off in that direction, toward the mouth of the alley. Where was Willow? There was still no sign of the Scoobies.

Angelus stood his ground, keeping himself between Buffy and the French Slayer.

"Use your special firearm!" shouted Darla.

The assassin reached into his pocket. Buffy didn't like this. Special firearm?

Franco produced a semiautomatic nine-millimeter from his pocket. This was not good.

He raised the gun toward Marguerite.

"I get to kill the other one," Darla told Franco. "I don't like her."

Buffy charged in the direction of the assassin, and Angelus leaped, cutting her off. He knocked her violently to the ground, and she bucked him off, flipping him to the side.

She had only a fraction of a second and knew that. In the corner of her eye, Franco took aim at Marguerite.

A deafening shot cracked and echoed through the alley. A gray blur streaked into view, knocking Marguerite over. A scream pierced the roaring silence following the shot.

She recognized the voice. It was Giles. He'd been hit.

As Marguerite struggled to her feet again, fighting against her bindings, Xander ran forward with a knife, cutting through the ropes.

"Shoot them! Shoot them!" Darla yelled, running forward.

Buffy jumped to her feet, kicking Angelus in the side before he could rise. Her leg burned with pain.

Darla reached the assassin. She demanded the gun, but Franco held on to it, too caught up in the fight.

Angelus rolled to the side, away from Buffy's reach.

Buffy ran for Franco and the gun. Angelus dashed for Marguerite. They reached their targets at the same time. Angelus shoved Xander away just as Willow ran into the alley. With a wicked backhand, he knocked her sprawling. Giles, shot in the arm, rose unsteadily to his feet and tried to tackle Angelus. Spinning, the vampire grabbed Giles's injured arm, sticking his thumb directly into the wound and twisting. He forced Giles to his knees.

Buffy grabbed at Franco's gun, struggling with him for control. Darla kicked her hard in the kidneys, but Buffy held on, gritting her teeth through the pain. She didn't let go. The gun went off once, twice, discharging harmlessly into the drizzling sky.

Angelus grabbed the weakened French Slayer, spinning her around.

Buffy kicked Darla to the side, then shoved the assassin into Angelus. He staggered back, releasing Marguerite. She ran to Xander and Willow, bending to help them.

"Don't worry about us!" shouted Xander. "Run out of here!"

"I will not leave you," she answered in accented English.

Buffy used the momentum of tackling Angelus to

send them spiraling backward, where she, Franco, and Angelus crashed into the opposite alley wall. She sandwiched Angelus between herself and the assassin. Franco's gun arm was now pinned against the wall, and she could see the very end of the barrel sticking out, shielded almost completely by Angelus's body.

"Shoot! Shoot!" Darla shouted again, recovering and racing toward them.

The assassin angled the gun up toward Marguerite. His finger started to squeeze the trigger.

Buffy hit the gun barrel with her fist, but it moved only a fraction of a centimeter. Angelus's bulk was too heavy for it to move much.

Franco continued to squeeze the trigger. Buffy tried to shove Angelus to the side but, grinning, he wouldn't move. He used his body as a shield. Buffy couldn't reach Franco. Darla grabbed her harshly from behind, choking her. She had only a millisecond before the gun fired, killing the Slayer and possibly Xander and Willow, too.

There was only one thing to do.

Letting Darla continue to choke her, Buffy pulled out the stake. Everything slowed. Franco's finger was almost fully depressed on the trigger.

Buffy thrust the stake into Angelus's heart. He vaporized, leaving only ashes. The stake continued on in its forward thrust, passing through the falling ashes and piercing the heart of the assassin. Dust exploded outward, showering her, and the gun clattered harmlessly to the ground.

"No!" shouted Darla, emitting a piercing scream

of rage and grief. Xander rushed forward, grabbed the gun, and pointed it at her.

"That won't kill me," she spat venomously, teeth bared in rage.

"No," said Marguerite, stepping forward. "But I will."

Sizing them up, Darla glared at them with simmering hostility. Then she turned and ran away. Marguerite started after her, her face gray and body trembling from blood loss. She looked on the verge of collapse.

"No," Buffy said, stopping her. "I'll explain this in a minute, but it's not her time to die."

Marguerite stopped, gasping for breath and staring angrily after the receding figure in blue. Then she turned to Buffy. "At least you got the other two," she said in her excellent English. "They grabbed me while I was sleeping in a shelter."

Yes, Buffy thought, *at least I got the other two.* She stared down at the dust, now drifting away in the evening breeze, mingling with the drizzling rain. *It wasn't Angel's time to go either.* She felt numb, unable to move, and sank to her knees. In an instant, Willow was beside her. "Buffy, what did you do?" she whispered.

Buffy looked pleadingly into her friend's eyes. "I didn't have a choice. . . ." She let the stake tumble out of her hands, clattering to the stones of the alley.

She stared at the dust that had been Angelus, her mind searing with an intense disbelief. "Couldn't you have—," Willow began, but didn't finish.

Buffy sniffed, her eyes welling with tears. "The Slayer would be dead if I'd hesitated even just another second." As she sank lower, Willow grabbed her arm, pulling her to her feet. Buffy wobbled on unsteady legs.

A cry of pain and some rather British cursing brought her back to the immediacy of the situation.

Giles stood a few feet away, his arm streaming with blood. Willow tore off part of her jacket to stanch the flow while Xander steadied him.

Buffy rushed to his side. "We need to get you to a doctor." So much blood was leaking out that she couldn't see the wound properly.

"Yes," he said, "but I'd prefer one from the twenty-first century. Fewer leeches."

Willow laughed, then looked at Buffy's expression and stopped.

There was no joy left in Buffy's heart. A silence fell over all of them. Buffy turned back to the drifting dust in the alley, her chin trembling. Willow hugged her.

Marguerite turned to them, confused. "But wasn't it good? To destroy both vampires?" she asked.

After a long pause, when no one else could speak, Giles said quietly, "One of them was different." He placed a hand on Buffy's shoulder and said, "Well, let's at least get Marguerite to an eighteenth-century doctor. We can explain this to her on the way."

"And then let's go home," Xander said, still clutching the gun.

"And then let's go home," Xander said, still clutching the gun.

"Are you okay?" Willow asked Buffy gently, squeezing her hand.

Buffy could only shake her head.

With Marguerite leaning on Buffy, and Giles supported by Willow and Xander, they trudged out of the alley, heading for the house of Marguerite's doctor, who lived on Rue Vivienne, on the far side of the Palais Royal.

Fifteen minutes and one painfully jarring hired carriage ride later, they arrived.

They woke up the doctor, who immediately went to work on Marguerite, treating her for blood loss. He laid her in the guest bed. While he cleaned and bandaged Giles's wound, Buffy sat at Marguerite's bedside and explained who she was. Marguerite found it miraculous. Because her English was so good, it made the entire experience simple. In a half hour the doctor appeared at the bedroom door with a rather pale-looking Giles.

"The bullet passed through the meat of his arm," he explained in heavily accented English. "Keep it clean, and it should heal."

"Good to know," Giles said.

"Hey, we match," Buffy told him. "Both of us were shot on the right side."

"Oh, how grand," he responded in a monotone.

"Now we go back?" Xander asked.

"Will Marguerite be okay?" Buffy asked the doctor.

He nodded. "She has lost much blood, but she will recover in no time. I have been her doctor since she was born, and she has always had a remarkable healing rate."

"How about that," said Xander.

"I will be fine now, thanks to all of you."

Buffy exchanged a secret smile with Marguerite and squeezed her hand.

They left, walking out to a back alley behind the doctor's house. Buffy remembered the incantations she'd stolen from Franco and pulled them out. She unfolded them, hoping there wouldn't be more time periods. There weren't. Franco held only the spell for 1792.

"Well, that's a relief," Giles said.

Willow spoke up. "That may be the end of the enchantments, but what about the artifact itself? We still don't know where it is."

Giles grunted in thought. "My guess is that it lies somewhere in the room Buffy discovered. I don't think Lucien would have let it too far out of his reach."

"But, Giles, Angel and I searched that room. It wasn't in there."

"Then it must be hidden."

"Oooh, I sense a trip involving metal detectors!" Xander chimed in.

Buffy glanced over at him. "Knock yourself out."

"That's Giles's job," Xander countered.

Giles shook his head in misery. "Very funny, Xander."

"I thought so." Xander looked at the stone buildings rising around them. "Are we ready? I've seen enough back alleys of Paris to last me a lifetime."

Giles spoke the incantation, and Buffy's heart filled with mixed emotions. She was finally returning to her own time for good. They'd foiled Lucien's plot. But Angel would not be there.

The portal opened, whisking them through dazzling light, dumping them out in 1998 Sunnydale.

But it wasn't the same Sunnydale they'd left.

The portal spat them out into hell itself. The air reeked of guttering fires and rotting flesh. Burned-out cars littered the empty streets. It was night, and vampires roamed in droves, trolling the streets for victims. They closed in when they saw Buffy and the others.

In the sky swooped huge, winged creatures breathing fire. One dropped a half-eaten corpse, which landed with a dull thud next to Buffy. She rose shakily to her feet.

This chaos, this hell, could only mean one thing.

The Master had risen.

And he'd opened the Hellmouth.

Chapter Forty-eight

As the vampires closed in, more than Buffy could possibly count, more than a hundred, maybe more than two hundred, she turned to Giles.

"Speak the incantation!" she shouted to him.

He still lay on the ground, groggy from the portal travel. Slowly he lifted his head, taking in the approaching throngs of hungry vampires. "What?"

"Send us back! Send us back!"

"Oh, gods," he breathed when he saw the red sky, the fires, the creatures jeering and closing in on them.

"Speak it!" shouted Xander.

Willow crawled over to Giles and pulled the incantation out of his pocket.

"What went wrong?" Giles said, his voice small.

"Say it!" Willow told him. She pressed the incantation into his hand.

He lifted the paper and read the incantation. The portal winked into view, sucking them up into the air. Three vampires dove in after them.

They landed with a thud on a cobbled street, with the familiar cries of *"Vive la nation!"* ringing up around them. Buffy struggled to her feet, pulling out the stake. While the vampires stumbled around, unused to the nausea of portal travel, she staked them quickly, one after another.

Then she helped the others to their feet, looking around to get her bearings.

They'd landed on the other side of the Place de la Révolution. In the distance, she saw two other portals opening in the sky, and figures pouring out of them.

Giles gripped her shoulder, steadying himself, wincing against the pain. He saw the other portals too. "That's us," he said.

"What?"

"That's us arriving, the first time. One portal for us, one portal for the assassins."

"This makes my brain hurt," she said.

"What are you going to do?" Willow asked her.

"I know what went wrong. I killed Angelus."

"You changed the time line," Xander said.

"Yes. Angel was the one who discovered Lucien's plot. He was the one who held Lucien prisoner while we stopped the assassins. With him dying here in 1792, he wasn't present for any of those things. The Master rose."

"What are you planning?" Giles asked.

"I've got to save Angel's life." She turned in the

direction of the now dissipating portals in the distance. "I have to tell myself not to stake him. You guys wait here, out of sight."

Xander grabbed her arm. "No."

She turned on him, impatient. "What, you're going to try to stop me? I know you're jealous, Xander, but this is the fate of the world we're talking about."

Xander looked stung. "It's not that," he said, hurt in his voice. "It's paradox."

"A pair of what?"

"You shouldn't meet yourself. The entire universe could implode. At least, that's what they always say on *Doctor Who*, even though he frequently met himself. Of course, that was in different incarnations, and—"

She raised an eyebrow. "Xander. Point."

"Right. Don't meet yourself. Avoid yourself. You have to think of another way." He turned to the others. "None of us can run into ourselves. The entire space-time continuum could collapse."

"Been reading Einstein?" Giles asked suspiciously.

"No. But I haven't watched *The Terminator* and *Back to the Future* for nothing."

"Of course." Giles rolled his eyes.

"Hey, don't take it lightly. You guys need to listen to me on this."

"Okay," Buffy said. "Then what?"

"What if you send Angelus a note warning him not to go to the alley?" Willow asked.

Buffy liked the idea.

"You already know what pub he's at," she continued.

"It took us hours to find it. You could go now and beat yourself there. If he's not there yet, he will be shortly. You could leave a note for him at the pub."

"I don't like the risk that he might not get it," Buffy said.

"Then wait for him to get there. We'll all stay out of sight, somewhere safe, while you go."

Buffy looked at Giles, at the sweat beading on his brow. He was in no condition to travel. "Okay. You guys stay here and watch over Giles. I'll go straight to that pub and send Angelus a message."

"Glad you have your notebook?" Giles asked.

"Yes, teacher, I'm glad I brought my notebook to class for once."

Giles smiled in self-satisfaction. Then he winced in pain.

"Wait," Buffy realized. "Why don't I just wait at the pub and stake the assassin when he shows up? Then we'll never have that confrontation in the alley with Darla and Angelus."

"No, Buffy," Xander said adamantly. "Then our other selves will never find the assassin, and we'll keep looking and looking. Eventually we might give up, but that wouldn't be for days, and then we'd be altering events again. Imagine if we jumped in here and never found the assassin. Wouldn't you just assume he was lying in wait?"

"Yes," she agreed. "So then we tell ourselves not to chase the assassin, to just go home."

"Now we're back to meeting ourselves again," Xander pointed out.

"Oh. Right. I could give us all a note instead," she offered.

Xander shook his head. "There are too many variables. When dealing with time travel, the best thing to do is make things simple. We know that we already successfully stop the assassins and save Marguerite's life. Now we need to do the simplest thing to ensure that Angel lives." He brought a hand to his forehead and added, "I can't believe I just said that."

Buffy ignored the remark. "Back to the original plan, then."

"Yes."

"Okay, then. I'm off." Around the corner, the crowd roared with malicious glee, and Buffy knew they were executing that family. She fought the urge to help. She'd seen firsthand how bad things could be if the original time line were altered. "I'll be back," she told them, then ran, leaving them behind.

Chapter Forty-nine

In the alley outside the pub, Buffy snuck a peek through the shuttered window. Angelus sat at a table alone, sipping blood from a glass mug. Perfect. She tore a sheet from her notebook again and wrote:

Angelus. If you value your life, do not go with Darla to any fight in an alley tonight. Make up an excuse. This is serious.

Signed,
A friend

Once again, she folded it into a paper plane and let it sail through the front pub door. It jabbed him in the back, and he turned, scooping it up off the floor. He read it, then immediately spun and scanned the pub. She ducked back outside. He had to take it seriously. *Please take it seriously.*

She hid behind some wooden crates outside the door and waited.

In a few minutes he emerged, glancing up and down the alley. He read the note again. He took out a pocket watch, glanced at the time, and replaced it.

Buffy crouched, tense.

Two minutes later Darla arrived.

She kissed him. "How shall we entertain ourselves tonight, my love?"

He hesitated. "I'm feeling a bit sleepy," he said in his Irish brogue. "Must have been someone I ate."

She laughed. "You're going to bed? This early?"

"If you don't mind," he told her.

"Of course I mind," she said. "You're supposed to entertain me."

Ugh. What a brat. Buffy could barely stand listening to her.

"Well, perhaps I'll bow out just for tonight. But if you want to come by later, I'll probably be recovered. I can entertain you then."

He grabbed her, kissing her deeply.

Buffy's stomach knotted.

Darla moaned with pleasure, then looked up at him coyly. "Until then, my darling."

They parted. Angelus exited the alley, walking past Buffy's hiding place. Darla entered the pub.

Just as Buffy prepared to leave, the assassin showed up. He pulled out a piece of paper, checking the pub name against it. Then, nodding, he folded the paper and entered. So Lucien really *had* planned this from the beginning. He must be having a laugh right now, guarded by the very person who was instrumental in his plot to kill Marguerite.

"Darla, I presume?" she heard him ask.

"Who wants to know?" she murmured in a sultry voice.

Buffy stood up. She ran down to the mouth of the alley and peeked around the corner. Angelus walked some distance away. He passed a different pub, then stopped. It was one of the many Buffy had checked for the assassin. Angelus turned back around. He gave a quick glance toward the alley, then walked inside the bar.

Buffy breathed a sigh of relief. Good. She'd just changed events. If he held true to form, he'd be in this different pub, drinking, for most of the night. If Darla went looking for him at home to join her in Slayer-killing fun, he wouldn't be there.

She'd done it.

She hoped.

Buffy darted out of the alley and ran back to the others.

They waited where she'd left them, Giles now leaning over and groaning in pain.

"He needs to get to a doctor," Willow said. "He needs some painkillers or something."

Buffy studied her Watcher's gray face and furrowed brow. "Well, I think I did it. I think I was successful. We can go."

Shakily Giles stood, and once again produced the

incantation to return them to 1998. He spoke it, unhaltingly this time, the spell practically memorized.

The portal emerged, spinning hypnotically. They dove inside, tunneling through space and time, somersaulting and spinning dizzyingly.

The velocity decreased, and Buffy braced for the launching sensation. She shot out, landing this time on soft grass. It was day, and she closed her eyes against the dazzling sun.

She rolled to a stop beneath a merry-go-round. Willow tumbled out, landing beneath a seesaw, and Xander and Giles were thrown into a patch of weeds near the sidewalk.

Buffy got to her hands and knees, peering out into a well-maintained city park. Sunnydale looked as it should. No burned-out cars. No swooping winged creatures. No stench of fire.

And Angel?

She helped the others up, then told Willow and Xander to get Giles to the hospital.

"Where are you going?" Willow asked.

"The library." She didn't need to explain more. Willow understood. Buffy had to see if Angel was alive.

"What if Sunnydale's all *Road Warrior* meets *Blade Runner*?" Xander asked her as she hurried away.

"Run," she called over her shoulder.

She covered the distance to the high school in a matter of minutes, leaping over fences and cutting through backyards. It was still the weekend, she guessed, seeing no cars in the parking lot.

She ran to the side door of the library, opened it, and ran inside.

Lucien paced in the cage. He looked up when she entered.

Angel sat in a shadowed corner, reading a book. His head lifted, and a broad smile spread over his face. "Buffy."

"Angel!" She ran to him, embracing him, kissing him. It had worked. She held him tightly, not letting go.

"Mmmm . . . you should travel back in time more often," he told her, hugging her back. She knew only hours had passed since he'd last seen her. But she had seen him killed and resurrected.

She held him, not letting go, and turned her head toward Lucien.

He'd stopped pacing and stood glaring out at her.

She thought of torturing him, forcing him to reveal the location of the artifact. But she would wait for Xander. Too bad.

Three hours later, with Giles resting at the hospital with Willow, Buffy and Xander returned to the small room. Xander powered up his metal detector, sweeping the floor and walls. Before long it beeped repeatedly, revealing the loose brick and the artifact within. He pulled it out, emitting a long, slow whistle when he took in the gem on top.

"Bring this to Giles," she told him. "He'll know what to do with it."

"Where are you going?"

"I have someone to dust."

"Have fun."

"I intend to."

They parted, and Buffy returned to the library, pushing through the double doors. Lucien looked up nervously as she entered.

"Your plan has failed," she told him. "And I'm afraid there's no reason to keep you alive any longer."

His glare melted away into fear. She walked to Angel and held out her hand to him. He reached into his pocket, produced the key to the cage, and placed it in her palm.

She strode to the cage and unlocked it. Lucien drew farther back inside, pressing against the file cabinets.

"Time for a suntan," she told him, grabbing his arm. He struggled, bringing his hand up to strike her. She blocked the blow, dragging him out. He cleared the door of the cage and she spun him around, using his own weight to wheel him outward. She let go and he stumbled with the momentum, grabbed a desk, and stopped himself, still in the shadows.

"Give my regards to oblivion," she told him and, leaping up, kicked him in the chest. He shot backward into a blinding patch of sunlight. Instantly his body caught on fire. Screaming, he flailed helplessly, then exploded into a plume of ashes.

She stood, catching her breath, steadying herself against a table. It was over.

Angel crossed to her in the shadows, pulling her into his arms.

• • •

That night at Giles's place, Xander and Willow sat with the wounded Watcher on the couch. Buffy sat next to Angel, balancing on one arm of his chair. He stroked her back.

Her leg gave a twinge, and Giles's arm hung in a sling. In front of him sat a cup of the hard stuff, Earl Grey.

"Next time, let's not get shot," she told him.

"Agreed."

"And next time," Willow said, "let's visit the Galapagos Islands before they've been discovered by humans, or take a nice, relaxing vacation on a virgin beach in Hawaii."

"A virgin beach that gets the Sci-Fi Channel," Xander put in.

"And has ancient ruins to explore," Giles added.

"At night," Angel put in. "You guys had all the fun this time."

"Fun," Xander said. "Last time I checked, fun was riding Space Mountain at Disneyland, not fighting for survival on an American battlefield, or almost getting sacrificed in blood rites."

"You were not almost sacrificed," Giles told him in exasperation.

"How do you know? They could have been working up to that just as we left."

"Yes, I'm sure they were, Xander," he retorted. "After being in your company for several hours."

"Well, I for one caught up on my reading," Angel said.

"Oh?" Giles asked. "Did you read Deserot's *Compendium of Bothersome Demons and Musical Instruments of the Third Century*? I left it for you."

Angel shook his head. "I couldn't get past the nose flute section. That whole bit on cleaning mucus out of—"

"Ew!" Buffy said. "Too much information."

"Yeah. That's what I thought," he said. "So I settled for *Tess of the D'Urbervilles*. You left it at my place."

"That book must be downright cheerful for you, Angel. Enough brooding in it?" she asked.

He gave her a wry smile. "Not quite. I'm reading *Les Misérables* next."

"Perfect," Willow said, grinning.

Buffy leaned back against Angel, who slid his arm around her. They'd done it. Here they all were, a little scratched, but alive. She'd not only met other Slayers, commiserated with them, and protected them, but she realized more than ever how valuable her friends were. Without them, she wouldn't be alive. As Angel stroked her arm affectionately, and she looked across at the others, she realized how much she had to be happy about.

And heck, this year she might even pass history.

ABOUT THE AUTHOR

Alice Henderson has been writing since she was six. She holds a master's degree in folklore and mythology, and she has studied the beliefs, traditions, and mythologies of many different cultures, from ancient Sumerian to Celtic and Mayan. In addition to several *Star Wars* video game manuals and strategy guides, she also wrote *Night Terrors*, a Buffy the Vampire Slayer title in the Stake Your Destiny series.

An avid reader, Alice regularly devours books. Her pet rabbit, Captain Nemo, also avidly devours books, but in a different way. She lives in San Francisco, where she is at work on her next novel. Please visit her at www.alicehenderson.com.

Buffy
the Vampire Slayer™

Into every generation,
a Slayer is born . . .

Before there was Buffy, there were other Slayers—called to
protect the world from the undead. Led by their Watchers,
they have served as our defense—across the globe and
throughout history.

In these collections of short stories written by best-selling
authors, travel through time to these other Slayers. From
France in the fourteenth century to Iowa in the 1980s, the
young women have protected the world. Their stories—
and legacies—are unforgettable.

Published by Simon & Schuster
™ & © 2006 Twentieth Century Fox Film Corporation. All Rights Reserved.